W9-BRI-272

The
Thief-Taker

Memoirs of a
Bow Street Runner

T. F. Banks

A DELL BOOK

A Dell Book
Published by
Dell Publishing
A division of Random House, Inc.
1540 Broadway
New York, New York 10036

ISBN: 0-440-23696-7

Reprinted by arrangement with Delacorte Press
Printed in the United States of America
Published simultaneously in Canada
October 2002
OPM   10 9 8 7 6 5 4 3 2 1

For
M. J. T.
and
K. R. N.

Acknowledgments

I cannot thank Ian Dennis and Sean Russell enough for tirelessly reading, rereading, and re-rereading the various drafts of this book. Without their invaluable contributions, THE THIEF-TAKER would never have got beyond the fantasy stage or, worse, might have turned into yet another dusty academic study.

The death of Halbert Glendinning will, in my mind, always be coupled to the great battle fought at Waterloo, and the extraordinary celebration within the city of London that June of 1815.

At about the same time also an odd little event occurred that I mention, not by way of name-dropping, but only because it, too, is forever linked in memory to the Glendinning affair. I had the good fortune to meet the famous Lord Byron, and under circumstances that you will hardly credit, for we did not meet at a salon—Bow Street Runners were not welcome at such gatherings. No, we met at a club I frequented: Gentlemen John Jackson's boxing club. Byron was a devotee of the manly arts, and we actually stood toe to toe and traded some pretty fair blows for a time. That was before the great scandal broke that drove the poet from England forever.

But I am getting away from my story. I recall this meeting because it was after our contest at Jackson's that a boy came to fetch me about this fellow Glendinning. It seems he'd arrived at a nearby house in a hackney-coach. All I knew about him then was that he hadn't paid his fare, and that he was dead.

But it turned out he was a poet, too, of sorts. . . .

—Henry Morton,
The Memoirs of a Bow Street Runner

June 1815

Chapter 1

Morton had all but finished dressing, and was basking in the glow of warmth and well-being, albeit moderated by a few stinging bruises, that followed his remarkable evening at Jackson's.

"Mr. Morton...sir?" a voice said breathlessly.

Morton looked up to find a boy, gasping in the doorway as though in the throes of an asthmatical convulsion.

"Henry Morton, yes."

"I've run all the way, sir..." the child managed. " 'Tis Mrs. Malibrant....Asks that you come directly." A few desperate breaths were needed. "I'm to say 'tis most urgent, sir. Most terrible urgent."

Morton tossed aside a towel. "Nothing has befallen Mrs. Malibrant, I hope?"

"Oh, no, Mr. Morton. 'Tis the gentleman, sir. The young gentleman who just arrived at Lord Arthur's." The boy straightened a little and shook his head. "He appears to be dead, sir. Most thoroughly dead."

It was but a short walk from Jackson's in Bond Street to their destination in Portman Square, but even so, Morton's long, purposeful stride soon had the boy out of breath again, precluding conversation. Following along the dimly lit street came the hollow echo of a tired horse and tradesman's cart, the owner shuffling numbly beside. A pile of cobbles and rubble forced Morton and the boy outside the line of iron posts that protected unwary pedestrians from street traffic. Here they found their footing with care in the foul street.

At this hour, near to ten Morton guessed, Bond Street was quiet but not empty, the shop windows dark, the signs over doors unreadable in the gloom.

He was trying to remember in what manner Arabella had said she was engaged that night. Was she not onstage this evening? He was sure she'd said she was, and Morton had a near-infallible memory. Very odd.

The gateman who protected the privacy of the occupants of the Square took notice of Morton's gilt-topped baton and let them through. "Ev'ning, Constable," he said, tipping his cap. "The disturbance be down there to the right, nigh on Portman House."

Along the line of elegant Greek Revival town houses, Morton could see one with its doors open, light and guests spilling out into the street, where carriages clustered in a throng. Rather too early for a dinner party to end, Morton thought, and as he drew closer saw that there was little gaiety in the faces.

The boy whisked him past the butler, who had barely an instant to cast a disapproving glare in Morton's direction. He was let into a small sitting-room, and there two gentlemen stood over a third who lay very still on a divan. A pleasantly greying man looked up, his face grim and pale.

"Henry Morton. Bow Street. Mrs. Malibrant sent for me."

The man nodded. "Arthur Darley."

Hadn't Arabella mentioned a Lord Arthur a few times? She had so many admirers it was difficult to keep them straight, and Morton usually didn't try, finding them an ineffectual lot. Though Lord Arthur was imposing enough. No fool, Morton surmised, and taking a man's measure was part of Morton's trade.

"Doctor?" Lord Arthur asked the second man, who glanced sourly over his shoulder.

"Well, I'm sorry to say it, sir," the other replied, "but this young man is beyond my powers to help. Beyond anyone's, in fact. He smells powerfully of strong drink and has aspirated his own vomitus."

Morton peered past the doctor. The dead man, who could only have attained this state very recently, still had some colour in his face. "His lips are not terribly blue for a man who has suffocated," Morton offered.

The doctor turned on him, eying him rather viciously. "And you are a medical man, sir?"

Morton held his preferred response in check. "No, I am a Bow Street man," he said, "but I've seen a few corpses in the course of my duties. His windpipe is blocked?"

"I have seen 'a few corpses' in my time, as well, sir," the little man said, his tone mocking and indignant. "I served with Wellesley in Spain."

"Army surgeon? Well, that would make you an authority on men drinking themselves to death. You don't mind if I have a look, do you?" Wellesley, indeed! As though this small man were a familiar of the Duke of Wellington's.

The doctor stood his ground a moment more, then

gave Darley a stiff bow. "I have given my opinion," he said haughtily. "I bid you gentlemen good evening."

"Thank you for your assistance, sir," Darley said, and accompanied him to the door.

Morton could see the dead man clearly for the first time: young, perhaps twenty-six or -seven, not strongly formed but hardly effete. He guessed him to be of good height, perhaps three inches shorter than Morton himself. His hair was straw-coloured. His eyes had been closed but they were likely blue. The rather square mouth was now rapidly turning to greyish-purple. His elegant evening clothes, fashionably dark, were covered in vomit. It even matted his hair.

Morton breathed in the familiar smell of death, but there was something more as well. Sickly sweet. He bent over, braced himself, and pressed on the man's chest, breathing in through his nose as he did so. He gagged and pulled a handkerchief from his pocket, covering his mouth. His eyes watered, but the contents of his own stomach stayed where they belonged.

Covering his fingers with his handkerchief, he distended the man's lips, then pulled on the teeth to open the jaw. As he thought. He wiped his hands energetically. There were no signs that the young man had been assaulted. His clothes, though soiled, were not torn or even appreciably askew. Morton gently turned the man's head, which rolled heavily to one side. No marks or signs of a blow. His hands and forearms bore no bruises or contusions. He had not defended himself.

A real doctor would have to make an examination, but Morton had seen enough to convince him. Quickly he went through the man's outer pockets and fob. A watch, some coins, a small ring of keys. He opened the jacket.

"What are you finding, Mr. Morton?" Darley had returned from seeing the doctor out, and now eyed the thief-taker rather suspiciously.

Morton's fingers encountered a small sheet of folded paper in an inner pocket. He stood up, turning to Darley.

"Nothing unexpected. To be honest, Lord Arthur, I am not sure why Mrs. Malibrant sent for me. I do not know how this unfortunate gentleman met his end but there are no signs of foul play. He doesn't appear to have been robbed. Though, at the risk of offending your friend the surgeon, I do not think he suffocated. Can you tell me who he is and the circumstances in which he was found?"

Arabella let herself in at that moment, and both men bowed to her. She was dressed in a gown of green silk that seemed to reflect the colour of her eyes, which were, Arabella liked to say, the hue of jade. Porcelain-pale skin and, about her lovely face, a cloud of cumulous red hair. Arabella Malibrant did not go unnoticed in a crowd.

"Mr. Morton," she said, nodding. "This is the man I spoke of, Arthur."

Arthur?

"So I assumed." Lord Arthur clasped her hands. "And how are you, my dear? Are you sure you wish to be in here? Shall I come out?"

Arabella's eye strayed to the dead man. "No, I'm well. I have just sent Miss Hamilton home with her brother. She did not want to leave but her friends prevailed. Poor thing," she said, her eyes glistening.

"Yes, poor Louisa," Darley agreed.

Morton felt his head shake involuntarily. Arabella Malibrant was no more a shrinking violet than Morton

himself. He was sure she could step over a corpse in the
street and not interrupt her conversation. It was not for
his benefit, this little display of feeling.

Silence for a moment, and then Morton cleared
his throat. "You were about to tell me, Lord Arthur,
who this unfortunate man was and how he was
found...."

Darley seemed to refocus. "Oh, yes. His name is
Halbert Glendinning. He arrived here, oh, some thirty
minutes ago in a hackney-coach. I was not there, of
course. But he... well, Mrs. Malibrant, you were there."

Arabella nodded, her mane of red hair swaying.

"I had arrived just the moment before and was on the
stair when I heard a fuss. Several servants were looking
into a coach where they had discovered this young man,
sprawled. There was a bit of a scene, as you might imagine. Arthur was sent for and arrived a moment later.
And then poor Miss Hamilton..." Arabella shook her
head. "I thought my heart would break when she called
out his name. No actress in England could have put
such feeling into it, and yet it was restrained." She
glanced at Morton, who must have looked impatient, for
she drew herself up a little, green eyes glaring. "All of
this was horrible enough, but I should not have sent for
Hen—Mr. Morton but for one thing. The jarvey was
frightened nigh unto death. I have never seen a man
look so ill so suddenly. And the moment poor Mr.
Glendinning was lifted from his carriage, the man was
gone. Not so much as a by-your-leave. Just vanished.
Without his fare! Can you imagine that? 'Now, that,
Arabella,' I said to myself, 'is as suspicious as anything I
have ever seen. Mr. Morton will want to talk to him.'
And I sent for you straightaway."

Darley looked oddly at Morton, and Morton knew

what the man was thinking. *And who, sir, are you to Mrs. Malibrant?*

A knock at the door drew Lord Arthur, who excused himself and went quietly out. Arabella stayed, as any lady certainly would not. She glanced again at the dead body, then at a painting on the wall. A number of things Morton might say ran through his mind, none of them appropriate to sharing a room with a gentleman who had so recently departed the pleasures of this earth. *"Arthur?"* he said at last.

"It's not what you think," she said quickly, but for an actress Arabella was a surprisingly poor liar. It was precisely what he thought. But, then, what could Morton say? They had an "understanding," of sorts, and gentlemen like Lord Arthur Darley were part of it. Gentlemen of quality. Likely married. A man who did not find his money chasing criminals through the streets of London.

Arabella raised her head and stared at him rather defiantly. Morton looked down at the scrap of paper he still held in his hand. Unfolding it, he held it up to the light and read aloud.

> *"It will find you soon enough,*
> *The empty night after the day.*
> *Brief and filled with sorrow,*
> *Love will rise and slip away."*

"What is that?" Arabella asked.

"I found it in his pocket."

"Well, he was no Byron."

Morton glanced down at the unmoving form of the young man. No, he was no Byron.

Arthur Darley returned at that moment, and his soft eyes came to rest on Glendinning. For a moment he stood very still, and Morton thought the feelings he saw in the man's face were not feigned.

"It is so tragic," Darley said quietly. "So many men lost in the recent wars, Mr. Morton, and more to come across the Channel, I fear. But one comes to think that we at home are safe."

Safe? Morton thought. Here was someone who did not see the side of London frequented by the men of Bow Street.

"Lord Arthur?" Morton said, interrupting the man's contemplation. "Have you any reason to believe this death is anything but natural?"

Darley looked up at the Bow Street Runner enquiringly. "You're really quite certain the doctor was wrong? That he didn't choke to death on his own gorge?"

"The doctor's examination was less than thorough, I think. You see this poor unfortunate? If he had asphyxiated, and I have seen many a man who has, hanged and murdered both, his airway would have been blocked or there would be signs of an assault upon his throat. And if you push upon his chest, as I did a moment ago, air passes freely out of his lungs. The passage is not blocked, nor is there vomit in his mouth. I have looked. Did the doctor open Glendinning's mouth and examine his airway?"

"I don't believe he did."

"I don't believe he did, either. Forgive me for asking again: Is there any reason to believe Mrs. Malibrant's fears are founded? Might Mr. Glendinning have expired of something unnatural?"

Darley glanced at Arabella, the question unspoken.

"Mr. Morton is entirely reliable," she told him.

"I'm glad to hear it," Darley said dryly. He stood for a moment, lost in thought, then he shook his head and sat down rather heavily in a chair. "I . . . I cannot quite catch up with what has happened. You see, Mr. Morton, someone tried to kill poor Glendinning earlier this day."

Morton and Arabella both stared at Lord Arthur, but Darley hesitated.

"What is it, Arthur?" Arabella said softly.

"Well, I don't suppose he can be charged with it now. . . . You see, Glendinning was involved in an affair of honour this morning. Your own people interrupted it, Mr. Morton. I don't think shots were fired."

"A duel with whom, Lord Arthur?" Morton asked.

"I don't know," Darley replied. "I can find out, perhaps."

"I don't much care to prosecute a duel, Lord Arthur, if that is your concern. And it seems no one was arrested."

"Peter Hamilton will likely know the story. He was Glendinning's friend." Darley stared down blankly at the corpse that lay upon his divan. "He was the kindest young man. A bit quiet, but liked by everyone—or so I thought. Poor Louisa."

"Who is Louisa, exactly?"

"Louisa Hamilton," Arabella said. "Peter Hamilton's sister."

"Louisa and Glendinning had come to an understanding recently, or so I believed. I had thought they might announce their engagement tonight." Darley shook his head again.

"If Mr. Glendinning really was involved in a duel," Morton said, "it casts Mrs. Malibrant's observation into a different light."

"You don't really think it's possible that . . . ?" Darley eyed Morton, perhaps hoping he would tell him that such things could not happen in his world.

"It happens daily, Lord Arthur. Daily, and sometimes in homes as fine as this."

Morton saw Arabella home, happy to find that she was going home. He was not overly prone to jealousy—far less than the next man. No one would ever catch Morton murdering a man over a woman, as perhaps had happened this night. It was often the reason duels were fought. He had seen it before.

The coach bounced through a pothole and the driver cursed. Morton gazed thoughtfully out the window.

Arabella sighed, signaling that he was not paying attention to her as he should. Morton turned back to her.

"Is it not the saddest thing?" she asked. "If you had heard poor Miss Hamilton cry out, Henry, you would have done anything to ease her pain. I tell you, it was wrenching. I could never duplicate it." She pitched her voice low and tried anyway. "*'Oh, Richard. Richard . . .'*"

"Very touching, I'm sure," Morton said. "There is only one problem. . . ."

Arabella raised one perfect eyebrow.

"His name was not Richard."

Chapter 2

"**Y**ou don't believe me, do you?" Arabella demanded as soon as she had shed her wrap. They had come to her lodgings in Theobald's Road.

"Don't believe what, pray?" Morton did not care much for her mood, which was combative and testy.

"About the jarvey."

"You said he was frightened near to death and fled without demanding his fare, which I admit *is* suspicious."

"Do not mock me, Henry Morton," she said coldly.

Morton regarded her seriously. She really was the most beautiful woman. "You should not knit up your perfect brow so."

"I shall crochet it if it pleases me."

Morton wanted to take her in his arms—somehow wanted it even more because he knew the timing was not right at all. Instead, he dropped into one of her comfortable chairs, and caught sight of himself in a looking-glass: a big man, large-boned, and lean from years of

Gentleman John's brutal "toughening." His brow was too heavy to appear refined, but his jaw was strong. Arabella said he had the eyes of a poet, whatever that might mean. "Soft and soulful," he guessed, but dark and inquisitive was his own assessment—too inquisitive.

"It is odd," he said more seriously. "Why was the jarvey so frightened, do you think? Could it have been merely the fear the poor feel when they think some accusation might be leveled at them? Glendinning died in the man's carriage, after all. Did he fear that these nobs would blame him in some way? If only for negligence?"

Arabella did not take a seat, but instead paced across the small sitting-room. Morton watched her go, hungrily, his own feelings not in tune with the mood. "No, I think it was something else." She struggled to give voice to what was in her mind. "It...it was not that kind of fear, Henry," she said at last.

Morton suddenly found himself listening. He was not sure why. As though his own feelings had been deafening him to what Arabella had been saying. Like most people of her profession, Arabella was an acute observer of human nature, and Morton had come to trust her intuition.

"I'm sure you're right," he said, "but it seems unlikely I will find him now. We might offer a reward for him to come forward." There were some thousand hackney-coach licences granted in London, not to mention those who plied the trade unsanctioned.

Arabella stopped her pacing. "Four-seventeen," she said firmly.

For a moment Morton stared at her blankly, then his face lit in a smile. "The coach number?" he said.

"Of course! After what I saw, you did not think I

would forget to note it? Mr. Morton, you do me a dis-
service."

"Not at all, my dear. Many a Bow Street officer has
cursed himself after the fact for not noting a hackney
number in the heat of the moment." He smiled at her,
hoping his praise would ease the tension between them.
"I shall find the man tomorrow, and speak with him, if
you think it worthwhile."

"I do, but don't wait until tomorrow. I tell you,
Henry, this jarvey will be gone by then. He was that
frightened. Gone, and then you shall never find him."

To Morton's distress she went directly to the door,
opening it like a matador flourishing a cape. "I will re-
serve tomorrow evening for you," she announced. "You
may fetch me directly after my performance and tell me
that I was absolutely right. That this young jarvey did
know something more, and that the death of Mr.
Richard Glendinning, or Halbert, if that was his name,
was suspicious in the extreme."

"But, Arabella . . ."

But Arabella would brook no argument.

She did give in a little as he passed, favouring him
with a most promising kiss—but it was a promise for the
future, not this night.

Morton found himself out on the street, his mood alter-
nating between amusement and chagrin. Arabella
Malibrant had him in thrall, as she did much of London
at the moment. At least he was not alone in his thralldom.

There was nothing for it but to locate this worthless
jarvey and find out why he bolted from Lord Darley's
door—for innocent enough reasons, Morton suspected.
And if he could not find the driver of coach 417 . . . Well,

he did not care to consider the price he would pay for failure.

The mists in the still-dark streets were heavy, and his footfalls echoed dimly in the muffled silence.

He could not go to the Hackney-Coach Office in Essex Street, to find out who held licence number 417, until it opened in the morning. But Morton had an idea that such a visit might not be required. He'd made this kind of enquiry before.

He walked the few blocks to the theatre district, where it took only a moment to locate a familiar coach driver.

"Evening, Willam."

"Evening, Mr. Morton. Where might I carry you, sir?"

"I'm not sure myself. I'm looking for a jarvey who was about in four-seventeen this evening."

The driver nodded and stroked the stubble staining his chin. "Well, Mr. Morton, most of the licences in the low four hundreds be in the hands of innkeeps in the City. Beyond St. Paul's, sir."

"The City it is, Willam," Morton said, tugging open the coach door. The warmth of a bed—first Arabella's and now his own—receded into the cool, distant hours of the morning. Sleep would be brief, if he managed any at all. Morton had an early, and unpleasant, appointment to keep: the hanging of a man and wife.

Finding coach 417 was not as easy a task as Morton had hoped, and, as always, the Londoners' natural suspicion of the police did not help. Finally a stableman Willam knew suggested they try the Scotsman Blenkinsop, proprietor of the Three Georges, Cheapside.

The courtyard of the Three Georges was silent and still when Morton arrived, the shapes of a dozen or so coaches filling most of its dark space. Only a small number would be out at this hour. But those that were would surely be due back soon, to let the day drivers take them.

The Runner found the ostler in the stables, cleaning harness by the dim light of a smoking lantern.

"Four-seventeen?" The wizened little man stood and released a small groan as he bent his spine, his hands pressed into the small of his back. "Oh, aye, Constable. That be one of ours."

"He in yet?"

"Nay. Be the only 'un that ain't. Should be here soon enough, though."

"I'll tarry, then," said Morton. He paid Willam his fare, and, tucking his baton of office into his belt, took a cheroot from his frock-coat pocket. The old ostler bore the lantern over and offered him a light.

"Mind the hay," he muttered as he shuffled back to his task, reseating himself with a sigh. "Come a cropper, has he, our Ralph?"

"Oh, nay," replied the Runner.

The other looked a little disappointed.

"Yorkshireman. Never know wif them, does one?"

Morton blew out a puff of smoke, and nodded sagely. "Not so bad as an Irishman, though," he said.

"Nay," agreed the other readily.

"You know this cully, driving four-seventeen?"

The ostler shook his head. "Keeps to hisself. Know his name, that's all. Ralph Acton."

But time was never to be wasted, so as Morton smoked, flicking his ashes out into the cinder-yard, he kept up an easy conversation with his new inform-ant, while the latter went on with his labour. The stableman's views, the success of the trade he was in, the personalities, the gossip and wrongdoings of his neighbourhood—all were fodder for Henry Morton's casual curiosity, and the other man was glad enough to tell. Most people, the Runner had always noticed, were happy to talk about even the most mundane details of their own lives. What was rare was someone prepared to listen; even a "horney" like Morton would sometimes do.

Perhaps three quarters of an hour passed in this way, before hooves and the rattle of wheels were heard, approaching from the east.

"Here he be, Constable."

Down Lothbury Street now slowly came clopping the tired horse, behind it the dark bulk of the coach, the hunched shape of the driver above.

Morton tossed away his fag end and sauntered out into the yard. The sallow, grey-jacketed man who looked down at him as the coach drew up knew at once what Henry Morton's profession was.

"Coach four-seventeen?"

The jarvey grimaced and jerked his head rudely downward toward the number plate nailed to the side of the carriage.

"Tell us about this gentleman you let down at Portman House, Mayfair, earlier this night."

The man blinked in surprise, then blurted out: "Wot of him? Bilker never paid!"

"The dead are notorious shirkers, Ralph," Morton said dryly.

"He was drunk, is all!" the jarvey protested. His voice had an irritating whine.

"And you didn't stay to collect your fare? Come down here."

"See here, you've no call to—" the driver began to object, but got no further. Morton reached up and jerked the man from his seat by his scruffy lapels and slapped him roughly back against the side of his coach, so that the little vehicle swayed and squeaked on its springs and the horse snorted and shook its harness. But the Runner's voice, when he spoke, was even.

"A dead man was found in your carriage this evening and the circumstances under which he died were not so innocent, now, were they, Ralph Acton?"

The little man began to shake. He kept opening his mouth as though to speak but no words followed.

Well, well, Morton thought.

"Speak up, lad. I'm all that stands between you and a cell at Newgate, for if you're honest with me I'll let you go home this night, and no one will be the wiser. Lie to me, and you'll meet the Magistrate at Bow Street, and then no one will care what happens to you. No one but you. You do care, don't you, Ralph?"

The little driver nodded.

"Good. Now, from where did you fetch him?"

All the coachman's resistance had fled. He gave off, at close range, a sharp, sour stink of unwashed clothes and fear.

"Picked him up in Spitalfields," he wheezed.

"Spitalfields. Where?"

"At the tavern there, in Bell Lane, by the brew'ry."

Henry Morton frowned in surprise. "What—the Otter? That flash house!"

The jarvey mumbled something unintelligible.

"Did you find him up at the Otter?" And Morton gave him another shake. The driver's imperfect memory was beginning to be intriguing.

"Seems so," the coachman muttered. "Appeared a common enough public house to me."

"You know bloody well it's a flash house," observed

Morton. "Or you'd have told me the name straight off. What was the man's condition when he boarded your coach?"

"He was half-seas over. Careens out of that public, and tells me where to take him. Fast as me poor nag can manage."

Morton stared at him thoughtfully a moment more, then released him and stepped back, dusting off his hands a little. Then he put his right hand casually into his frock-coat pocket. The pocket where gentlemen would generally keep their silver.

"So the man was alive . . . ?"

"I told you so, yer honour."

". . . and moving under his own power when he entered your coach?"

The jarvey looked particularly anxious, his eyes on Morton's buried hand. But he answered.

"Happens, maybe, some culls about the Otter helps him out. A bit. He were right cut. But he were sober enough to tell me the address in Mayfair."

"These culls—did they take anything from him?"

"Not as I saw. But they could have done, couldn't they?"

"Who were they?"

The man shrugged, glancing down at the cinders. He was terrified: Morton could see that, but it wasn't Henry Morton that inspired the fear, now. There was something else. Arabella had been right.

"Did you know, Ralph, that someone tried to kill this same gentleman earlier today?"

The jarvey looked up, eyes flaring from fear. He shook his head in denial.

"Why didn't you stay at Portman House?" Morton pressed.

"They was all saying he was dished," said the man. He shrugged. "I thought they might be looking to blame someone...." he said weakly.

"Why would they blame you?"

"That's the way of things, ain't it? Blame the one wot's least able to defend hisself."

The jarvey was keeping something back, but Morton doubted he could be made to tell. There were things in London more frightening than a Bow Street Runner, or even Newgate Prison.

He was satisfied, however, that Acton had only driven Glendinning from Spitalfields to Mayfair. The coachman had no part in whatever had happened—but something had indeed happened.

"Where do you dwell, Ralph Acton?"

Acton hesitated.

"The innkeep knows where to find you, does he?"

The jarvey's shoulders sagged. "Off Cartwright Square," he said. "Up the east alley."

Morton mulled it over a moment more. "What is it you're not telling me, Ralph? You know who these men were?"

"Nay, nay. They were no one to me." The jarvey shifted from foot to foot.

Morton stared hard at the man, but it had only the effect of causing him to shift more rapidly. The Runner drew out his hand, with a single shilling in it, which he turned reflectively in his fingers.

"I will find out what happened to Mr. Glendinning, Ralph, you may be sure of that. Now, you heed me. I'm Henry Morton of Bow Street and I know who you are and where to find you. If any of this proves false you can be sure you'll see me again."

"T'ain't false," said the man, low and bitter.

Henry Morton held out his hand and dropped the coin into Acton's open palm. "No, it isn't all false, that's certain. It's what you aren't telling me, Ralph; that's what worries me. For you know how things work—you said it yourself. If Glendinning didn't die a natural death, they'll be looking for someone to swing for it. If you're hiding as much as I think you are, that could be you, Ralph, for you'll look guilty, won't you? You might wish you'd told me the truth then. Think on it."

Chapter 3

For the second time that morning, Morton set off in search of a hackney-coach, though on this occasion he was perfectly indifferent to any number-plate it might bear. The air, for the time of year, had fallen cool, and the Runner tugged up his collar against the chill. Morton was normally fastidious in his dress, but that morning he had donned a stained and ancient greatcoat that would allow him to escape notice in a crowd. Where he was going, Bow Street Runners weren't welcome.

The hour was not so early that the wheels of commerce hadn't begun to turn, and on Shaftesbury Morton found a hackney-coach disembarking its fare.

"Number four, Bow Street," Morton called out, and settled back in the seat. He closed his eyes and felt that odd sensation, as though sinking, that lack of sleep brought on during moments of respite. He remembered the hackney-coach driver he'd spoken with earlier, and wondered again what Ralph Acton had been hiding.

Morton drifted into an odd dream where he wandered

lost through dim, ruinous alleys, noisome and narrow.
Wraith-like inhabitants lurked silently in the shadows,
eyes sunken and hostile—and fixed on him.

The Runner awoke as the carriage rocked to a stop.
The facade of the Bow Street Magistrate's Court
loomed out of the gloom. A figure loitering on the stair
stepped out into the faint morning light.

"Morton?"

Morton pushed the carriage door open. "Yes, come
along, Jimmy. We've something to see to."

The coach swayed as the newest Bow Street Runner
pulled himself aboard and settled opposite Morton in a
dissonant squeaking of carriage springs. In the faint
light Morton could barely see his young colleague, but
his great bulk could be sensed. Morton rather liked
Jimmy Presley: a costermonger's son, strong as an ox;
someone you'd like to have at your side if things got
roiled. But Jimmy was still finding his way, still coming
to understand he had some decisions to make about the
kind of officer—and the kind of man—he wanted to be.
It was to this end that Morton had arranged their morning's outing.

Presley leaned forward a bit, out of shadow, and in
the soft grey light appeared even younger than his
twenty-some years: broad-faced and boyish.

"Have we a profitable bit of business lined up?" he
asked, and smiled.

"Profitable? Perhaps. But not in the usual sense."

Presley raised an eyebrow.

"Have you ever been to a hanging, Jimmy?"

The young man's voice faltered a little. "Nay, Morton,
I've not. Nor ever wished to."

"Well, that is about to change. We're off to Newgate
to see those sad cullies, the Smeetons, dance on air for

their sins." Morton eyed his companion. "Mr. Townsend did me the favour of taking me to witness the hanging of the first criminals I ever nabbed. 'Best to see what your efforts have wrought, Morton,' he said. 'If you haven't the stomach for it, then you'd better find yourself another trade.' It is a part of your education that I thought George Vaughan might neglect."

Vaughan was another Runner, and apparently Presley's mentor at Bow Street.

Jimmy Presley said nothing, but turned away from Morton, toward the window where the city of London was emerging from the dark of night into the grey of day.

Some distance from Newgate they were forced to continue on foot; the crowds were too thick for the coach to make progress. Morton cast his gaze up at the watery overcast, and wondered if the sky would shed tears for the Smeetons, and any other unfortunates who would come out the "debtors' door" that day.

Morton noticed that Presley carried his baton, the gilt top gleaming in the dull light. "I'd put that out of sight," Morton said, nudging him. The older Runner had his own baton tucked away in a pocket inside his greatcoat.

Presley looked a bit surprised, but slipped his baton into his belt and pulled his coat over it. They jostled their way along Newgate to within sight of the prison. Here the crowd grew very dense, and Morton and Presley had to force their way forward.

"Look to your purse, Jimmy," Morton warned in a low voice.

"Here?" Presley turned toward Morton, wondering if the older Runner was practicing on him.

"Oh, aye. Within sight of the hangman."

A few paces farther on, Jimmy waved a hand down

the street. "Look at them! There must be ten thousand, if there's a man."

"Twenty-five, even thirty thousand, it's said." Morton pointed up Ludgate Hill, past St. Sepulchre's Church. "Not so many years ago they had a panic here—no one knows what set it off—but when all was said and done nigh on thirty people had been trampled to death: men, women, and children. Scores more lay injured. But the very next day the crowds were back—just as large—as though it hadn't happened at all. Oh, they're great admirers of our work, Jimmy."

This did not elicit even a smile from Presley.

Morton nodded to the houses lining the street across from the blind edifice of the prison. There were people sitting high up on the roofs. "Two sovereigns it would cost you for such a view."

"Nay!" Presley protested.

"It's the truth. Three guineas to watch from a window."

Pie-sellers and grog men began their bark, and a low, continuous rumble rose from the crowd pressed into the street before Newgate Prison.

Earlier, dray horses had pulled the wheeled gallows into position and carpenters and their assistants had set the posts in place and erected barriers around the black-draped base.

At a quarter of eight the City Marshall made his slow way on horseback through the pressing masses. Following on foot were the officials of the prison, the court, and the police. Immediately, parents began passing their children forward over the heads of the crowd so that they would be assured of a view.

Morton and Presley were still some way off, but their height allowed them to see. The younger Runner drew a long breath, and looked around, as though searching for a means of escape. It was a cruel thing Morton was doing, dragging this young man to such a spectacle.

The chimes of St. Sepulchre's started to sound the hour, and were answered by the dim ringing of the solitary bell deep within the walls of Newgate. The black debtors' door swung open and a party emerged onto the platform.

"Hats off! Hats off!" people began to cry, not out of respect, Morton knew, but so that no one's view should be blocked.

Before the sombre party came the Ordinary clergyman, in full canonical dress.

"There he is," Morton said softly to Presley. "The man who enriches himself by publishing the *Calendar*." The clergyman used his privileged position to record—or invent—an endless stream of lurid last confessions. "The man in the dandy green jacket is Calcroft, the hangman. See the flower in his buttonhole? He says that as he's not an undertaker he won't dress like one. Oh, he's a rare wit, he is."

People in the crowd began to shout and jeer; Calcroft tipped his hat to them. Behind the hangman came his assistants, conspicuously bearing ropes, then the warders, and between them, heads bowed and hands bound, a man and a woman.

Presley straightened, his attention entirely focused now.

During the brief course of English justice, and the few days of their incarceration, the Smeetons had changed utterly. Where they had been but forty years of age when Morton and Presley apprehended them, they appeared sixty now. They shuffled forward, bent and ruined, faces pale as new-quarried stone. Morton could see the woman's cheeks glisten, but there was no sound of sobbing above the hush of the crowd. The man and woman came before the clergyman—like bride and groom, Morton thought.

Just as the nooses were to be set in place, the man took a step forward and raised his head. Morton saw despair written there, but defiance as well, and anger.

"Here's a pleasant diversion for you," the condemned man hurled out, "watching old Caleb Smeeton and his good wife hang! Thieves, you think us!" He paused and Morton thought the man would break down, but he went on, strangely calm. "But how did those fine Bow Street men know where to nab us? Just where to be, and at what hour? Our 'friends' helped them, now didn't they?" he bitterly answered his own question, and glared out at the crowd. "Friends like *you* . . .

"Aye, one of our own peached on us . . . the same as told us about the panney, and what hour the owner would be away. The friend who said, 'It'll be safe, sure. Take your wife to help! Never mind she don't want to. Take her!' And her a God-fearing woman, who'd ne'er do such a thing for all her life!" He glanced over at her, and she met his eye, tears still slipping silently down her face.

The crowd was hushed as well. This was one of the reasons they came—to hear what the condemned would say, though often they were disappointed and the criminals uttered not a word, or were too distraught to speak. But Caleb Smeeton had a kind of guileless loquacity, and even Morton found himself listening without his usual scepticism.

"A fool they took me for!" Smeeton went on. His head dropped a little. "And a fool I was. But not so simple as I can't see now what was done to me. My so-called friends were closer to Bow Street than to me—" One of the warders had come forward and took hold of the man's arm. As he was pulled back, Smeeton raised his voice for the first time. "Well, take pleasure in your forty pounds, George Vaughan!" he shouted. "And you, lily-white Henry Morton! You murder a virtuous woman to-day! You too, Jimmy Presley, you murdering bastard!"

Morton felt Presley flinch beside him, and heard both their names called out in fury on all sides, mixed in with cries of rage against the hangman and the judges, and, over and over, against the despised Runners from Bow Street. The noose was dropped over Smeeton's head and the crowd boiled in indignation, cursing and shoving the constables who held them back from the gallows. Morton and Presley were pushed and jostled this way and that, as though they stood in a surging surf.

White hoods were drawn over the heads of man and wife; the nooses inspected a final time. The woman collapsed suddenly, her knees giving way, and she was suspended by her neck a moment, before the warders pulled her up. But she was only on her feet an instant before the traps were sprung, and the two figures fell. And hung, silently, side by side.

Presley stood mute, staring raptly at the slowly spinning bodies. It was long over. Morton reached out and tugged his coat sleeve.

"Come along, Jimmy," he said softly, feeling, himself, both sorrow and guilt.

Half-reluctantly, the young man turned away, and they pushed through the crowd, which was suddenly abuzz with chatter, and even laughter. But neither Morton nor Presley shared in this odd sense of release.

They went quite a distance before a hackney-coach presented itself. Morton quietly gave the driver the address of the Bow Street Magistrate's Court, not wanting anyone in the crowd to hear.

The two Runners settled themselves into the poorly padded seats, not saying a word. Morton wondered if Presley was cursing him silently. The young man had pulled his baton from his belt and now sat with it across his knees staring at it quietly.

The older Runner tried to recall what he'd felt toward Townsend the morning they had made this same journey. He'd not felt anger, that was certain, but then he'd respected Townsend enormously, and still did. He wasn't quite sure that Presley held him in the same regard.

The boy had to see it, Morton told himself. This was how the criminal classes were kept in check. And how the Bow Street Runners made their living—from rewards for convictions. And some of those convictions led to hangings—too many, some thought. Not near enough, others insisted.

Presley leaned his head back and closed his eyes. He remained like that for some time, his big hands rising to cover his face a moment, and then falling away.

"It's an ugly business, Jimmy," Morton said solicitously.

"Aye. There they were alive one minute, and dead the next. Limp as rags..."

"I was talking about our business: thief-taking."

Presley reached back and knocked on the small sliding door that separated them from the driver. "I'll step down here!" he called out, and then to Morton, "I'll walk the rest of the way."

Chapter 4

At the Bow Street Magistrate's Court Morton began asking around to discover who had interrupted Glendinning's duel, and was surprised to learn it had been Presley, accompanied by George Vaughan.

Morton found the two Runners with their faces buried in copies of *Hue and Cry* and *The Morning Chronicle*. As he dropped his gilt-topped baton into the umbrella rack beside theirs, the two looked up and nodded.

" 'Tis a leisured life these Runners live," Morton said.

Vaughan dropped his eyes to his reading again. "Don't go spreading it abroad, Mr. Morton. We'll have the gentry in here wanting our places."

"Isn't that the truth, Mr. Vaughan. The envy of the world, we are." Morton sank into a chair and picked up a *Hue and Cry*.

"I hear you took our Mr. Presley out to see a necktie party," Vaughan said from behind his paper blind.

Morton did not respond.

"There's a pair won't be stealing away the living of hard-working shopkeepers," Vaughan went on.

Presley kept his face hidden behind his sheaf of paper.

"No, they won't be doing that," Morton agreed, and glanced at the first page of his own journal. "I hear I missed a show yester morning out on Wormwood Scrubs...?"

Presley let forth a small, forced laugh, looking over at Vaughan, who continued to flip through his paper. "A bit of target practice, was all. Pair o' cullies, though. Couldn't hit the stable door if their lives depended on it! And it cost them dear, didn't it, that little stroll on the grass!" He laughed again, but it sounded forced and artificial. Morton wondered what Vaughan had been saying to the young man.

"Did it?" asked Morton. He had no opportunity to say more, however, as the side door opened and the Chief Magistrate, Sir Nathaniel Conant, strode in, followed by his clerk and several helpers. The early session of Bow Street Police Court had just gone into recess.

But the "beak" wanted to know about the duel, too.

George Vaughan was smoothly reassuring. "No blood spilt, my lord, and no harm done. Mr. Presley and I were on 'em before they'd taken up the matter in earnest."

Sir Nathaniel Conant leveled a hard gaze at the veteran Runner, but the latter met his eye steadily. "I am informed, Mr. Vaughan, that shots were fired."

"Well, sir, if so, it must have happened before we arrived, which I can hardly credit."

The Magistrate scowled as he lowered himself into his seat behind the polished satinwood writing-table, a massive man hunched over a delicate stick of furniture.

"How did you know of it?" he demanded.

"Mr. Presley received a tidy little warning," Vaughan said. "An abigail came by—"

"Who?"

"A lady's maid, my lord. And Mr. Presley took charge of the matter, promptly found me, and was good enough to carry me up to the Scrubs with him. Most commendably direct, he was."

"Who was she?"

Morton caught just a flicker of a glance from Presley to Vaughan before both men shrugged.

"Didn't say," answered Presley. "Nor named who sent her, neither."

"And the principals in this affair were...?" Sir Nathaniel looked from one Runner to the next. "Morton? Were you part of this?"

"Nay," said Henry Morton. "I was in Whitechapel all morning."

"Mr. Vaughan?"

"A Mr. Halbert Glendinning," said Vaughan. "Up against our Colonel Rokeby. Seconds: for Glendinning, a Mr. Hamilton. For Rokeby, his toady-man Pierce, as ever."

While they spoke, Sir Nathaniel's factotums busied themselves about the chamber. Briefs and order papers were stacked in the cabinets lining the wall behind the Magistrate; the wig was lifted discreetly from his head; a goblet of Madeira was decanted and placed comfortably to hand on the table.

He sipped his wine. "This bloody man Rokeby's killed five times; isn't that what's said?"

Morton noticed a look of considerable surprise pass over young Presley's face at this. But then he swiftly composed himself again.

"At least." Morton himself quietly answered the question.

"And you did nothing?"

"We warned 'em very firm, Sir Nathaniel" was Vaughan's ready retort. "I'll warrant they took our meaning, too."

"Oh, aye, I'll warrant they did. I'll warrant there was some handy giving and taking."

Vaughan's eyebrows raised as though this suggestion of impropriety impugned his honour.

Perhaps Sir Nathaniel realised he had overstepped a bound as well. If he was going to make accusations against a Runner they would have to be in a court of enquiry. The Magistrate swallowed again from his glass and one of his assistants whispered urgently in his ear.

Presley caught Morton's eye and with a small grin rubbed his thumb and forefinger together. The little gesture, Morton realised, did not go unnoticed by the portly man seated behind the table, who then returned his attention to the Runners.

"No felony was committed," said Vaughan evenly. "We performed our proper duty."

"What was it over, this duel?" the Magistrate asked, ignoring Vaughan's defense.

"Mere idle talk, sir. Hot words, is all," replied Presley disdainfully, but Vaughan drew himself up and eyed the Magistrate darkly.

Sir Nathaniel Conant regarded him a moment, reflecting. "In future, sir," he said coldly, "when men discharge weapons at one another, you are to arrest them and bring them before this Police Court, as a case of attempted murder. The panel, not you, shall be the judge of the seriousness of the infringement on His Majesty's peace."

"As you say, my lord," drawled George Vaughan.

There was enough defiance in this laconic response to make the Chief Magistrate hesitate an instant, but not quite sufficient to draw him into further confrontation.

"There is a complication," announced Henry Morton. All their eyes went to him. "Last night, the same day as his interrupted duel, Mr. Halbert Glendinning turned up dead."

"Cor!" blurted Jimmy Presley. Sir Nathaniel Conant stared.

"What on earth do you mean, sir, 'turned up dead'?"

"I mean, my lord, that he arrived at a social function in a hackney-coach, and he was dead when the footman opened the door."

George Vaughan cleared his throat. "I heard he was drunk. Choked on his own puke."

It was now the turn of the other three to look in surprise at him.

"You know of this, too?" demanded Sir Nathaniel.

"Town's full of it, my lord. I had it from an informant of mine—member of the serving class, but reliable."

"Was this person there?"

"Spoke to one who was, appears."

"I admire my brother officer's sources," remarked Henry Morton a bit sourly, "but I was in Portman House last night myself, and I am less certain the man's death was natural."

George Vaughan looked at him wordlessly, but it was evident to Morton that the man was far from pleased to be contradicted. Nor was this the first time the two of them had been at odds.

"Why?" demanded Sir Nathaniel Conant.

"There are several suspicious circumstances," Morton replied. "He had not choked on his vomit, as his mouth and throat were clear of it. He was young and in apparent good health. But more to the point, not only had someone aimed to kill him earlier that morning—our notorious Colonel Rokeby—but he had come to Portman House from one of the worst criminal dens in London. I tracked down the hackney-coach driver who brought him, and the man was frightened out of his wits. Something transpired at this flash house, and I think the driver knows or suspects something of it. I gave him a bit of time to mull it over."

"Which flash house was this?" grunted the Chief Magistrate.

"The Otter House, Bell Lane, Spitalfields. I think there should be an investigation, my lord, and the coroner called in to authorize a postmortem examination."

Sir Nathaniel scowled in distaste. "And what is it you think happened to him, Mr. Morton?"

"I am not sure, sir, but it seems very likely he was murdered, and it would not be difficult to guess who had this done."

The Magistrate eyed him. "Have you a witness?"

"I have not. Not yet."

Sir Nathaniel shook his head. "A man who frequents a house like that," he remarked, "courts such a fate. And perhaps deserves it."

"Lord Arthur Darley, his host, assured me that Glendinning was a man of modest deportment, and excellent character, not given to such . . . practices. The body, incidentally, lies at his house for the moment. I asked him to wait upon our warrant."

"What are you suggesting we do?" Sir Nathaniel demanded impatiently.

Morton drew breath. "I would like to have Sir Benjamin—"

"Oh, your precious Brodie, again," scoffed Vaughan with a glance at the ceiling.

Sir Benjamin Brodie was undoubtedly England's foremost, indeed single, expert on poisons, and had lectured on the subject with great authority in London, as well as at Cambridge. But Henry Morton was the only man at Bow Street who believed that such knowledge could be of use in police detection, and Sir Nathaniel had had only too much experience with the fate of Morton's supposed "evidence" at Sessions Court. Never once had their lordships accepted it, and he'd had to listen to many a stern lecture on its inadmissibility. The simple truth was that there was no reliable test for the presence of even a single kind of poison in a dead body. Quack chemists had completely muddied the waters, rendering any such claims doubtful. Convictions were only ever obtained with direct, corroborating testimony.

"Spare me your alchemical lore, Mr. Morton," the Chief Magistrate told him.

"The death was suspicious," repeated Henry Morton.

As Sir Nathaniel Conant mused, his glance shifted from Morton to Vaughan to Presley. The impression came unbidden into Morton's mind that there was something more than he entirely grasped going on amongst the people in this little room. But he was far from understanding what it was. An intuition, a vague feeling, was all he had.

"Very well," decided the Chief Magistrate. "I will summon Sir Charles Carey and we'll go to Portman House together to view the remains, after I adjourn my court for midday. Send word to Lord Arthur not to

make any arrangements until our arrival. We shall need
to speak with the man's family. Offer my condolences
and ask if they would wait upon us there at, what? Half
noon?"

Morton dipped his head in acquiescence. The Magistrate moved on to another topic.

"The matter of the two Smeeton miscreants...went
off duly?"

A curious way to ask if being suspended by a rope
around the neck had had its usual effect, Morton
thought.

"It went off..." he answered bleakly.

"There was some difficulty?" asked Sir Nathaniel, in
response to Morton's unspoken reservation.

"The condemned man made certain accusations from
the scaffold."

George Vaughan released a snort of contemptuous
laughter, but Morton noticed that Jimmy Presley only
looked rather pale.

"It is hardly the first time," remarked the Chief Magistrate.

"He named the officers of police involved in his capture," went on Henry Morton. "He accused us of profit-
ing from his death and his wife's, of bringing them
about, even, for our own gain. He cursed us and claimed
that his wife was innocent—"

"Innocent!" scoffed George Vaughan.

"The populace seems to be predisposed to listening to
such cant," Sir Nathaniel said. "But we have our duties
to attend to."

Morton joined in the little chorus of agreement. But
then, as they all began to rise and reach for their hats, he
said: "I should say, Sir Nathaniel, the hostility toward us
is strong this time. Decent and respectable common-folk

are angry, and this makes the rabble bold. I caution you, Mr. Vaughan, Mr. Presley: We should be on our guard."

George Vaughan shook his head. "You be on your guard, Mr. Morton, if you think you have reason," he said. "I have none."

Chapter 5

Jimmy Presley came up beside Morton as he stood at the little writing-stand in the Public Office antechamber, drafting his note to Lord Arthur Darley.

"So," the younger man said with an effort at carelessness, "Mr. Vaughan tells me that every fumbler who meets the hangman claims his innocence and blames us."

"Well, Jimmy, that's not precisely true," responded Henry Morton sympathetically, setting down his quill and reaching for the blotter. Presley stared in a distracted way out the latticed window onto Bow Street.

"They're always innocent when they're in the dock at the Old Bailey, of course. But by the time they come out the debtors' door, it's often a different matter. I've only heard of accusations like Smeeton's once or twice before."

"But now the people believe they really were. Innocent."

The great roar of disapproval and anger came back into Morton's ears, the heated words flung out, the red faces of the men surging against the barricade below the scaffold. He looked thoughtfully at his young colleague for a moment, and then went back to his writing.

"Ah, well, Jimmy," he remarked evenly. "Maybe George Vaughan's right. A man's not for this calling if he gives a fig what 'the rabble' believe."

But the young man looked distinctly unhappy anyway, so Morton went on.

"You and Vaughan had the Smeetons dead cold to rights. They were seen on the premises the day before the robbery, looking it over. They turned up at the place right on time in the middle of the night, jemmy and skeleton keys to hand, and they used them. As neat and tight a case as you'll get in a year."

"Then why didn't the people see that...that there was nothing else to be done?" Presley couldn't quite name the thing he had so recently had a part in bringing to pass.

"The people, as you style them, really aren't very fond of us, Jimmy, let's be plain about that. They don't like the police system, and they especially don't like the Bow Street Runners." Morton smiled a little. "They'd rather live in a green and pleasant England where the constables are all unpaid, and where stout yeomen seize upon malefactors and are only incidentally rewarded for their efforts. Unexpectedly, as it were, and all the while blushing and pulling their forelock and saying they'd have done it anyway, m'lord, reward or no. I can't really blame them. I'd like to live in an England like that, too. Better still, why not an England where there are no thieves like the Smeetons? No murderers. No whores or vagrants. And no need for police, either."

Presley grimaced, and slapped his newly acquired baton restlessly against his gloved hand, saying nothing.

"I've noticed that people don't mind when the navy men get their bounty for the French ships they capture," Morton went on. "They're heroes. But when a Bow Street man gets his pittance for gaining the conviction of a proven criminal, that's 'blood money.' How often have you heard it said that we'll chase a man into the City and nab him there where the rewards are greater? Some days I think there's more sympathy out there for the flash crowd, Jimmy, than there is for you and me—until a man gets robbed. Then he'll speak to us a little more respectfully—at least for a day or two." Morton stopped. His resentment on this subject was like to get out of hand, and Presley didn't look as though he were listening.

"But, Morton, there *was just* something about the way..." It came out in a little rush, and then the young man paused, as if suddenly aware of the implications of what he was saying. "About the way we caught 'em," he finished, very low.

Morton felt a slight tickle run down his spine, and he turned to look hard at his companion.

"It was just so... neat, how we knew exactly," Presley murmured. "Exactly where and when to find them, and exactly what they were going to steal."

"Your peacher told you all that, didn't he? Where would we be without our informants?"

And of course, those informants got paid, too.

"He wasn't my peacher," confessed Presley unhappily. "I'd never met him before that night, I mean, the night when you and I nabbed the Smeetons. In fact, I've never met him, ever."

Morton stared. If Jimmy Presley hadn't helped develop the information that led to the arrest, he didn't deserve any more of the credit—or the reward money—

than Morton himself did. But Presley and George Vaughan had received seventy pounds each. Morton was given only twenty, for participating in the final arrest.

"Vaughan let them believe I was part of it, so that I would get the appointment to be a Runner. He and I were friendly-like, when I was in the Worship Street Patrole, and he said he wanted to have me as his brother officer. He told me, after, what to testify."

Morton considered carefully. As his own role in the matter had been limited, he had not attended much of the Smeetons' trial. He had never heard the testimony of the two other Runners on the subject of their informant. But, really, the informant was hardly crucial; the panel, for example, was unlikely to insist that his or her identity be revealed. The Smeetons had already broken into the draper's shop when he and Presley moved in. Someone had betrayed them, sure enough, but that was as common as theft itself in this city. It was their bad luck that they couldn't trust their underworld friends, and that the owners of the shop they'd chosen to burgle belonged to a prosecution society, so that the rewards offered were substantial enough to make it worth extra effort on the part of an officer like Vaughan.

"George Vaughan just told me he had this peacher," Presley went on in a numb voice, "and he told me where and when I was to show up and arrest them."

"Well, that's normal enough, Jimmy. But you're mad to testify to something—anything—in a law court that you don't know to be true yourself. They'll give you a rope of your own for that."

Presley nodded miserably. "Aye, aye. But it was just to be this one time, so that I would get the appointment."

"Well, in any case," Morton's voice relaxed, "the

information Vaughan gave you was correct. He wanted you to have the chance to perform the arrest, and I happened to be in the Office that evening, so we did it together."

"Nay, not exactly." And Presley, looking wretched, seemed to turn a shade paler. "You see, Morton, hearing what that cull said...up there, has made me turn it all over in my mind again."

"What do you mean, not exactly?"

"I asked George Vaughan to come with me, to make the arrest. Two officers, you need two officers. Isn't that normal?"

Morton nodded, watching him steadily.

"But George Vaughan didn't want to do it. He says, 'No, you go by Bow Street before and get Sir Galahad there, and take him.'"

"Sir Galahad," murmured Morton bleakly.

"You, Morton. I suppose you know that's what he calls you. And he knew you were at Bow Street. Then he says, in a voice as if he wasn't talking directly to me, or really, as if he didn't care if I heard, he says, 'They'll never doubt *him*.'"

"And what," said Morton, rather coldly now, leaning back and regarding him, "did you think that meant, Jimmy?"

Presley avoided his gaze, and looked again out the window. "Some sort of a joke between you, I suppose," he muttered. "That's what I thought then."

"And what do you think now?"

"I don't know."

They both stood silent, rapt in very different trains of thought. Henry Morton was remembering the night of the Smeetons' arrest. Why indeed had he been at Bow Street? Was it not some tip, now that he thought on it,

that Vaughan had casually given him? The chance of a
rich piece of work from some wealthy barrister, who
was supposed to be coming to the Office to hire a Runner? The barrister had never appeared, but the Smeeton
matter had turned up instead, to the solid benefit of his
pocket. Morton saw now that something he had been
avoiding, something he had not even really admitted to
himself he was trying to avoid, was in a fair way to becoming unavoidable.

He had never doubted that George Vaughan, like
quite a few other Bow Street men over the years, took
more money for his services than the statutes specified.
That he took bribes, and favours from low women, and
had disreputable friends among the flash crowd he was
supposed to be policing, Morton had long assumed. But
what was emerging in Presley's account was something
more, something on rather a larger and uglier scale.

Presley looked up at him now, appealed to him,
Morton thought.

"Take heed, Jimmy," he finally replied, low and full of
meaning. The other stared back at him, his face working
with suppressed feeling.

"There's nothing to be done now about the Smeetons,
that's sure," Morton continued. "But it's time for you to
do some thinking. Men like George Vaughan might
dance a fine jig on the right side of the law, thinking
they'll never misstep, but if Sir Nathaniel ever gets
proof of it, Vaughan'll be dancing at Beilby's Ball instead. And I'll tell you this, George Vaughan will throw
them anyone he can to save his own neck. Don't let that
be you, Jimmy. I'd hate to see that. I'd regret it more
than I can say."

Chapter 6

When Morton boarded Sir Nathaniel's carriage the Chief Magistrate nodded to him over the edge of a neatly folded newspaper.

"We are without the coroner, I see," Morton observed.

"We shall collect Sir Charles as we go." Sir Nathaniel turned his attention away from his reading, letting the paper drop, then striking it once with the backs of his fingers. "Have you seen what Peel has to say of us, Mr. Morton?"

The thief-taker shook his head.

Sir Nathaniel lifted the paper. "Before Parliament yesterday. The Runners are, and I quote, 'a closely knit caste of speculators in the detection of crime, self-seeking and unscrupulous.' He admits that they are sometimes 'daring and efficient,' but *only* 'when it coincides with their private interest.'" He let the paper drop again. "Mark me, Mr. Morton, we shall see an end to the present system of rewards and incentives, and sooner than some might wish. I for one have wearied of defending the reputations of my Runners." He shook the paper once. "And while *this* is being spoken in Parliament, we have Mr. Vaughan and Jimmy Presley out proving that Mr. Peel is right on every count!"

Sir Nathaniel turned his attention to the passing scene. The sunlight falling into the carriage illuminated the Magistrate's long, pale hands, still clutched tightly around the morning news. After a moment he turned back to Morton. "I regard you as a person of principle, Mr. Morton, and I'll not say that for all your colleagues. You're an adept at your profession, yet I'd like to believe you take no more than is your due for it."

"I thank you for your confidence," murmured the Runner.

"You and your comrades have interrupted affairs of honour before?"

"Many times."

"Then tell me, sir, how much does it cost a man to fight a duel in the environs of London and not find himself before a panel of Magistrates?"

Morton smiled a bitter inward smile, though he regarded his superior with a level gaze. How much, indeed. Who was doing the dueling? Who was doing the arresting?

The Chief Magistrate had been in his position at Bow Street for a little more than a year. He would stay perhaps another year or two, and then go on to another government appointment, courtesy of some other well-connected friend. Henry Morton would work with men like George Vaughan and Jimmy Presley all his life.

Did Sir Nathaniel realise what he was asking of Morton?

"Whenever I've interrupted a duel, sir, I've brought the principals before my Magistrate, you may be sure. But occasionally we do find that reconciliations have occurred before our arrival. Perhaps apologies have been tendered. Gentlemen do occasionally resort to their own better instincts. In such cases a warning is all that's required—indeed, there is little more we can do."

Sir Nathaniel gazed at him for a moment, shook his head, and leaned back in his seat.

"Very well, Mr. Morton," he replied coldly.

Sir Charles Carey, the coroner, was waiting for Sir Nathaniel and Morton on his front step and they went directly on to Portman House. After they had viewed the body in the small sitting-room, Lord Arthur Darley introduced them to Sir William and Lady Caroline Glendinning in his library. The dead man's parents were already dressed in silken mourning suits, cut to a style of the last century more commonly glimpsed now in the country than in London. Both had powdered hair. They sat on Lord Arthur's elegant sabre-leg chairs with a rigidity that Morton guessed reflected both repressed grief and a deep distaste for the conversation they were about to endure.

"I'm sure that the gentlemen from Bow Street do not require Lady Caroline's attendance," murmured Darley in considerate tones.

"Thank you, Lord Arthur," she replied, "but I will stay."

Sir Nathaniel cleared his throat.

"The question before us is whether or not my officers should be directed to make further enquiry into this un-happy event." Sir Nathaniel glanced at Morton. "It is Mr. Morton's opinion that your son's death is of a some-what...anomalous nature. His whereabouts before his arrival at this house last night are...uncertain, the causes of mortality...imperfectly understood."

Morton could see the effect of these words on Lady Caroline. It was the first she had heard of such things, he felt sure.

Lady Caroline raised a handkerchief to her mouth. "But what are you suggesting?"

"Only that the matter might bear looking into," Sir Nathaniel said.

"I do not mean to distress you, Lady Caroline," Morton said, fearing Sir Nathaniel was being too delicate. He addressed both parents. "I'm quite certain we know where your son was before he took a carriage for Portman House, and it was a particularly notorious criminal den, where—"

"How can that be, sir?" Sir William interjected. "What are you suggesting about my son? That he consorted with criminals?" Like his wife, he had a faint north country or Scots accent.

"Indeed not, sir. Your son is said to have been a man of character. That is why I have suggested we look into this matter a little more. What was Mr. Glendinning doing in such a place just before his end? And what might have happened to him there?"

"You are very certainly misinformed, sir!" Sir William cried. "My son was a gentleman. A man of letters. Not an habitué of low houses."

Morton started to respond, but Sir Nathaniel cut him off with a gesture. "Your son's character is not in question, Sir William, let me assure you. But it *is* very suspicious that he fought a duel in the morning and...died later the same day."

"His honour had been impugned and he defended it,"

Sir William said, drawing himself up a little, proud of his son. "His untimely passing was a sad coincidence. Nothing more."

"Perhaps," agreed Sir Nathaniel, "but we do not know what caused this untimely passing."

"I have spoken to the surgeon who attended poor Halbert upon his arrival here, and I am satisfied that there was nothing untoward about his death. His constitution was ever delicate," Sir William said. The pride disappeared from his face, however, and he slumped down a little. His wife reached out and gently placed her small hand over his.

Their son was dissolute, that is what they believed, Morton realised. They thought he'd drunk himself to death in a bawdy house, and they wanted it to go no further.

"Sir," Morton said. "I was present at the time of this surgeon's examination and can tell you that it was less than thorough. Your son did not choke. I am quite sure of it. A proper examination might tell us the cause...of this unfortunate event."

"Such a thing hardly seems necessary, Mr. Morton," Sir Charles Carey interjected, "if, as you admit, a medical man has seen to it already. You are hardly qualified to overrule him."

Lady Caroline gave the coroner a sad look of gratitude.

Morton felt his anger rising. The Glendinnings did not want their son's name sullied. And bloody Sir Charles did not want to commission an autopsy and risk finding nothing—in which case the King's Bench might refuse to pay the fee, leaving Sir Charles to cover it himself. He and Morton had fought this battle before.

Morton made an effort to keep his eyes straight ahead

and his voice level. "It is, Sir Charles, the Chief Magistrate's decision to make."

For the first time Sir William looked straight at Morton. His voice was icily deliberate.

"I know you, fellow, for what you are. You seek to profit from my son's death. And if there were no crime, where would you find your thirty pieces of silver?"

He looked back to Sir Nathaniel.

"There will be no investigation, sir. Lady Caroline and the rest of my family have suffered enough. I forbid it."

"You will pardon me, Sir William, but in cases of possible felony—"

"I forbid it! I will not cooperate with it. I will not prosecute it, even if you produce a case. There was no felony, and your little flock of carrion-crows will not pick over my son's good name to the benefit of their pockets!"

He rose quite suddenly, drawing up his wife after him, and with her leaning on his arm, they went out.

The four remaining looked one to the other as Morton seethed inwardly. *Thirty pieces of silver!* That the man who risked getting his skull cracked in parts of London these people had never seen should get slapped across the face with such an insult...! And by a man who had achieved his place in the world by being born under the right blanket!

"Mr. Morton," Darley said quietly. "Are you so sure?"

Morton scowled and nodded. "I spoke with the driver of the coach who brought Glendinning here. Mrs. Malibrant's intuition was correct. Something untoward happened. I am certain of it."

He noticed Sir Nathaniel staring at him thoughtfully at that moment, and did not like what he read into that gaze. Doubt. Doubt that Morton himself had

contributed to in the carriage on their way here. And
that Sir William's accusation had only encouraged.

"Lord Arthur," the Magistrate said, bowing to Darley.

Out on the walk, as they awaited their carriage, Sir
Charles Carey turned on Morton.

"You know perfectly well, Mr. Morton, that the lords
of the King's Bench do not approve of idle inquests!"

"I saw that man within a quarter hour of his death,
sir, and he did not die of choking."

"A doctor examined him before you, sir," the coroner
fumed. "And you would have me hire another to draw
the same conclusion. I will not do it."

"So it is about *your* expenses, is that it?"

Sir Charles balled his hands up into tight little fists
and his face turned suddenly red. "And can you guaran-
tee me, sir, that at the end of quarter sessions I will be re-
imbursed for the expense of hiring a surgeon? No, sir,
you cannot. The Chief Justice will scrawl *needless* over
the writ, and I shall be out of pocket every shilling of it.
Would you care to pay for it yourself?"

"Gentlemen, enough!" Sir Nathaniel glared at his two
companions until they fell silent. Then he said: "There
will be no inquest, and no investigation of this death."

The two men looked at him, their expressions in stark
contrast.

"You have no evidence, Mr. Morton. Glendinning's
constitution was delicate, he drank too much, perhaps
in reaction to the earlier events of the day, and he died. If
we investigated every man who died of drink in London
we should do little else. No, we will chase this no further. His family have sorrow enough."

"They are trying to protect his character," objected

Morton. "They don't want it known that he was at the Otter—"

"That is probably so," Sir Nathaniel interrupted. "Would you? I expect their fine Halbert was something of a bounder. It is enough that they shall have to live with this knowledge; there is little need for the world to know."

Their carriage drew up and Carey climbed in, smiling in triumph.

"Nonetheless, I think a brief visit to—"

"You shall do nothing of the sort, Mr. Morton! That is all I have to say on the matter, sir. Devote your energies to that theft of antiquities from Burlington House."

Morton's impatience with the previous interview boiled over, and he replied with poorly judged asperity.

"There is no point in any further investigation into that particular matter. The thieves have the goods secured. As I have explained before, there are very few ways for them to make a profit on such unusual material. They, or their fence, will have to sell it back to the owner. There is nothing for us to do but wait for them to make contact, place a notice in the newspaper, or use some other familiar device. I have no appetite for more fruitless digging in the cold ashes of this crime."

It was the second time that day Morton had refused to cooperate with his Magistrate. Sir Nathaniel turned on him.

"You have no appetite for it? You will develop the taste, sir, and I'll thank you not to speak back to me in this manner!"

Sir Nathaniel climbed into the carriage beside Sir Charles and pulled the door sharply closed behind him, leaving Morton standing by the kerb as the coach jounced once, then went deliberately on its way.

Chapter 7

You may begin by admitting I was right," Arabella said as she caught sight of Morton in her mirror. He had just let himself into her dressing cabinet backstage at the Drury Lane Theatre. She continued applying her face powder with studied care.

"You were undoubtedly right, Mrs. Malibrant," Morton said mildly. "About what, pray?"

Arabella smiled, but then recomposed her face. "Do not try your charm on me, Henry Morton. You doubted me, and should not have. Is that not what you have come to say?"

"I never doubted you for a moment," Morton said, pulling up a joint-stool. "You are never wrong. Not even the time you had me nab the footman for stealing Lady Ellington's bracelet. He just did not have it in his possession at that moment—or ever, if my memory serves."

"I do not claim always to be right," she said, crinkling up her brow.

Morton laughed. "Nor do you ever admit to being

wrong, but in this case, my dear, I believe you were right. Though no one but you and me seems to believe it."

"And why is that?"

"I don't know. I told them that I had it on good authority from Mrs. Arabella Malibrant, but they seemed not to care. I was somewhat taken aback."

Arabella's frame of mind had apparently improved, and she only made a little grimace in response to this sally. "I hope you challenged them all to duels. Who were these doubters, pray?"

"Halbert Glendinning's parents, Sir William and Lady Caroline; my Magistrate, Sir Nathaniel Conant; the coroner, the ever-worthless Sir Charles Carey. I am not even certain your Lord Arthur believes me."

"Oh, he is not mine," Arabella said quickly. For a moment she concentrated on her eyebrows.

Morton watched the transformation. He always marveled that what looked so garish up close became something quite ethereal at a distance.

"Do you know," she said, sitting back and examining her efforts with a critical eye, "they used to whiten the face with lead powder, but now folk say it is poisonous and like to kill you. Do you think we could convince Mrs. Siddons to try it?"

"Certainly she is no rival to you."

"Hmm," Arabella responded, beginning now on her lips. "It was Rokeby, of course," she said.

"Who had everyone using lead powder?"

"Who killed Glendinning. Or had him killed."

"He is the obvious choice," Morton agreed, "if Glendinning was indeed killed."

"He was. Rokeby is a rogue, and a murderer, too. I wish someone would shoot him, but he seems to shoot them all first. Could you not shoot him, Henry?"

Why this sudden antipathy toward Rokeby, he wondered. "Officers of police are not allowed to duel. It is illegal, if you remember."

She raised her eyebrows, angled her face this way and that, and then turned in her chair to look at Morton. "You look worried, Henry. What is it?"

"It is something Jimmy Presley said to me this morning. Do you remember the Smeetons?" He proceeded to relate his conversation with the younger Runner, and then what he'd learned from the jarvey, and lastly the interview with the Glendinnings and his altercation with Sir Nathaniel.

"Why is this affair with George Vaughan any concern of yours? If he is corrupt, what of it? It is not for you to police your fellow officers, surely."

Morton drew a long breath. Arabella was not one for taking on the responsibilities of the world. Let others worry about their own transgressions, or the sins of their brothers. Arabella was only concerned if such sins touched her or someone of her circle. Beyond that the world might cheerfully annihilate itself, Morton was sure.

"What is it Rokeby has done to you, my dear?" Morton asked on impulse.

"Me? Nothing. I should never be so foolish as to succumb to such calculated charms. But I know several women—I cannot name them—toward whom he has been most cavalier. If no man can shoot him I might have to do it myself."

"He would not duel with a woman."

"Oh, I would not use anything so crude as a firearm," she answered sharply.

Morton smiled and shook his head. "The formidable Mrs. Malibrant."

"Why, so I am. But I *am* surprised to see you here this evening."

Morton did not like the sound of this, nor the tone. "You promised this night to me," he said, his suspicions growing in spite of himself.

"Tomorrow night, Henry. I am otherwise committed this night."

"I'm quite sure we agreed to this night."

She knew his memory was almost infallible. Morton was somewhat famous for it in police circles.

"Could I have misspoken myself?" she asked innocently. "Well, let us not make a Trafalgar of it. Tomorrow night I will pledge to you. No, truly, Morton. Don't look at me so."

Morton continued to look at her just so.

"Very well, I confess. I committed myself to two engagements on the same evening. It was a mistake honestly and innocently made. A lapse of memory—not everyone's is so perfect as yours."

"Lord Arthur?"

She nodded sheepishly.

"Is he not married?"

"In name only—his wife lives in the country. Their children are grown. Now, Henry, you know we have always agreed..."

Morton held up both his hands, rising to his full height. "Do not waste this soliloquy on me, who knows it by heart."

But the room was small and she put herself between Morton and the door, her absurdly made-up face close to his, green eyes gazing out from a field of cool, white Lille powder.

"Tomorrow night I promise to you—no, Henry, I promise. And there will be no mistakes." She watched his face to gauge the effect of her pledge. "Now don't go running off—I have something for you." She searched around her table and finally produced a leather-bound volume.

"There; by your pugilistic friend, Byron."

"Hardly a friend," Morton protested weakly, too aware that she patronised him. It was the new book, *Hebrew Melodies*.

She pressed it into his hands, and he felt his fingers close around the smooth calfskin. New volumes of poetry were rare, and expensive, pleasures.

"Will you stay for the performance?" she asked softly.

Morton wondered if anyone ever refused the wilful Arabella.

"Through the first act, at least."

"Well, come see me then and we can visit until curtain call."

There was a knock on her door just then—alerting Arabella to her entrance. She leaned forward to kiss Henry, remembered her face paint, and smiled as only Arabella could. Then she was out the door and hurrying off to her assignation with a full house of admirers.

Morton looked down at the book in his hands, opened it to the title page, and there, in a fine, legible hand, found:

> *To Mrs. Malibrant:*
> *Whom I have long admired from afar.*
> > > > *Byron*

Morton laughed. He could do nothing else.

Chapter 8

Morton sat reading Byron's newest work, though his concentration flagged. Not enough sleep the previous night, what with Arabella sending him off to find that worthless jarvey. And then her "forgetting" all about their engagement. She hadn't forgotten at all, she'd just had a more interesting offer. Why did he even...?

But there were reasons.

He sighed and tossed down the poems, picking up the morning *Times* again and running his eye down the close columns of advertisements. Had he simply missed the inevitable little notice that indicated the thieves of Lord Elgin's antiquities were prepared to sell them back to their owner? At least he'd have that to lay at Sir Nathaniel's feet.

Not that the swag was very much: a few scraps of carved marble pilfered from the casually guarded heaps of the stuff in and about a shed in the inner courtyard of Burlington House. Elgin's supposedly magnificent collection, shipped back from Greece, was gathering dust there as the government tried to decide whether to purchase it and thus whether—and this was much worse from the point of view of those parsimonious gentry—to spend the money to build a proper museum to house it. A British Museum. What an extravagance.

Sir Nathaniel Conant was, by and large, a man Morton esteemed. He was perhaps a bit naive in the ways of the criminal classes, but he would learn—if he stayed at Bow Street long enough. It bothered Morton to have offended him, and he rather badly wanted to make it right.

Despite combing the columns twice, Morton found no reference to the missing marbles. In disgust, he opened the paper to news of the more common variety. That fraud Mesmer had died, apparently. *"The discoverer of animal magnetism,"* the editor named him. Morton snorted. He'd thought the man dead for years, so obscure had the once-celebrated doctor become.

Inevitably he found his way to the accounts of Wellington's army and the looming conflict on the continent. The reports were several days out of date, of course; news from Belgium and France never appeared less than three or four days after the events. The *Times,* however, was usually fairly reliable and gathered information from disparate sources.

The foreign news was gathered under various headings. DUTCH MAIL, or FLANDERS PAPERS. Official accounts invariably appeared under the headings WAR DEPARTMENT or OFFICIAL BULLETIN, the latter sometimes subtitled "Downing Street." Nothing new here.

But under the banner FRENCH MAIL Morton found a brief item originating from Paris regarding "the Emperor" (the *Times* itself, unlike its continental correspondents, never honoured him with this title but always called him "Buonaparte"). *"It is creditably believed that the Emperor left Paris on June 12 ..."* Morton read, and then paused.

Everyone knew that the allies were gathering their armies for a thrust into France, and here was Napoleon leaving Paris, perhaps for Ostend, it was speculated. Morton felt a small, cold wave of apprehension wash through him. What if "the Emperor" had no intention of waiting for the allies to combine their forces?

But obviously Wellington would have better intelligence than the *Times,* Morton thought, and turned his attention back to the paper, poring over the various reports.

As he read, his manservant Wilkes slipped into the room, collecting the remains of Morton's tea. Wilkes had been rescued by Morton little more than a year ago. For many years he had served in a prominent household, but then had developed a noticeable shake in his hands—the palsy, it was feared. Morton had taken him on out of kindness. But there was also a part of the Runner—a part he was not unaware of—which took some satisfaction in employing as a gentleman's gentleman a man who had served an earl. Morton himself was only a "ha'penny gentleman," someone who wasn't born to the life, but used his barely adequate income to keep up the appearance.

Fortunately Wilkes's condition had not seemed to worsen with time, and though he did break a bit of glassware now and then, Morton found him otherwise beyond criticism. And he learned a great deal from Wilkes, a great deal about gentlemen and their habits—not all of it flattering. Which also rather pleased him, in a different way.

He and the old man had developed an odd...

friendship. Morton could think of no other word for it.
They had come to like each other. They did not, after all,
have class standing between them.

Which is why Wilkes could say, as he did now, "You
look troubled, sir."

"Do I?" Morton asked, then let the paper fall. "Yes.
Yes, I suppose I am." He gestured to a chair. "Have I
spoken to you about George Vaughan?"

"A fellow Bow Street man?"

"Yes." And Morton found himself repeating the concerns he had earlier shared with Arabella. His manservant's response was rather more satisfactory.

"You think this man Vaughan corrupt, sir," Wilkes
concluded.

"Oh, yes, he's corrupt. But I would have said only
in the manner and degree of his time. What Jimmy
Presley's story suggests is something more."

"Perhaps you should speak to Sir Nathaniel."

"Yes, I likely should. Though do not forget that young
Jimmy Presley was also involved—as was I, for that matter, for Jimmy and I made the arrest. It was all very tidily
arranged." Morton shook his head. "I doubt we could
make a case of it. I'm sure Vaughan could produce someone claiming to be his informant in the matter, and who
could gainsay him? Certainly not the Smeetons, that is
certain. No, if Vaughan did arrange the whole thing he
managed it carefully. And Jimmy Presley might be in
more trouble than Vaughan—after all, he swore to things
of which he had no direct knowledge."

As Morton gazed down into the rain-washed street
below, the old man asked: "And this other matter, sir—
of the young man who was killed?"

"I don't know for certain that he was murdered, but
there is something very odd there."

"What does Lord Arthur Darley think?"

"Why do you ask?"

"He is an astute man."

"Do you know him?"

"I know of him, sir. He is a man of parts, they say. He is well respected."

Morton sipped his port. "What else can you tell me?"

"He is the younger son of the Earl of Cardiff. Served in the Home Office for a time, if memory does not fail me. A brother made the ultimate sacrifice at the Battle of the Nile. The present earl, Lord Arthur's older brother, is a buffoon whom Lord Arthur keeps afloat. Lord Arthur is a man known for his loyalty. His acquaintance is broad, though his sympathies lie with the artistic set. Frequents the theatre. The opera. Can shoot, ride to the hounds, and play the violin."

"A man of parts," Morton agreed. Darley sounded a little too much to be true. "You don't know the Glendinning family, by chance?"

Wilkes shook his head. "I'm sorry, sir."

Morton gazed out the window again, over the glistening peaks of the houses opposite. Somewhere beyond, across the Channel, Wellington was seeking Bonaparte on the fields of France. It made everything else seem inconsequential. If Bonaparte could defeat the armies of Britain and Prussia... Well, there might be a need for another battle of Trafalgar, and there was no longer a Nelson to fight it. How much would the death of Halbert Glendinning mean then?

There was a light tapping from beyond the door, and Wilkes rose immediately to see who it might be.

Every Bow Street Runner had his own corps of informants, and it had taken the old man a while to get used to the people who appeared at Morton's door of an evening. Every kind of riffraff they must have seemed to his eye, always with some unsavoury secret to disclose or comrade to betray. Such folk must have called rather infrequently on his previous master. Wilkes watched over Morton's silver with a certain fixity whenever they appeared.

But Henry Morton had chosen his lodgings in Rupert Street exactly with his informants in mind. Comprising the upper floor of a rambling wooden structure, a former inn from Jacobean times, the rooms were eccentric and unfashionable, but private. While his front doorway was guarded by his suspicious landlady, he also had a more secluded entrance, up two flights of outside stairs from a back lane. Mind you, it was not just peachers who ascended these stairs. Arabella or, be it admitted, her predecessors often came up the same way.

Neither the landlady nor her porter and other servants in the lower regions of the house had ever discovered Morton's occupation. As someone who bore at least the appearance of a gentleman, and could pay a gentleman's rent, it was not necessary that he have an occupation at all. Only Wilkes was familiar with the visitors his master entertained.

Now the manservant reappeared at the sitting-room door.

"One of my saunterers, Wilkes?" asked Morton.

"Not at all, sir. It is a lady." The old man's voice had taken on a suitably grave tone. Clearly, this was a respectable female, too. "A Miss Louisa Hamilton, sir."

The name seemed familiar, and then Morton remembered why. *"Poor Louisa,"* Darley had said, and now here she was.

"Please, show her in."

Morton rose from his chair in time to greet a tall

woman, veiled and richly dressed in deep mourning. Beyond the door another female silhouette hovered, but did not enter.

He introduced himself. "May I...express my condolences at your loss," he murmured politely. It was not necessary to assume he knew who had died, given her garb.

The veiled head dipped in acknowledgement, but she said nothing.

"Do come in, Miss Hamilton," he said even more gently, and smiled and gestured with one hand. "Make yourself at ease."

"Thank you," she whispered, and then, to his surprise, gently pulled the sitting-room door closed on the two servants before taking the upholstered reading chair he indicated. A suggestion of unfamiliar perfume reached him.

Port-wine would not do for a woman, but Morton had some decent Portuguese sherry, and went to his sideboard and poured a glass. This he set down on the marble-topped pedestal beside her before resuming his own place. There was a moment of awkward silence, during which Morton had time to feel his curiosity begin to stir. It was really most odd.

Suddenly Miss Hamilton reached out and laid a hand on the book Arabella had given him earlier. "Ah, you are reading Byron," she said, almost with relief, he thought.

"I've just begun," Morton said.

"It seems to me that, in this collection, there are lyrics that belong among the best in the language." She caressed the reddish-brown morocco and took her hand slowly away. Morton mentally took his hat off to his titled sparring partner. Byron must have every educated female in London reading his books—and dreaming of

him, too. Even Arabella, apparently: though who was
the admired there seemed uncertain.

But Louisa Hamilton had not come to discuss Byron.

"I have spoken with Lord Arthur Darley," she finally
began.

When she turned her head a little Morton could make
out a silhouette beneath the veil. Dark-haired and blue-
eyed, with a generous mouth. There was something else,
but he could not say what it was. Something in the way
she looked at him, her head turned slightly away.

"He told me you believe Halbert Glendinning's death
to have been . . . unnatural."

Morton made a noncommittal gesture with one hand.
"I do not know how Mr. Glendinning died, only that he
did not choke, as the surgeon at Portman House suggested."

"But there is more, is there not? Lord Arthur intimated that there was, though he would not say what."

"Well, Mr. Glendinning did go out in an affair of honour that same morning. It is a coincidence with obvious
implications." Morton hesitated. Was Darley right? This
woman and Glendinning were set to announce their engagement?

"I fear you are protecting me from something harsher,
Mr. Morton. As was Lord Arthur."

Morton breathed deeply. He should say nothing
more. After all, who was he to impugn the dead man's
name?—exactly as his family had feared. But then there
was the little matter of the truth. Henry Morton had a
certain stubborn streak about it. "I spoke with the jarvey who carried Glendinning up to Portman Square. He
had collected him from a particularly notorious flash
house in Spitalfields, I am sorry to say."

"Pray, pardon my female ignorance. What is a flash house, Mr. Morton?"

"A den for criminals—we call them 'flash customers' or 'flash coves.' Actually, that's what they call themselves. It's a public house, usually, employed by a criminal gang as a base of operation, and for . . . their entertainment. There are dozens in London, sometimes in ill neighbourhoods, but sometimes not. At times they face streets of perfect respectability, and could never be guessed at by their outward show. In fact," Morton smiled wryly, "there is one directly across from the Bow Street Public Office, called the Brown Bear. We use it from time to time to lock up suspected persons."

"And you are sure that Halbert Glendinning was in such a place?"

"I am quite certain."

She shook her head, looking down at her gloved hands clasped on the black-and-grey lap of her dress.

"People have been whispering," she said. "What is it about this place you are not telling me, Mr. Morton?"

It was a question Morton was not eager to answer. He said nothing.

After a moment she looked up at him directly and the light from the lamp seemed to penetrate her veil. Two things struck him. She was a very comely woman. But, yes, there was something else. . . .

"Mr. Morton. Please do not spare my feelings. The whisperings are worse than the truth, I fear."

Morton hoped she was right. But he doubted it. "The Otter, for that is the name of the place, is a house where men come to fulfill some very base appetites."

She closed her eyes. "Go on, Mr. Morton," she whispered. "You may say it."

One of Henry Morton's ideas about truth was that if people said loudly and clearly enough that they wanted to hear it, they should.

"They go there to consort with children, Miss Hamilton. Little girls."

For a moment she was very still, and then her eyes sprang open. Even behind the veil their gaze was startling.

"*Never,*" she breathed. "Never could Halbert have done such a thing."

"Doubtless you're right," Morton said softly. He half expected her to denounce him next, denounce him and his precious truth. But she did not.

Instead, Louisa Hamilton drew herself up. "Halbert Glendinning was of the simplest, finest character," she began.

"So Lord Arthur assured me."

"Hear me out, Mr. Morton. Halbert was the gentlest soul I have ever known. He could bring himself to hurt nothing. He was entirely free of the sort of odious inclination you have just named—I can say it with certainty. It is utterly inconceivable in him." And something in her manner did in fact go a distance toward persuading Morton. She was certainly intelligent, and perhaps not quite so unworldly as many females of her class. But she was puzzling, too, with this combination of shyness and strength, stiffness and sudden protective passion.

"Understand, Miss Hamilton, that I never suggested—"

"Of course, Mr. Morton. I realise you didn't, but still . . . you did not know him. He wrote poetry and worshiped art. . . ." She shook her head, for a moment unable to say more. Then, very quietly and firmly, she went on. "What you have told me, Mr. Morton, makes me even more certain that my fiancé died unnaturally. I am here to engage you to discover his killer, and to aid in that person's prosecution."

Morton's surprise left him speechless.

"You do take on such work, don't you?" she asked. "When I spoke with Mrs. Malibrant at Lord Arthur's, she assured me that you did."

"You saw Mrs. Malibrant at Lord Arthur's... this evening?"

She nodded.

Morton felt his mood lower a little. "Well, yes, I do," he answered her question. "I am paid only a small retainer by the Magistrate at Bow Street." Morton was embarrassed to say it was but five shillings a day. "Like my brother officers, I earn my living largely through rewards for convictions, and private work. I used to attend the Drury Lane Theatre, for instance, so that ladies might feel comfortable wearing their jewelry. I made Mrs. Malibrant's acquaintance that way."

"And how much would you earn for gaining the conviction of a murderer?"

"For a murderer, nothing. That is a duty."

"For other crimes?"

"Theft over fifteen shillings—forty pounds."

"I am prepared to pay you ten times that much. Half immediately."

Morton reached for his port-wine. Four hundred pounds was a good year's income for many men. Poor Louisa indeed!

"Will you take up this task?" she asked.

"I can do nothing else," he replied. "You offer far

more money than I can imagine turning down. You should pay me less."

"I would pay you more, if it made success any more likely."

"It wouldn't."

She smiled.

"I believe I have made a good choice in you, Mr. Morton," she said quietly. Then she looked again at the book on the table.

"You seem to be an educated man, if I may say so," she remarked. "How many officers of police read the latest poets?"

"Too few."

She laughed, and her indirect glance met his for an instant through the veil. Then Morton had it, what was strange about her: She had a wandering eye. Only very slightly so, but detectable all the same. A woman who never looked quite directly at the world.

Even so, he thought a little flicker of understanding passed between them. Then they both looked down, and when she raised her handsome face again her expression was businesslike once more.

"How will you begin?" she asked.

"I will likely speak to the jarvey again. Visit this flash house in Bell Lane. Talk to anyone who might have seen Mr. Glendinning the day of his death. Try to discover all of his movements and activities that day, and indeed for several days before. I will want to know more of this duel...." A lamp guttered, and Morton reached out to adjust the wick.

"Mr. Morton?" she asked quietly. "Members of my family, and of Halbert's, are concerned for my...well-being. They feel the whole matter should be forgotten as quickly as possible. Were I known to be doing this, there would be a very strong effort to dissuade me. If you could keep the identity of your commissioner hidden during your enquiries, I would be greatly obliged."

"Yes, certainly. But I'll need to speak to you and pose some questions."

"Indeed, I will want to answer them, when an opportunity presents itself. But let me send my maidservant Nan to you tomorrow; she can provide you with almost anything I could myself. She is closer than a sister to me."

Morton nodded his agreement. But there was one more question that he wanted answered before he began, and he wanted the answer from no one else.

"Are you acquainted with Colonel Rokeby, Miss Hamilton?"

He thought she blushed, though through the veil he could not be sure.

"I understand," she said, "how the Colonel must be your first concern. The duel makes that necessary."

"Runners from Bow Street interrupted that contest," noted Morton, "after a warning delivered by a lady's maidservant."

She nodded. "Yes, I sent Nan."

"And how did you learn of the duel? From Mr. Glendinning?"

"No, in fact, I found out quite by chance. A servant said something. I could not quite believe it. Halbert despised such things. But it was true. Nan confirmed it through the manservant of my half-brother."

Morton nodded. She had nimbly dodged his original question. "Colonel Rokeby and yourself, Miss Hamilton?"

She sat for a long moment, looking past him. Then she turned her head again.

"To come here at all, I suppose I must trust you, Mr. Morton." She met his eye in her oblique way, then dropped her gaze and began speaking in a low, expressionless voice. "In an earlier period of my life, under the pressure of . . . events, I did some very foolish things, Mr. Morton. I was . . . acquainted with the Colonel, briefly. But I soon broke off any connection between us."

Morton thought Arabella would likely be proved right again—which she would no doubt be delighted to hear.

"How did he accept this rejection?"

She shook her head. "I really have no notion. Until this duel, I had not thought of or spoken to the Colonel in many months."

"And your acquaintance with Mr. Glendinning began when?"

She stared blankly.

"Miss Hamilton, you can see the relevance, surely. Was Colonel Rokeby angry enough, or jealous enough, to have wanted to revenge himself upon your fiancé? How long ago did your relations with the Colonel come to an end?"

"A year—eighteen months ago. Halbert began to call not long after." She looked up at him. "Is there more, Mr. Morton? I must return to my home."

Morton hesitated.

"Can you not simply proceed?" she almost pleaded. "Need I say more about events I am loath to admit even to myself?"

Morton felt the propriety of pressing her no further, at least for now. If he had no solicitude for her feelings, he ought to have for his four hundred pounds. He bowed silently.

"I will send Nan to you tomorrow, with a draught on

my bankers." She rose and stepped toward the door, but then turned. "Mr. Morton? Did I bring this upon poor Halbert? Did my treatment of Colonel Rokeby cause...?" She could not bring herself to say it.

"Even if it were Rokeby, Miss Hamilton, the blame is not yours. Rokeby's actions are his own to account for. No one else's."

She nodded once, seemed to waver where she stood, then held out her gloved hand, which Morton touched to his lips. Wilkes saw her out.

Morton picked up his glass again, noticing that his guest had not touched her own. Had Rokeby actually taken the step of murder? Certainly the man was a killer, but so far his killings had always been "honourable," if not strictly legal. Had he killed Glendinning to have revenge on Louisa Hamilton? And had this same woman just engaged Morton to take her revenge upon Rokeby? Was he to be her champion? Sir Galahad indeed?

Morton stared down at her untouched glass and suddenly had the feeling, unbidden, that, for all her grace and refinement, Miss Louisa Hamilton was capable of such a thing.

Chapter 9

Morton descended from his hackney-coach in Petticoat Lane, just south of Highgate Street. The rain had finished and it was clear now, with a bright half-moon shining, so that he could see a long way up and down London's most notorious market for prostitutes. Even well after midnight it was as crowded with figures as a normal street in daylight, women and men moving busily up and down, and the shrill voices of drag-tailed Sally and her sisters began at once to urge him from several sides.

News that there was a "horney" in the neighborhood would spread quickly, so Morton pulled the brim of his topper down over his brow, bent his head, and strode resolutely away. Opposite the East India warehouses he entered Parker's Alley and passed through into the dingy silence of tiny Cox Square. In a few moments he came out into narrower, less frequented Bell Lane.

Here it was much darker, and completely still. The lightless bulk of Constitution Brewery loomed above, blocking out the moonshine. All the old, nondescript buildings on this cheerless street were unlit, except for a dim yellowish glow deep behind the dirty glass of number 12, midway along. Toward this pale beacon Morton made his way, wondering what had brought young Glendinning to such a place. Was Louisa Hamilton utterly wrong in her belief in her fiancé's honour? Many women were.

No signboard marked the Otter, but it was a public house for all that, and its door was not latched or guarded. Two stone steps down into total obscurity, around a narrow corner, and then, removing his hat and bending, he passed through a low archway. Just as he did he encountered a fat man dressed like a shopkeeper, who was coming out. Something about Morton seemed to alarm him and he ducked his jowled head shamefacedly, brushing past and out into the street. Morton went into the taproom. Small lamps glowed in the corners, but it took his eyes several moments to adjust to the dimness. He was immediately aware that there were people in the place but, uncannily for a tavern on a normally busy night, there was no movement and no sound. Gradually the forms of low benches along the walls emerged, and two small, freestanding tables. A plank bar ran along one side, behind which, on his stool, sat the hunched, motionless figure of the barman. Behind him, rising over his barrels, a set of steep wooden stairs led upward into even deeper obscurity. At one of the tables two other men sat, looking steadily at the newcomer.

Hat still in hand, Morton made his way across to the empty table, pulled up a flimsy chair, and sat down. The publican very slowly stirred himself and presently arrived at his side.

"Yer pleasure, sir."

"A line of the old author. And a candle."

The man shuffled to the far side of the room and fetched one of the small, smoking pewter lamps and set it down before Morton. He was a dry, balding man, perhaps fifty years old, slight of build and dressed in a loose white smock and threadbare trousers. As he slouched away again Morton looked about himself. When his eyes met those of the two men at the other table, they looked down at their hands. He saw now that another figure—apparently a man—lay motionless on one of the benches along the stone basement wall, one arm trailing down with its knuckles in the dirty sawdust covering the floor. Otherwise the room seemed empty. But Morton sensed other presences, other eyes watching him, and set about discreetly trying to find them.

By the time the barman had finished uncorking the dusty bottle and pouring out his glass, Morton had discovered a pale shape in the shadowy corner below and to the right of the bar. There seemed to be some sort of recess in the wall there, perhaps an old root- or ice-cellar, and peering from its depths there was, he saw now, a small, motionless face.

"Lucy!" harshly barked out the keep in a dry, coughing voice. "Where's that little wagtail? Lucy!"

The small face vanished back into its obscurity and then, moments later, a miniature female figure emerged from behind the wall quite on the far side of the bar. There must, Morton saw, be some connecting passage joining the two places, perhaps only large enough for a child to slip through.

For a child was the owner of the face he had glimpsed, and who now dutifully approached his table, bearing his dram carefully in two hands. Dressed in an utterly filthy dun-coloured scrap of robe, her dust-grey hair chopped short and sticking out in tufts around her head, she looked to be nine or ten years of age. But Morton knew how deceiving such appearances could be, here where a lifetime's knowledge of good and evil could be compressed into a year or two, and where human beings matured quickly, or not at all. The girl set the clouded glass down cautiously before him, and then made an odd awkward dip, a kind of hurried curtsey. Dark, curious eyes looked up at him, set in sharp, strangely knowing features. Then she wheeled and was gone in a little rush back into the gloom beyond the bar.

As his glance followed her, he caught sight of others. Partway up the wooden staircase, three little crouching forms, three more female faces, peering down at him. The instant he noticed them, they scrambled silently upward out of sight.

Henry Morton drew a heavy breath, and drank down half his glass in one swallow. He made a peremptory gesture to the keep, calling him over to the table.

"So," Morton addressed him in the language of the streets, "this be a nanny-house?" And he inclined his head toward the stairwell.

"It may be. You hanker for a bit of a curtezan, do you? A little kinchin-mort?"

Morton could hardly contain a grimace. "Courtesans" seemed rather a grotesque term for the pitiful little females he had glimpsed on the stairs.

Before he could put another query, however, a new voice spoke, clear and deliberate.

"Guard yerself, Joshua. He's a horney."

Morton twisted round in anger. It was one of the two men at the other table, the larger, burlier one, who gave him one hard, defiant stare, then looked down again.

"We've a lawful public, here," the barman protested,

backing away. "Drink yer swig and leave us be." It was true enough. Morton knew that formal justice was largely powerless to stop the overt business of a house like this. The only charge that could even be laid was that of creating a "common nuisance," and with no one working the sidewalk outside the house, this would be impossible to sustain. But there were other pressures that could be applied.

"Come back here," he ordered the man, dropping the pretence of being an ordinary customer. "I've some questions for you, and you'll answer them smart if you want to continue vending drink in this parish."

The tapster edged back, reluctantly. Only a tiny percentage of the tens of thousands of public houses in London actually possessed the required licence. But if an officer suddenly insisted on one, he could, at least for a time, make some misery for a place.

"Last night you'd another gentleman in here," Morton told him, watching him closely as he spoke. "He was well dressed, in black pantaloons and a dark green coat. He left in a hackney-coach, somewhere around the hour of ten."

Joshua mumbled something to the effect that he'd served plenty of customers yesterday, and how was he to remember—

"He drank more than was good for him," Morton interrupted, "and someone from this house helped him into his coach." Joshua's rheumy eyes flickered over to the other table, to the man who had warned him that Morton was police. The other man stared back impassively now, saying nothing. His companion gazed off as if distracted.

"Plenty of coves as drink too much," said Joshua.

"Yes, but this man stood out. You don't get his sort

often—very finely dressed, like a dandy. I've no doubt you remember him."

Another flicker of the eyes in the direction of the other table. At the other table, the same impassive stare.

"I don't recollect him. But I haven't always been here, have I?"

"He left by hackney-coach. The driver took him from your very door." Morton decided to bluff. "He said one of the men who helped him into the coach was the publican."

He watched the man's eyes, which slid away toward the others. "I don't recollect such a man."

Morton turned in irritation to the second table.

"What about you two? Did you see the gentleman?"

"We wasn't here yesternight," responded the burly man.

"No, I'm sure no one was here," Morton muttered. "And why would that be, I wonder?"

He did not offer to pay for his brandy as he stood, and the keep did not make any effort to remind him of it. For an officer of police to pay for something at a flash house would be to grant it a degree of legitimacy, and neither Morton nor any of his brother officers ever did. An honest house was quite another matter.

"If I were a cully, like some I see here tonight," he announced generally, "I'd give some serious consideration to my liberty and my livelihood, and to what I might be able to do to help the officers charged to keep His Majesty's peace. I'd take some time, for example, to think over what passed here yesternight, so that I could tell them next time they asked. Because they'll be back to ask again, sure."

"This here's a lawful house," objected Joshua. "And Bow Street knows it, even if you don't."

"I am Bow Street," said Morton.

To this Joshua grunted unintelligibly and the men at the second table both looked mutely down into their mugs again.

Well, he could get no more from them. He gave his hat a brief, contemptuous brush with one hand, as if to rid it of the contagion of their presence, and went out.

Chapter 10

Morton was restless after his visit to the troubling streets of Spitalfields, and had consequently not been in his bed nearly as long as he might have liked when Wilkes woke him to announce that Miss Hamilton's maid Nan was waiting to speak with him.

"Damnation," the Runner mumbled emptily, and swung his feet over the side of his bed. Wilkes had at least thought to accompany these tidings with a hot bowl of *café au lait*—many of Morton's tastes in the pleasures of life were defiantly Gallic—so while he sipped he asked:

"Did she say anything interesting last night, this abigail?" Morton assumed that Wilkes had entertained the servant in the kitchen while he'd talked to her mistress.

"She is discretion dressed and walking, our Nan," replied Wilkes. "Actually, sir, she made it rather clear that any man who served a mere police constable was beneath her notice. She was not about to tell me anything."

"Well, I wonder what hope I have. Being the mere police constable himself."

A few minutes later Wilkes ushered the visitor into the parlour. Morton very politely saw her to a chair, offering refreshment as he did. His attentions were received with minimal courtesy, and a barely civil refusal to taste his food or drink.

Nan was a slim woman of middle years with a sharp, long-nosed, narrow countenance. She was well dressed in an Indian muslin day dress, over which was artfully arranged a silken blue pelisse and cape with, of course, the proper black mourning ribbons. Morton guessed that such clothes had been passed on to her by Miss Hamilton, so perhaps they really were as close as sisters. At any rate, her manner certainly suggested she viewed herself more as a gentlewoman than a servant.

She perched on her seat as if unwilling to make herself comfortable and peered back at Morton with the kind of suspicious air he knew only too well. From top to bottom of British society the very idea of a police was distrusted and resented. He half expected to be treated to the usual speech about the liberties of free-born Englishmen. Instead, she said: "I am to give you this." She passed him a neatly folded paper. Morton opened and ran his eye over it quickly, just long enough to pick out the reference to *Two Hundred Pounds Sterling,* then casually set the bank draught aside. God knew, the Runners were suspected of greed enough as it was. Nan's palpable disapproval of her mistress's proceeding burned like a hearth before him.

"Thank you."

"And I am to answer your questions. If you have any."

"I do." Morton smiled encouragingly. "Your mistress," he said, "lodges the most complete trust in you."

"She has known me long."

"It reflects very well on you, I think. When did you begin with her?"

"When she was but a slip of a girl. I have served her near all her life."

Morton nodded appreciatively.

"Do you remember a Colonel Rokeby, who might have visited your mistress at one time?"

Nan nodded, saying nothing—unless one took into account her manner, which said a great deal. *These things were none of Morton's business.*

"Can you tell me anything of the nature of their...acquaintance?"

"Surely, sir, you realise that—"

"Let me be clearer: Was their acquaintance such that Colonel Rokeby might have cause for jealousy after the fact? Did he regard your mistress in a way that would lead to this?"

"The workings of the mind of a person like Colonel Rokeby are a mystery to me." She said it with a certain bitterness, Morton thought.

"And to me. But would he have felt an implied promise had been broken? Did Miss Hamilton's rejection of him raise his ire?"

"I wouldn't know, sir. I am hardly in the man's confidence."

Morton sighed under his breath. But she was in Louisa Hamilton's confidence, or was supposed to be. He changed his tack.

"You carried the note to Bow Street that warned the officers of the duel?"

Nan nodded again, regarding him warily.

"How did you first learn of the duel?"

"From the servants. Master Peter's man had let it slip."

"And you told Miss Hamilton?"

She nodded again.

"When was this?"

"When was what, sir?"

"When you learned of the duel?"

"The evening before it was to take place."

"And Mr. Glendinning had not come to your mistress's house at all that day?"

"No, sir. He had not."

"What did Mr. Hamilton have to say of the affair afterward? I trust you heard something from his servant."

"Only that Runners from Bow Street had interfered where they should not have. That they had no regard for a man's honour, but only their pockets."

"He was angry, then?"

"Yes, sir."

"Do you know, Nan, if Mr. Glendinning was proficient with a pistol?"

"I don't, sir, but it would surprise me."

"Why is that, pray?"

"He was not inclined to sport, sir."

"Tell me about Mr. Glendinning. Did you approve of him?"

"Indeed, sir, he was very kind and respectful of Miss Hamilton. A gentleman from heart to head."

"Then you thought them a good match?"

"It is not my place to hold opinions, sir."

Morton almost laughed aloud at the notion of the woman sitting before him being without opinions, on this or on any other matter. Perhaps he ought to ask for her views on Bow Street and the men who toiled there.

"Do you know what caused this duel, Nan?"

She shook her head.

"Mr. Hamilton's manservant knew nothing?"

"He would not speak of such a matter to us, sir, nor would we ask."

Morton rather doubted that, but decided to let it pass. Instead he set to work to find out as much as possible about Glendinning and Miss Hamilton. In this, Nan was forthcoming. The particulars of the Sussex circle, which both families were part of, the names of Glendinning's servants, his solicitor and his London friends, and the details of his habits were soon committed to Morton's comprehensive memory. Everything she told him served to support the picture Louisa had provided of her dead fiancé. When he tried to probe his possible dissipations, Nan's response was little different from that of her mistress.

"I know nothing of his private doings, Mr. Morton. But the maidservants in the Glendinning houses, both town and country, reported nothing amiss of him in the way of improper familiarities. I asked them particularly, when it began to seem Miss Hamilton might regard him with favour."

"You take good care for your mistress's welfare, I think. If you had heard that he had in fact behaved in ... an indiscreet or reprehensible way, would you have reported this to her?"

Nan's response was unhesitating. "Indeed I would. And to Master Peter."

Morton made an approving sound, then posed the question that had been nagging at him.

"Do you know if Mr. Glendinning's familiars called him 'Richard'?"

Nan responded slowly. "Not that I ever heard."

"Who is 'Richard,' then, Nan?"

She looked steadily at him, considering. "I can't think of anyone by that name who could be relevant to this matter, sir. But it is a common enough name."

"I suppose it is. Did Mr. Glendinning have any detractors?"

"I would hardly know, sir," Nan said. "He was very mild in his manner and congenial to all, so far as I knew."

When she was gone, Morton examined the banker's draught with more care and found, to his own amusement, that his pulse sped up slightly as he did. How often did even the great John Townsend receive a sum like this? But once before, a letter of this sort had proven fraudulent, and in the end Morton had only been able to dispose of it for a few pence on the pound. He'd best cash this one before he invested too much time and energy in the matter.

Then he sat, tapping the paper on the arm of his chair, and thinking out his strategy. By rights, he ought to report to Bow Street now. But he felt, as he had told Arabella, that he might do well to keep himself out of Sir Nathaniel's view till the Chief Magistrate's ire had cooled. Let him think he was searching for the Earl of Elgin's stolen antiquities.

In fact, as regarded that matter, there really was nothing he could do but wait. He had mined all his sources of information in London and uncovered nothing. Whoever had stolen that particular swag was being very quiet.

Not for the first time, Morton wondered who the thief

was. Elgin had enemies, and his plundering of the
Parthenon was controversial—Byron, for one, had spoken out bitterly against it. Were the Greeks trying to recover their heritage? Or had a wealthy collector
commissioned the crime—that would at least explain
why the goods weren't being fenced. But, no, the most
likely explanation was still some opportunist amongst
the flash crowd. He'd make his move soon enough.

Wilkes came in then bearing a tray with Morton's
usual morning fare, as well as a second bowl of *café au
lait*.

"Ah, Wilkes, you are a rare treasure, I must tell you."
Morton took up the bowl. "Well, we were right about
Nan. She was not about to offer much knowledge to the
likes of you and me."

"This man Glendinning, sir ..."

A bit despite himself, Wilkes had begun to find himself attracted to his employer's profession. Morton
smiled.

"Yes?"

"Was there a reason for someone else to kill him?
Someone, I mean, other than Colonel Rokeby? I don't
suppose there was a convenient will and an indebted
nephew?"

"To be honest, I know very little as yet. But it's true
that the reasons for murder are seldom subtle. Do you
know what Townsend says? 'When you hear hoofbeats,
assume horses, not zebra.' Someone tried to kill Mr.
Glendinning in the morning—I hardly think it was
someone else who managed it later the same day."

Wilkes continued to ponder the thing, however, hovering halfway between the table and the doorway to the
kitchen, the tray with Morton's empty bowl on it trembling precariously. "Even so, sir, the manner of it does

seem odd. Why the Otter? But then, if someone in the flash house murdered him in the usual way, why was he not robbed and his remains dumped into the river Thames? Why would they poison a man and then put him in a hackney-coach?"

"Questions I have asked myself. Mind you, it appears young Glendinning did get into the coach under his own steam—more or less. It seems more likely that the man who murdered Halbert Glendinning did it for revenge, not profit. A gentleman would have no need of a watch or a man's pocket money—not that Rokeby is much of a gentleman. But the question remains: revenge for what?"

"Or upon whom?" Wilkes said thoughtfully.

Morton stared at his companion wordlessly, rather struck by that particular question.

Chapter 11

After a very satisfactory visit to his banker, Henry Morton set out for the West End with the kind of spring in his stride that only a healthy bank balance can give a man. Nan had told him that the Hamiltons were due to leave for Sussex early in the afternoon, and he wanted a chance to interview Peter Hamilton, Louisa's brother, before he departed.

Hamilton was unmarried, and in London he and his sister shared an elegant redbrick terrace house on the east side of Hanover Square. Morton presented himself at its door just after ten o'clock, and was ushered into a small salon on the ground floor to wait.

It was quiet, and sun shone brightly through the silks of the elaborately dressed window. Against one wall a massive eight-day clock, taller than Morton himself, ticked with a clear, jeweled ring on every beat. On either side of the timepiece were mounted several small, exquisite silverpoint studies from Canova.

Somewhere above him, he supposed, Louisa Hamilton was preparing for her journey. Or perhaps she was merely sitting alone in the window light with her grief, waiting. Had word drifted up to her that he was here? Might she come and speak to him?

The door opened, and a young man came in.

As Morton turned, the new arrival bowed very slightly and stiffly, then clasped his hands behind his back. His rather heavy face was dark and unhappy.

"Mr. Morton?" His voice was surprisingly harsh, as if it were the voice of someone much older. This was the brother of the gracious Louisa Hamilton?

"Mr. Hamilton," replied Morton in a civil manner, "I greatly appreciate your receiving me, at what must be a difficult moment."

Another slight bow greeted this speech.

"I am an officer of police," Morton went on, "and have been commissioned to make some enquiries into the death of Halbert Glendinning."

Peter Hamilton cleared his throat. "But it is my impression, Mr. Morton, that the Bow Street Magistrate has spoken with Sir William and Lady Caroline Glendinning, and that they have declined to have this matter enquired into further."

"I am fulfilling another commission, Mr. Hamilton, for a private party—partly with a view to clearing away any unfortunate imputations that might cloud Mr. Glendinning's name. I gather that you and he were close friends?"

Peter Hamilton breathed deeply, as though restraining strong feelings. As Morton watched him, waiting, he could see how his face, with its broad brows and large, soft eyes, did after all show a resemblance to Miss Hamilton's, even if his voice and manner were strikingly different.

"Who has given you such a commission, Mr. Morton?"

Morton had not forgotten what Miss Hamilton had said about the concerns of her family and friends.

"I am not at liberty to say, but you may trust it is at the command of one who wishes Mr. Glendinning's name well. Such proceedings are common and entirely legitimate."

"It seems a bit irregular to me, considering the wishes of Halbert's own family."

"Which is why I have been asked to carry out my enquiry with the utmost discretion. Did you not think it odd, Mr. Hamilton, that your friend was involved in a duel in the morning and then died the same evening?"

Hamilton considered a moment—perhaps debating whether to answer at all. "Well, I suppose, Mr. Morton," he remarked, "that life is full of strange coincidences, most happier than that one, thankfully." The man gestured to a chair and then sat himself. He sighed heavily. "But yes, it is odd, as you say." He looked directly at Morton then. "Do you believe there is reason to think Halbert's death... questionable?"

Morton nodded.

"But did a surgeon not see him and pronounce it to be of natural causes?"

"He did, but I was there as well and thought his examination less than methodical. I also discovered that Mr. Glendinning had come to Portman House from a particularly odious establishment."

Hamilton looked down, nodding. "Yes," he said, "I had that from Lord Arthur." He shook his head sadly. "I shall miss Halbert terribly. And poor, poor Louisa..." He looked up at Morton, appealingly. "By all means, let

us erase any doubts about his passing. It shall be difficult enough for us all to get over as it is. But always to
wonder if there was foul play... How may I assist you,
Mr. Morton?"

"I am given to understand you were his second in the
duel with Colonel Rokeby."

Hamilton nodded.

"What was this duel about?"

The other man stared back at him for a long moment.

"Colonel Rokeby," he said very deliberately, "made
remarks, in public, of a character no gentleman may
brook. Halbert Glendinning issued a challenge. However, as you are perhaps aware, your *colleagues*," and
here Hamilton's graveled voice betrayed a hint of anger,
"intervened, and prevented satisfaction."

Morton tried to conceal his surprise. *Glendinning had
challenged Rokeby!* That verse of the dead man's poetry
came back to him, with its tone of despair and pes-
simism. *It will find you soon enough.*

"What was the subject of these 'remarks'?" he asked
Peter Hamilton.

Hamilton took a breath and let it out in a tired sigh.
"They made reference to Halbert himself, and to my
half-sister, Louisa. You will forgive me if I do not repeat
the remarks themselves."

Morton nodded. "Where did Mr. Glendinning go after the duel was interrupted? Do you know what he did
with that day?"

"Not with all of it, no. After the duel, Halbert and I
parted immediately, agreeing that we would see each
other again at Portman House that evening. He was exhausted, and shaken, and I urged him to return to his
rooms and rest. I had never seen Halbert so, Mr. Morton,
so I stopped in on him later that day, to be certain he was

well. His manservant said he was asleep, and I thought it best not to wake him. I never saw him again until they bore him up the steps at Lord Arthur's. Have you spoken with his manservant? Perhaps he knows more."

"I haven't yet, but I shall."

Hamilton closed his eyes for a second. "Before the duel I looked at Halbert thinking it might well be the last time I saw him alive. But after it was interrupted I trusted the danger past. And then..."

"Was Mr. Glendinning skilled with a pistol?"

The man shrugged. "I never got a chance to see. When he requested I be his second I asked him if he was confident, and he claimed he was."

"Had he no idea who Colonel Rokeby was? The man is as proficient a killer as you will find, Mr. Hamilton."

Peter Hamilton nodded grimly. "The Colonel's reputation had preceded him."

Morton waited, but Hamilton said no more. His silence seemed a kind of testament to his late friend's courage. Or perhaps to his desperation.

"I am told that Mr. Glendinning was normally a man of moderate habits, as regards strong drink," prompted Morton after a moment.

"His habits were those of ... many gentlemen, in this regard."

"His family seem to feel he was rather less the *bon vivant* than many gentlemen."

Hamilton smiled wanly. "His family did not, of course, know his every action. He gave them no overt cause for concern, in his domestic manners."

"But, from time to time, outside the circle of polite company, his behaviour was ... less restrained?"

"He was a young man, Mr. Morton, given to the

habits of young men. But I never felt that his dedication to such pleasures would bring him to ruin, as it has so many."

"Had you ever seen him drink himself insensible?"

"No, although I confess, I have seen Halbert imbibe enough that he required some assistance on stairs and entering carriages."

Morton decided to go back to the duel. "You are familiar with Colonel Rokeby, I take it?"

Hamilton scowled. "Yes, he courted Louisa's favour for a short while. But she quickly saw through to his true nature."

"Do you think her rejection of him could have led to a desire for revenge?"

Peter Hamilton raised his hands slightly in a gesture of helplessness. "It is hard for me to say. The Colonel's words were . . . cruel and rather calculated, I think, when I look back on it. Certainly they indicated a bitterness and resentment. I suppose it's not impossible. Perhaps even likely, when one thinks of it."

"Where were these provocative remarks of Colonel Rokeby made?"

"At a private dinner at the Guards Club."

"Were others present?"

Hamilton had risen and walked a few paces, agitated. "Some few officers, whose names I cannot recollect. Perhaps I never did know them." He turned and faced Morton then. "Mr. Morton, I hope you will excuse me. We are to travel to Sussex today, Louisa and I, to attend Halbert Glendinning's funeral. I would certainly be pleased to continue this at another time. . . ."

Henry Morton rose.

"Thank you for your patience, Mr. Hamilton." Morton bowed and started for the door.

"Mr. Morton?" Hamilton looked at him, his eyes glistening slightly. "What do you think befell my friend?"

"I do not know for certain, Mr. Hamilton, but I think it likely he was poisoned," Morton said flatly.

"If you were to catch the miscreant who did this, would you have any hope of conviction?"

"It depends, Mr. Hamilton. There would have to be very hard evidence, as our only authority on poisons is not much credited by their lordships of the Old Bailey."

Peter Hamilton took this in for a moment.

"I do hope you find the man, Mr. Morton." He paused, and then the hint of passion returned to his voice. "And if it is Rokeby, I hope you hang him."

The hired horse shambled along, its tired head hanging low, occasionally taking swipes at tufts of orchard grass along the margin of the path. Dragonflies hovered in the warm still air, the blur and glitter of their wings awhir in the soft morning sunlight. Morton let the horse have its head as the path plunged down a small embankment, the beast's shoulders bunching up and rocking him from side to side as each hoof landed hard.

The path ran on smoothly then, and arrived at a crude gate. Morton let himself through, and emerged from the trees onto a narrow lane. A half hour along this and the weathered roofs of a small village appeared among oaks and massive beech.

His mother's cottage was the last dwelling but one as you rode south of the town. It lurked behind an unkempt, ancient hedge of laurel, thick spirea, and hawthorn. Morton gave a boy a coin to water his horse, and mind it while it browsed by the stream. Pushing open the creaking gate, he entered the garden.

For a moment he stood, staring around at the tangle of flowers and weeds, colours tumbling one over the other, out of the borders of the beds and onto the gravel path. He could hear the rasp of something scraping in earth, and then a softly rendered old country air. Morton cleared his throat.

Rebecca's face appeared among the hydrangea, a straw sun hat pushed onto the back of her head. Her startled expression gave way to a smile, and she brushed back a strand of hair with a soil-stained hand.

"Well, if it isn't Gentleman Jim! 'Enry!" she cried. "Oh, I've forgotten your h'aitch," she added, laughing. It was an old jest, a reminder of a woman they'd once known.

She came out of the garden bed, wearing a farm labourer's boots, the skirts of her dress hitched up a little into a sash. There was a smudge of brown beside her freckled nose, which wrinkled up as she smiled. She kissed him lightly on both cheeks, rising up to her toes to do so.

"Don't take my hands," she said, "they're all over dirt from the garden. But you've come just in time. Something is thieving my carrots."

"Is it a person?"

She gazed thoughtfully at the rows of vegetables. "No, I suspect it isn't."

"I fear my skills are limited to the apprehension and prosecution of men."

"What is the point of having a thief-taker for a son if he can't protect even your garden? Oh, well. I shall have what the thieves leave, I suppose."

His mother led him to a small table set beneath the trees, and Morton lowered himself, with some misgivings, into a decrepit wicker chair. His mother disappeared inside to make tea, and Morton sat watching her pass back and forth before the window. She had once been a very comely young woman, and some echo of that remained as she aged. Not that she was old—only seventeen years older than Morton himself. But her life had been a hard one.

Still, her hair, now silvery white, retained its lustre, and her face was not deeply wrinkled, but etched instead by myriad wire-thin lines. Through the window, she still appeared youthful, for she had so far avoided the stooping and slowing that overtook people as they aged.

A moment later she emerged. "Kettle's on," she announced, and lit in the chair opposite. The sun dappled down through the leaves onto her face and dress.

"How's your new thatch?" Morton asked.

"It's as good as magic. Not a drop can find its way through." She bobbed her head to him. "And I thank you again."

"You shouldn't thank me, Mother."

"Then you shouldn't bring it up," she said, and Morton laughed.

From some distant corner of that summer afternoon a cuckoo called, and both Morton and his mother fell silent, listening. He looked up and found she was gazing at him, her face shadowed now by her hat brim.

"You've grown to look remarkably like your father," she told him. Morton's reaction to this did not go unnoticed, and she reached out to press her now scrubbed fingers to his wrist. "But let's not speak of the devil," she added.

Tea was soon made, and they sat drinking Old Gunpowder as around them bees hummed and pushed their determined way into trembling blossoms.

"I've been engaged in the most lucrative commission of my career," Morton said, realizing how awkward that sounded. The problem was he wanted to leave his mother some money, but her pride wouldn't abide it. Not unless he could convince her it wasn't money he needed himself.

"The tailors of London will rejoice," she said.

"I'm not really such a dandy. You've just not seen the way gentlemen are dressing in London these days. But I've no need of another frock-coat or pair of breeches."

His mother played with the tassel of her shawl. "No doubt you'll find some use for it," she said quietly. "Do you still see your actress?"

"When time allows," Morton admitted.

His mother raised her cup and saucer, but said, "She does not treat you as you deserve."

"No mother's son has ever been treated as he deserves," Morton replied, and saw her quick smile before she sipped her tea.

"And what of Mr. Townsend?"

"He is well."

"You'll take him my regards?"

"Indeed, just as I'm sure he would have sent his, had he known I would visit."

Setting her cup on the table, his mother leaned her head against the high back of the chair, closed her eyes, and inhaled the fragrance of her garden. "I worry about you, Henry," she said. "You don't know what it's like to be a parent and have your only child chasing about London after footpads and murderers."

"It's the footpads you should be concerned for," Morton said.

She smiled. "But even so, I wish you'd gone into the church as we'd planned."

"The church was never a plan I was party to. Anyway, you forget that I had to leave the university when Lady Beaufort died."

"I forget nothing, Henry," his mother said—and it was true. It was from her that he'd inherited his remarkable memory and whatever wit he might claim. From his father he got only his appearance, apparently.

"It was unfortunate that she didn't live a few years more."

"I'm only sorry that she didn't die sooner," Morton said.

His mother opened her eyes. "Now, Henry, where would we have been without her?"

"I don't know. Someplace where you wouldn't have had to atone for your 'sin' twice daily. Someplace where we wouldn't have had to shoulder the blame for her brother's transgression." Morton took up his cup, calming himself. "But it's all past," he said.

His mother grinned suddenly. "You don't miss your evening Bible readings? What of the inestimable—and inexhaustible—works of Hannah More? I can hear you reading them still. Did a word ever register in your mind?"

"I do remember being particularly struck by the word 'salubrious,' one day," Morton said. "Evangelical literature, however, did give me a great desire for other books. *Any* other books. And it taught me to pray. 'Please Lord,'" Morton intoned, "'deliver me from the writings of Hannah More.'"

His mother cuffed him gently on the arm, but laughed. "Amen," she said. And then more seriously: "But you received an education you should not have otherwise."

"Yes, I suppose I should thank her for that—incomplete as it was."

This promise of education had been the reason his mother had swallowed her pride a dozen times a day. It was the chain that had bound them both to that cold, proud woman. Pride, Morton noted, was a sin, yet the supposedly pious Lady Beaufort had exhibited it in a manner and degree that Morton had never before encountered.

In Lady Beaufort's house, however, no one else was allowed pride. Certainly not his mother—or Morton. Lady Beaufort had found them, when his mother had been forced to leave her employment after being got with child by her much older and more worldly employer. She had been sixteen.

She had had no family to go to. Only this remote and haughty widow—sister to Morton's blood-father—who took her on out of charity and to see her atone for her wickedness. Which Rebecca did twice daily, kneeling and asking God for forgiveness, while Lady Beaufort looked on. And then any number of times more in the way she was treated. She had stayed because of the promise that her son—Lady Beaufort's bastard nephew—would receive an education. That a position would be secured for him in some small parish. That he would have some kind of legitimacy in the end.

But Lady Beaufort had died and no provision had been made for either Henry or Rebecca Morton in her will.

"It is odd, isn't it?" Morton said. "The twists and turns of a person's life?"

His mother turned her head a little toward him, widening her eyes. "If we'd not met John Townsend, you mean?"

"I suppose. Or to go back one step; if Lady Beaufort hadn't been robbed."

"Yes, and if the old crone hadn't suspected us," his mother said bitterly, "as though we'd ever given her cause to think us thieves."

The scarlet face of a panting girl appeared over the gate at that moment, and then the gate sagged, and a small, serious boy lifted his head into view.

"It's time, ma'am!" the girl gasped. "Mamma's screaming something terrible and said to beg you hurry."

Morton's mother swept up out of her chair. "I am sorry, Henry. But I must bring another howling human into this world of misery. I pray that you won't be chasing after this one in a few years' time."

She hurried into the house, and emerged a moment later carrying a cloth bag. She drew up before Morton, looking suddenly as though a tear might fall. Reaching out a hand, she straightened the lapel of his frock-coat.

"Look at you," she said, her voice rich and deep. "Turning yourself out so. But even with your perfect manners and your educated talk you'll not fool them for long. Remember that, Henry. They'll always find you out." She put her cheek against his, then kissed him quickly and went out through the gate, taking the frightened children in tow.

Morton stood for a moment looking at the opening in the hedge. Then he gathered up the remains of their tea and carried it inside, leaving some small sum of money on the tray.

Chapter 12

As the midmorning sitting at Police Court would be under way by now, Morton decided he could hazard a brief visit to Bow Street without much risk of encountering Sir Nathaniel. He found George Vaughan lounging in the front chamber, a small ruffian with a bleeding nose slumped disconsolately beside him—doubtless awaiting their interview with the Magistrates. Morton threw himself down on the bench across from Vaughan, stretching out his legs and crossing them.

"This cull looks ready for a hearty choke-and-caper sauce," he remarked, and smiled cheerfully at Vaughan's prisoner. It was an underworld witticism for hanging, and Vaughan chuckled, his lean, hard features relaxing a little.

"Jack Ketch'll have him for breakfast, sure," he agreed. "He's hardly a mouthful, though. Likely get stuck between his teeth." And they laughed together at the other man's obvious discomfiture. Even so, Morton sensed a particular wariness in his colleague. Did

Vaughan know that Morton's knowledge of his doings
had recently been augmented by Jimmy Presley?

Even at the best he and Vaughan had never been in
sympathy, and this little exchange of rough police humour almost suggested that both were trying, for some
reason, to pretend otherwise.

Vaughan continued the bantering mood.

"So, what's this particular Bow Street Runner chasing today?"

"In fact, I've been thrown a scrap of work regarding
this swell, Glendinning."

"Oh, aye?" Vaughan's studied casualness was under-
standable now, of course. Was Morton trying to find out
about the bribe that must have been paid to Presley and
Vaughan to avoid prosecution? But Morton had no interest in that, and he wanted Vaughan to see it directly.

"Just as to what set him off. A modest gent, by all reports, faint-hearted even, some might say. But here he is
trying to get his brains blown out by a man like Rokeby,
then drinking himself into an early grave in some bor-
dello. I've been asked to see if I can find out why."

The other Runner gave a brief laugh.

"The answer to your question is simple, Mr. Morton.
The man was an ass. Though I don't suppose your people paid you to learn that."

"No, I don't suppose they did. You and Mr. Presley
were at this little dance. What was that quarrel about,
after all?"

George Vaughan shrugged. "You know our Colonel
Rokeby. He's an unfortunate tendency with his jaw,
hasn't he?"

"He has indeed. But I don't think I'd be for getting
myself killed over a few words."

"You'd need to be a gent to understand," George

Vaughan drawled. "And, Mr. Morton, nor you nor I is such a thing, it seems."

Morton straightened the seam on his perfectly tailored breeches. "So it would appear, Mr. Vaughan. So it would appear. But this man Glendinning," he went on, "was he up to the task, do you think? Would he have done for our man Rokeby if he'd had the chance?"

Vaughan scoffed. "He looked ready to swoon when we arrived. Had the vapours, he did. No, the Colonel was the horse to bet on."

"I wonder why Rokeby bothered at all with such a little fop? Why not just sneer him back to his lady-friend? It's not as if the world would start calling a man like Colonel Fitzwilliam Rokeby of the First Guards timid."

Now Vaughan smiled at him a moment without answering.

"Well, Mr. Morton, I suppose there be men as don't much care whom they shoot, or why. But I see the way of your thinking. Best ask the good Colonel yourself, I'd say. Best ask him straight out: Did he pour a hogshead of brandy down this cully's throat, to finish up what Mr. Presley and I so inconsiderately interrupted?"

Morton smiled back.

"I will ask him just that."

Presley would probably be a better source. But Presley was not about, so Morton decided to pay a visit to the Guards Club. He was getting little of value with his vague enquiries. Perhaps, even as Vaughan said, it was time to do the obvious.

The Club stood austerely behind a row of white Doric columns set back from Upper Grosvenor Street. Morton, of course, got no farther than the porter in the front vestibule, and indeed, had it broadly hinted to him that he ought by rights to have made his appearance at the back with the other trades. But he was properly dressed, behaved with pointed self-respect, and loudly mentioned the words "police" and "Bow Street," and was thus shown into a small, dark waiting-room for nonmembers. There was, he suspected, an airier and better furnished one for nonmembers of blue blood. But this would have to do. The porter allowed as how he would enquire into Colonel Rokeby's availability.

The irony of it, Morton reflected, as he looked over the rather poor daub that hung on the papered wall—apparently a representation of the Foot Guards at Talavera in '09—was that Rokeby's birth was probably as low as, or lower than, his own. The Colonel's commission, if he ever really held one, was unlikely still to be active. He had probably won it gambling. Could one do that? If anyone ever had, it would have been Rokeby. Well, if he had not won the commission outright, he doubtless won the means to purchase it, fit himself out in a splendid uniform, then promptly sell up. What Rokeby had really done was master the ability to look his part, and to lie with the most polished effrontery of any man in Europe. That, and kill with a dueling pistol, which had the tendency to discourage contradiction.

Many weary minutes later the porter sidled in to say that Colonel Rokeby was not, as it happened, available to be seen. Before he could start to show Morton the door, however, the Runner asked for Captain Pierce instead. The porter looked irritated, but went off again.

Morton expected an even longer wait, but within a remarkably short interval the door opened again and Pierce himself sauntered in, alone.

"Good day, Constable, good day!" the little man

cheerfully greeted him, one hand extended, the other
dangling a cigar. "It's been many a month, has it not?"

Morton returned the proffered salutation with
concealed distaste. If there ever was a definition of the
unkind moniker "toady," it surely began and ended in
the person of "Captain" Archibald Pierce. Rokeby's
diminutive follower must have had even fewer military
credentials than his master, and displayed in addition
the most irritatingly ingratiating manner of any man
Morton had ever known. Why on earth did the real
military men who presumably ruled this Club not rebel
and throw the two of them bodily out their door? It was
one of the mysteries of the Regent's London, though,
this unpredictable permeability of the most supposedly
"exclusive" barriers. Why, for instance, had the fashionable world from the Prince down allowed themselves
to be dominated by such a miserable and low-born
specimen of the human animal as the dandy "Beau"
Brummell?

Part of Pierce's talent, of course, was his bonhomie
and his shameless willingness to flatter. He quite neatly
complemented the inveterately insulting Rokeby: Once
the pair of them had what they wanted of you, either
you allowed the Captain to smooth you over with his
honeyed tongue, or you objected and the Colonel shot
you dead.

"How can I assist His Majesty's most loyal officer of
police today?" Pierce glibly enquired. Such absurdities
flowed so naturally off the man's tongue that they almost sounded reasonable. Morton told him he wanted to
speak to Rokeby.

"Not here, my friend. Not today. Tomorrow perhaps,
but then, maybe I can help you instead. You know with

how much of his confidence the Colonel honours me. What might it be about?"

"I'm wondering what passed between the Colonel and Mr. Halbert Glendinning, that it should have come to an affair of honour."

"Ah, ah," said Pierce wisely, "unfortunate business, that." He drew deeply on his cigar, and luxuriously emitted smoke. "Most unnecessary, really. Puzzling, in fact."

"Why?"

"Well, Constable, the Colonel had not felt himself offended by young Mr. Glendinning. Not in the least. Indeed, he hardly knew the man."

"But words passed between them."

"Not to the Colonel's recollection. That's what was rather surprising about the thing."

"Come, come, Pierce. There was a dinner, here, at this Club, and Mr. Glendinning went away from it so deeply angered as to be ready to wager his life."

Pierce stood a moment, cannily eyeing Morton, and smiling imperturbably.

"Not a bit of it, Constable," he finally said. "Not as either the Colonel or I recollect it. Now, as you well know, the Colonel's conception of honour is such that when a challenge arrives, be it from whomsoever, he is your man. Pistols for two, coffee for one. Unless of course," and Pierce lightly laughed, "you fellows get wind of it. Granted, of course, that it's formally illegal, but where honour and law collide..." He made a delicately helpless gesture.

"You are telling me that Glendinning issued the challenge and you did nothing to find out why?"

"Not at all. The entire matter was so mysterious that the Colonel dispatched me to make a little bit of an enquiry with this young gentleman's second. Not to cry off, of course, nothing near. But just to know a bit better what the matter was."

"Mr. Peter Hamilton?"

"Yes, that was the gentleman."

"And you went? What came of it?"

Pierce's voice lowered, in pretentious solemnity. "I received from that interview the mention of a lady's name. When I mentioned this name to the Colonel, he seemed to know it, and to understand somewhat better the nature of the offence. Even so, he said to me, 'Pierce, I don't mind telling you'—these were his words—'that the thing is hardly a killing matter, for all that.' He evinced a certain...disrespect for the quality of the understanding of the two gentlemen who opposed us."

"But he was prepared to kill Glendinning anyway."

"Now, Constable, as I'm sure you're aware, there was no duel at all, when it came to the point. The young gentleman's subsequent and unhappy end can hardly be laid at our door. He seems to have been a fellow of low habits and acquaintance."

"Now, how do you know that, Captain Pierce?" wondered Morton.

"Ah, but there are many ears in London-town. Many ears, and many tongues."

The Runner considered this answer a moment. There had been a good number of people at Portman House that night, and Lord Arthur's servants seemed to lack discretion, considering that Vaughan, too, had quickly found out what went on. Unless Glendinning's dissipations were both real and well known.

"Tell the Colonel I still want to talk to him. I'll be here tomorrow, at the same time."

"I've no knowledge of the Colonel's engagements this week," smoothly replied Pierce, "or even whether I will have the pleasure of seeing him myself this evening."

"Tomorrow," repeated Morton, and went out.

Chapter 13

Arabella Malibrant and Henry Morton sat again in the second-floor drawing-room of her tidy little house at number 7 Theobald's Road. It was a place Morton had sometimes wondered about. Was it left to her when her husband fled under a financial cloud back to his native Italy, or had she bought it of her own earnings? It was doubtful that even the most celebrated actress would be quite so well rewarded, at least for her work onstage. That some "patron" was behind it—or several—was an unavoidable possibility.

Such thoughts always caused a little burn of dyspeptic resentment in the heart of Henry Morton. This was usually followed by a sinking feeling. With application, and a little luck, he might yet earn enough to safely call himself a gentleman. But he had to admit that no number of lucrative commissions would ever enable a mere Bow Street Runner to provide a woman a house like this.

But it was a pleasant place, and he enjoyed being

there. Arabella had decorated with a somewhat more flamboyant hand than Morton himself would have wielded—like many women with hair of the same colour, she was rather too fond of red. The Turkey carpet was good, the shiny pink cushions... well, perhaps. But the heavy crimson window-drapes were too much. Not that she ever asked his advice.

Indeed, it was more Mrs. Malibrant's way to offer advice than receive it.

"I hear doubts, Henry Morton," Arabella said, patting her lips with a fine linen napkin.

They were drinking smuggled French wine and eating fresh oysters on the half-shell.

"It is part and parcel of what I do—doubt everything and everyone."

"Except me, of course."

Morton smiled as he speared an oyster with his fork. He was sure he felt it wriggle as he swallowed, and reached quickly for his wineglass. "If Rokeby wanted to do away with Glendinning he would merely have issued a challenge himself, on some pretext or other. What you suggest seems too elaborate and too subtle for our Colonel. And then to lure Glendinning off somewhere and poison him...? Aside from the fact that it isn't his style, he must surely have realised we would suspect him."

"But, Henry, had I not been at Portman House and been alerted by the jarvey, the doctor who saw him would have had the final word: died of excessive drink and choking on his own bile. It seems a crime with little risk, to me. Rokeby could hardly have predicted that a woman of my observational abilities would be on the stair."

Morton smiled. Arabella could not be flattered

enough. "You are a marvel," he murmured dutifully, pursuing another slippery morsel about its shell.

Arabella's rich throaty laugh filled the room. Perhaps it was the wine, or perhaps it was something else, but Morton could not help noticing that he was in rather better favour this night than he had been on the previous two.

"You might at least try to sound sincere, you dog!" she scolded. "And grateful. I sent Miss Hamilton your way. Where are my thanks for that?"

"I have just made a small remittance," Morton replied, "with more to follow."

"Oh, I see. Your favours have worth, but what of mine?"

"They are beyond price."

Arabella smiled, fixing a bemused gaze on him. "It is lucky that you are a handsome rogue, Henry Morton, for otherwise I should never have taken up with anyone so common as a Bow Street Runner."

Morton laughed. Their eyes met over the raised rims of their wineglasses, and Arabella's were dancing with amusement and affection. Yes, it did seem tonight was going to end more pleasantly.

Arabella's face turned suddenly serious. "She is an odd woman," she said.

"Miss Hamilton?"

Arabella nodded distractedly. "Arthur said he thought her a person whom tragedy would visit again and again."

"Yes," Morton said, surprised by the rightness of this. "I had that sense. As though she is aware of it herself and only struggles on. She is so joyless. I thought it merely the recent events, but perhaps it is more."

Arabella looked up at him. "Now, Henry, don't you go to rescuing her. You know where that leads...."

Morton grimaced and sipped his wine.

"Find out what you can of Glendinning's death, and then leave well enough alone."

Morton nodded, only half listening. "Do you think she was wrong about him?—Glendinning? Was he dissolute? You know how well these London men hide such things from polite society. And from their families."

She held out her glass and Morton poured more wine. "Yes, I suppose it's quite possible. One of the several things you shall have to find out. Who was Halbert Glendinning... and why did Louisa call him Richard?"

"Do you remember that verse I found in his pocket?"

Arabella shook her head. "It was not memorable."

Morton went to his coat and dug out the scrap of paper. Returning to his chair, he read:

> "'It will find you soon enough,
> The empty night after the day.
> Brief and filled with sorrow,
> Love will rise and slip away.'"

"'It'?" Arabella said.

"Death, one might infer: 'The empty night after the day.' Does it not sound like a love affair gone bad?"

Arabella took the paper from his hand and pondered it a moment. "It is most certainly about the loss of love. 'The empty night' alludes to that as well." She looked up at Morton. "I wonder if Arthur was wrong. He thought them about to announce their engagement. But what if the opposite was true?" She glanced at the verse again. "Did Louisa know how Glendinning felt?"

Morton shook his head. "I wonder. It is terribly despairing, isn't it? And think of what then occurred: He challenged the most feared duelist in London. It does look a bit suspicious, especially when you consider that Glendinning apparently had no skill with a pistol."

Arabella put her glass down and gazed gravely at Morton. "Self-murder. That's what you're suggesting?"

Morton shrugged. "I don't know. But what if his love affair with Miss Hamilton had come to an end, or he felt it was about to?"

"But why was he in the Otter?"

"When dying to defend her honour failed—and remember he is of a romantic disposition—perhaps he'd learned he could procure poison at the Otter. Or meet someone there who could procure it for him."

"Miss Hamilton is not paying you to learn this."

Morton nodded. He left his chair and went to the open window where the slight breeze touched him. The street was very quiet. He felt a tension in the city, now, with Bonaparte returned to the continent. All of England seemed to be holding its breath. He thought of Wellington, and had a sudden image of the Duke bent over a map by lamplight. What a terrible weight of responsibility on one man's shoulders.

Arabella came and stood beside him.

"I have need of some assistance in this matter, I now see," Morton said.

"Hmm."

"There are a few people in proper society who might be more forthcoming if they were approached by someone with more subtlety than I could ever manage. Someone they greatly esteem and have no doubt long wished to meet."

"Such a person would be difficult to find. And what

would such a helper's share of the four hundred pounds be, I wonder?"

"Madam!" Morton said. "The sort of person with access to the circles I speak of cares nothing for gain."

A voice cried out in the darkened distance and they both leaned out, listening intently, but it was only a domestic dispute, not someone shouting news from France. A familiar male uneasiness stirred in Morton, as it had so many times before. Should he not be there, with the others? Facing what had to be faced? Yet here he lingered. Fine wine, fine food, a beautiful mistress. Comfort. Safety.

Perhaps Arabella sensed his mood, for she laid an arm gently over his shoulders, which few women were tall enough to do. For a few quiet moments they stood gazing out together. Then they turned and faced each other, slipping into the more familiar male-female embrace, Arabella's arms sliding luxuriously around his neck as his own encircled her shapely waist.

He started to speak. "I should be—"

But she silenced him with a kiss. Her breath was warm, faintly redolent of wine. "No," she murmured, brushing her lips across his cheek and down over his bare throat. "You have your duties here. It comes for us all, as the poet said, and soon enough. We needn't go seeking it." She pressed her face close to him a moment. "Soon enough," she whispered.

Chapter 14

Next morning Morton rose early and made his way to Cartwright Square. Enquiries around the shabby neighbourhood led him to a ruinous rookery in a narrow passageway on the east side, just as Acton, the hackney driver, had said. Stepping gingerly to avoid the sewage that trickled in the gutter running down the center of the alley, Morton picked his way through the crowd of staring urchins and hollow-looking women who inhabited this miserable warren.

Here and there a figure sat on a stone step, head bent, lost entirely to the world, while others leaned out of the low windows, gazing at him with empty curiosity, staring blankly at the baton of office he carried in clear view in his hand, so that he needn't guard his pockets at every step.

Whenever Morton entered these parts of the city, he felt uneasy, almost at odds with himself. Part of him stiffened in resistance, as if against some kind of contagion, the contagion of poverty and social oblivion. He felt a kind of anger at these people, with their silent misery, their fecklessness, their lack of hope. The criminals, who tried to seize what they wanted from life, were almost better. But he also couldn't help feeling a certain sympathy for the gutter-folk, even pity, and a sense of bafflement. Morton, too, had been born without fortune, but he had made something of his life.

"Here but for fortune," he whispered.

He asked for the jarvey by name.

"Oh, aye, yer worship, Raff Akin dwelt here, he did. But he's off now, an' his wife and kinchins gone wif him."

A little crowd had gathered round and was staring up at Morton. Their spokesman was an almost inconceivably dirty little male person with the face of a grotesque dwarf and an indeterminate age somewhere between six and sixty.

Morton wondered if Acton had really left or if this was a lie—merely the common suspicion of police. "Unfortunate; I had a small reward for him," Morton said. "But he's gone, you tell me?"

"Oh, aye, yer worship; yesternight."

"Where to?"

"Didn't say, yer worship" was the listless reply.

"Back to Yorkshire," someone else volunteered. "That's where he hailed from, Raff did."

Morton tapped his baton on his gloved palm, perplexed, hardly noticing that the ragged people around him watched this little movement as if fascinated.

"Why?" he mused, as much to himself as to them.

"Hardly any wonder, yer worship, what with horneys coming about for him," suggested someone at the back of the crowd, and everyone nodded.

Morton reached into his pocket and took out a coin—

a silver one. "I mean no harm to Ralph Acton," he told them. "I will give this to anyone who can lead me to him."

He was offering enough for anyone hereabouts to give up a neighbour, but no one stepped forward. Acton, Morton guessed, was really gone.

He exchanged the coin for a few coppers, which he distributed randomly. The jarvey had not told all that he knew, but even so, it was a surprise to find the man had fled. Something had happened at the Otter—or Ralph Acton believed so. And whoever had been involved frightened Acton enough that he vacated the city, or at least Cartwright Square—not that it would likely have taken much to frighten the little driver. Whatever the truth, it made Glendinning's death more peculiar.

Nan had provided him with the temporary address of Halbert Glendinning's valet. The man, whose name was William Reddick, was staying at a cousin's tenement in Whitechapel as he searched for a new situation. In a cramped and stuffy little parlour also occupied by a toothless grandmother and several crawling children, he and Morton sat and talked.

"I am commissioned by a friend of Mr. Glendinning to look into his death," Morton explained.

Reddick nodded expectantly.

"Can you tell me what happened with Mr. Glendinning that day? Did he speak of the duel?"

"No, sir. He said only that he would go out to an affair of honour in the morning—this was the night before—and he gave me orders as to what clothes he would wear."

"Did he say why he would fight this duel?"

"No, sir, only what I said, and I didn't ask more. He was not one for explaining himself, Mr. Morton. He was a bit dark, was Mr. Glendinning."

"And the day of the duel?"

"He had me wake him earlier than usual—much earlier—though I don't think he had slept much the night before. I'd heard him up pacing late into the night and then in the morning he were very pale, sir. I brought him his usual breakfast but he barely touched it. Drank his coffee, dressed very neat, and went out. Gave me five pound when he left and said I'd always been a good gentleman's gentleman. It were most affecting, sir. Most affecting..." Reddick paused to brush at his eyes with the back of his hand.

Henry Morton murmured that he was sure it was. And thought, did men with vile appetites awaken this kind of affection in their servants?

Reddick continued. "I fretted the morning away, sir, as you may imagine. Mr. Glendinning had not seemed at all confident when he left, you see. But at half eleven he returned. He were not at all happy looking, though, even if he were still alive. Indeed, sir, he looked more melancholy than when he had left. He gave me orders that he was not to be disturbed, and went directly up to his study. And he were very quiet up there, Mr. Morton. I thought he might have fallen asleep on the divan, as sometimes he did.

"Mr. Hamilton called in the early afternoon, but I told him my master was asleep and not to be disturbed. He asked after him, and then went on his way, saying only that he'd meet up with him at Lord Arthur's that evening. A little later I heard Mr. Glendinning up, pacing the floor. There were certain floorboards that creaked tellingly. But he never came down, nor did he ring.

"Just shy of five, a boy appeared with a note. I took it up to my master and found him awake at his desk. He took the paper and I saw nothing more of him until he rang and had me draw a bath and lay out his clothes for Portman House later that night. He went out about nine or a little past, and that was all I ever knew until one of the servants from Lord Arthur's came by to say that... he was gone." The man drew his hand over his face.

"Do you know whom the note was from? Did you see its contents?" Morton asked.

Reddick sighed deeply and shook his head.

"I don't suppose this note was left in his study?"

"I wouldn't know, sir. His family took all of his effects, so you must ask Sir William."

Morton nodded. He'd likely get nothing from Sir William Glendinning, especially if the note said *"You can find what you want at the Otter House."*

"Was the note-bearer known to you?"

"Nay, sir. He were just a boy as you might see about the street."

"William, was your master of a melancholy disposition, would you say?"

The man hesitated. "Well, sir, he and Mr. Hamilton, Mr. Peter Hamilton, were men of letters. Their book-learning led them into all manner of strange notions, and to ask peculiar questions. I sometimes heard their discussions, sir. They were as like to question the morning, Mr. Morton. I had never heard such things. They were queer on these poets: Sir Walter Scott, Mr. Wordsworth, and Lord Byron. Talked about them for hours. Mr. Glendinning was beside himself with joy to have Lord Byron visit, though it were for barely a half an hour, sir.

Read some of Mr. Glendinning's poems, and was very complimentary, Mr. Glendinning said. Thereafter, my master and Mr. Hamilton took to getting themselves up in dark clothing, as though someone had died." He shook his head. "I thought it was this man Brummell they were in imitation of but it was Lord Byron, I came to realise."

Morton concealed a smile at the perplexity of this simple serving-man over his betters' fopperies.

Reddick continued. "I suppose I never really understood what they were about, sir. But it seemed to me t'were a romantical kind of sadness they worked themselves into. As though there were some pleasure to be had from taking such a dark view of the world." He shrugged. "He were a happier man before he discovered Lord Byron and those others, Mr. Morton."

Morton considered how to phrase his next question.

"Do you think, in this mood of romantical sadness, it's possible your master despaired to the point of...not wanting to go on?"

Reddick sat back and looked at Morton gravely. "Do you mean self-murder, Mr. Morton?"

"It might have been that his relations with Miss Hamilton were, perhaps, not quite as he wished them?"

Reddick sat back in his chair, glancing once at the old woman rocking a baby in the corner.

"It would help me to know these things, William. It would help the person who commissioned me to know the truth."

Reddick looked down at the ancient planked floor. "It were always hard," he said softly. "Not that she isn't a good, kindly lady, Miss Hamilton, but even so...Mr. Glendinning seemed always...confused. One day atop the world, the next in the depths, if you know what I

mean." He looked up at Morton suddenly. "He lived and
died by that young woman, Mr. Morton. That were the
way of it."

Morton found Jimmy Presley in the Golden Apple in the
Strand, a favourite haunt of the Runners. The younger
man was poring over a well-thumbed conduct manual,
which he swiftly tucked away when Morton sat down.
They greeted each other in friendly enough fashion, although the shadow of their last conversation still hung
over them.

"Now, Jimmy, tell me about that duel you and George
Vaughan broke up. I'm doing a little looking into that
Glendinning cove who was in it."

"Who's having you do that?" Presley immediately
wondered. "I heard Sir Nathaniel said we'd go no further."

"This is private work," calmly answered Henry
Morton. "Now, on Wormwood Scrubs that morning..."

"Aye, then." But Presley looked worried. "What
would you know?"

"How did things stand when you got there?"

"We heard the shot—"

"One shot?"

"Aye, just one. I don't know who told Sir Nathaniel
otherwise. We heard it as we were coming up through
the woods, to the south of them. George Vaughan
cursed, and we started to run. We had the constables of
the Horse Patrol with us, you understand, dismounted."

Morton nodded.

"So, as we came out into the clearing, we found them
there, smoke hanging in the air. George Vaughan commanded them to stand down, and they did. That's really

all there was, Morton. There was the seconds, and a cove who was probably the surgeon. Two carriages."

"Did you get the name of the surgeon? I'd like to talk with him."

Presley looked embarrassed. "Nay, we never did ask."

Morton frowned. If the police officers hadn't found out, certainly none of the dueling party would betray their doctor, who was also breaking the law.

"Did they object, when you stopped the fight? Did Rokeby and Pierce object?"

Presley considered. "Not that one would take note of. 'Twas all very gentlemanlike. The Glendinning cove looked like you could push him over with a feather, so we wondered if he'd been hit, after all. But he hadn't. Colonel Rokeby, he was cool as ice, and said as how his pistol had hung fire and only went off when he lowered it. And that was all there was."

Morton smiled at his young companion's obvious lack of relish for the next part of the story.

"Not quite all, Jimmy, now was it? Didn't you and Vaughan talk to them? Make certain arrangements?"

Presley shifted uncomfortably in his seat. "Now, Morton—"

"Never fear, Jimmy," Morton interrupted him. "I'm not concerned about the amounts, and I've no mind to peach to Sir Nathaniel about any of this. Not that it would surprise him. It's all done, that part. But I want to know what words passed between you, and how these gentlemen appeared."

Presley released his breath and shrugged. "It was George Vaughan, mainly, as handled it. You should ask him."

"I want it from you."

"Well, Glendinning and Rokeby both went back to

their carriages. And Vaughan had words with Pierce and the other second."

"Peter Hamilton?"

"Yes, him."

"Had words with them both, together?"

"Nay, each of them, private-like. Pierce first, then the other. And I talked to Pierce, after."

"What did he say?"

"A lot of not very much," said Presley with a laugh. "This is a cove with a jaw! But of all I remember, he was saying how the Colonel wasn't really angry against the young swell, and that he didn't see how there had to be a bother over the duel, and how something would be worked out so that everyone was satisfied, including us officers, for our trouble."

"Did you hear anything of Vaughan's conversation with him?"

"Nay, they stood apart a bit. But at the end, he says something to the effect—Pierce does—we'll meet by and by, Mr. Vaughan."

"What did he mean?"

Presley shook his head. "Maybe only that the Colonel was likely to be fighting more duels, and us Runners were likely to be interrupting them again. The notion didn't seem to worry him very much."

"What did Vaughan say to the other side? To Peter Hamilton?"

"I heard little enough of that, either. But I think they arranged something, so . . . we could have our . . . what he called our consideration. He said he hadn't enough on his person to satisfy us."

"Why did Hamilton pay it, and not Rokeby? Or were they both going to contribute?"

"I know not," said Presley. "Hamilton spoke low."

"So, they met later, Hamilton and Vaughan? Or was it Pierce and Vaughan? Or both?"

Presley shrugged again. "All I know is George Vaughan gave me my share at Bow Street that afternoon."

Morton mused.

"I know you saw very little of Halbert Glendinning. Did you get any chance to judge of his character, Jimmy? What manner of man he was?"

"He was dressed the gentleman of fashion, all in dark cloth as the young swells fit themselves out now. That was all. And he seemed as weak as a woman, for a man whose opponent's pistol missed fire."

"If it actually did," muttered Morton.

"Why would the Colonel bother to lie about that?"

"Maybe to keep himself just exactly on the lee side of the law. Or maybe so that it'd never be known he'd actually missed his mark. Someone obviously spread news that there were two shots, and it reached the Chief Magistrate that way. Perhaps you weren't close enough to hear the first report."

Presley conceded the possibility. Or perhaps the rumour had originated with a member of the Horse Patrol, who had simply got it wrong.

"It's a strange business, isn't it, for two gents to try to kill each other when they're not even angry? Maybe 'twas all for show," Jimmy Presley suggested then. Morton smiled once more. In which case, there hadn't been much of a crime, or any reason to feel guilty about accepting a "consideration" not to report it.

"Maybe it was," he agreed. "Maybe it was all for show. But one of them ended up dead anyway, didn't he?"

Chapter 15

As Morton started up the steps of the Guards Club, someone in a little knot of men lingering about the wrought-iron gates called out to him.

"From the continent, sir?"

Morton turned in surprise, not understanding.

"Have you news?" asked another.

"Oh, nay," replied Morton. They must have hoped he was a military man carrying word from Europe. "Is something afoot?"

"Bony's afoot, that's what," replied one of the men.

"Oh, aye?" Morton was startled.

"He's crossed the frontier, that's the word."

As Morton recalled the rumour in *The Times,* several of them nodded sombrely. They seemed to be of all walks—gentlemen, apprentices, tradesmen, even domestic servants sent to wait for word to bring to their employers. Morton experienced a moment of fellow-feeling with this random group of Englishmen, all sharing the same thoughts and fears.

"Well . . . God bless them, gentlemen," he said.

There was even a ragged little cheer.

"Aye, God bless them!"

"The Duke and all who serve!"

In the vestibule of the Club there was a different atmosphere as well, an electric charge that seemed to hover in the air. The porter had a look of almost unbearable self-importance and various military men of different ranks stood about without any apparent purpose, talking to each other in solemn voices. The camaraderie displayed in the street did not extend to Morton here, however. Once it was clear he had no new information, that he was not a member, and that he only wanted to speak to Colonel Rokeby, he was sent off to his usual little waiting-room without further ado.

This time Captain Pierce made no appearance, and Rokeby kept Morton waiting a very long time indeed. The porter went first to see if the Colonel was available, and returned with the message that he was expected directly. A weary while later, Morton was informed that the Colonel had in fact arrived and would see him "after luncheon." This was, apparently, a leisurely meal, and Henry Morton was made to recognise just how little consideration he or any policeman was due as it dragged slowly on somewhere deep within the exclusive confines of the building. But Morton was patient, and had slipped his Byron into his pocket in anticipation of delay, so that when Rokeby finally made his languid appearance at the door of the waiting-room, he was able to rise with an appearance of equanimity and affably bid him good morning—or was it now afternoon?

Fitzwilliam Rokeby stood tall, erect, and resplendent in his glittering scarlet and gold. He regarded Morton with silent, heavy-lidded hauteur.

"I am enquiring into the death of Mr. Halbert Glendinning," Morton told him. "His activities on the day he died are of particular interest to me, and I am informed that he went out to meet you early that morning."

Morton gazed at the officer in apparently cheerful expectation of his ready response.

Rokeby had a thin cigar in one hand, and with extreme deliberation he raised it to his lips. After a long puff, he slowly lowered it again.

"I did meet the man. But there was no duel, and I never had the misfortune to see him again."

"What precisely led to this encounter, Colonel?"

Another long pause, and application to his cigar. Then Rokeby very coolly and precisely said: "Anything that might have passed between Mr. Glendinning and myself was a private matter between two gentlemen, and no concern of yours."

Morton looked down at the single ring he wore, turning it on his finger as though it were the most interesting thing in the room. Even in anger his hands did not tremble. Then his gaze snapped back up to Rokeby. "Colonel, let me be perfectly clear. A man died in peculiar circumstances on the same day on which you tried to shoot him. Do not take what passes between us in this room lightly."

Rokeby became very still. "Do you suggest—?"

"I suggest nothing!" broke in Morton. And then more evenly: "I merely do my duty, and at this moment I am looking into the activities of Mr. Glendinning on the day of his death. You dueled with him—men from Bow Street witnessed it. For that alone you could be brought before a Magistrate. But I have no intention of doing so unless you refuse to cooperate. Do you refuse?"

This was a bluff, and Rokeby did not answer but only regarded Morton with those famously cold and steady eyes. An image flashed before Morton of those same eyes staring at him down a gun barrel.

Morton took silence for acquiescence. "There was a dinner here, at this Club, where Mr Glendinning took offence at some remarks of yours. What was said?"

All of Rokeby's responses were prefaced with long, contemptuous pauses. "In fact," he eventually said, "I have no notion what led that gentleman to consider himself offended. I believe him to have been some manner of fool."

"Did you not make light of the name of Miss Louisa Hamilton?"

Just a flicker of expression might have traveled across Rokeby's mask of a face. He drew on his cigar. "If ever I had occasion to speak that lady's name," he replied, "it will have been with exactly as much gravity as it deserved."

"Then you did offer such insult before Mr. Glendinning?"

Rokeby stared unflinchingly at Morton. "The first time I ever laid eyes on that fop, Glendinning, he was standing at twenty paces' distance, shaking like a leaf. He was not present at any dinner in this Club. And if you have come here to suggest otherwise..." Rokeby stopped, seeming suddenly to check his temper. Killers could not afford such emotions—if they could afford any emotions at all.

But Morton's own anger was rising. "If I have come to suggest otherwise, what, Colonel? Would you challenge me to a duel? I will arrest you if you do."

"Gentlemen," Rokeby said, "have only to do with other gentlemen."

"Of course." Morton was unable to keep an edge of mockery from his reply. "And how do gentlemen deal with insults from their inferiors? They thrash them, is that not it? I can be found at Jackson's in Bond Street every Thursday night... Colonel."

And without allowing Rokeby either the last word or any further demonstration of his indifference, Morton brushed rudely past him and strode out.

Chapter 16

Morton was still turning this interview over in his mind when the hackney-coach drew up before his lodgings. But he was startled from his reverie by the sight and sound of his landlady, sallying out into Rupert Street to meet him, berating him and shrilling incoherently.

"For God's sake, Mrs. Budworth, tell me what this is about."

"None of your rough language, sir! I am a lady, even if you be no gentleman! I do not habituate the places you and your filthy police do, nor, as my Saviour blesses me, shall I ever!"

"Calm yourself, Mrs. Budworth. And speak plainly."

"You have deceived me, with your fine clothes and your fine airs! But all the while you were going about London-town hanging poor, guiltless folk, and ripping the hearts from the breasts of widows and grieving parents!"

"Madam, I've never ripped a bodily organ from anyone, least of all a *widow*. I have been slandered."

"You have not! Not a tittle, sir, no, you have not! And now you bring the rabble of folk upon us screeching and hooting and offering harm to my house! I'll not endure it! You'll leave me, sir, upon the instant!"

By now Morton's manservant had heard the commotion and descended, his face set in a stately expression that Morton instantly suspected of concealing a certain amusement.

"Wilkes! Can you give me some idea what this is about?"

"Mrs. Budworth has been alarmed, sir," Wilkes said.

"I can see that! What has alarmed her?"

"What has alarmed me!" cried his landlady in deep indignation. "What has alarmed me!"

"A mob of ruffians have only this half-hour departed, sir. They have thrown cobblestones, broken some windows, and threatened worse," Wilkes added.

"They said they would fire me!" cried Mrs. Budworth, almost in tears now with consternation and fright. "They said they would burn my house to the ground!"

Morton looked from her to Wilkes, demanding explanation.

"So they did, sir," agreed Wilkes. "They found you out somehow and threatened their revenge upon you."

"And upon me!" cried the landlady. "Who've never so much as—"

"Revenge for what?" demanded Morton in frustration.

"Oh, for the hanging of their comrades, sir, the two late miscreants named Smeeton." Wilkes was rather enjoying himself, Morton could see. The old man had taken on an air utterly different from his normal manner in order to impress Mrs. Budworth. "These disorderly folk claim to believe these innocent of the crimes for which they were condemned. I fear, sir, that they publicly impugned your motives as an officer of justice. They implied an undue interest in monetary gain."

Morton sighed with disgust as Mrs. Budworth thrust herself before him, her face red and her eyes fairly popping with rage.

"You was a *horney*! And you never said it!"

"How much damage was actually done, Wilkes?" enquired Morton. "You will be fully compensated, you may be sure, Mrs. B."

"I may be sure! I may be sure!"

And Henry Morton reached with resignation into his pocket for a down payment.

There could be no question of being driven away, but Morton was deeply irritated to find his dwelling place had been discovered—and by a mob! It had been one of his best-kept privacies. It was true that he was occasionally visited by his informants from the London underworld—but only by those few he considered reliable. How had the mob found him? And, he wondered, were they serving Vaughan and Presley the same way?

Presley they could probably locate easily enough, although the young Runner's dwelling and relatives were as poor as those who would attack them. But Vaughan was another matter. Even Morton hadn't the slightest idea where, or in what style, George Vaughan dwelt.

The whole idea of assailing the homes of officers was new. Protests had usually only happened at the hangings themselves, although on one or two occasions people had hurled refuse and angry words at the front door of number 4 Bow Street. Now and again, as he had warned Presley, assaults had also been made against officers in the street.

Thought of that conversation made Morton's heart sink. He saw that, despite his own warning to his brother officers, he had been trying to forget about the Smeetons. But it was becoming difficult.

He dispatched Wilkes to Bow Street to warn Presley and Vaughan, and then to arrange for the tradesmen needed to replace the broken windows. Then he had another placating conversation with Mrs. Budworth, whose anger was considerably soothed by the medicine of a few more sovereigns.

Arabella arrived later and found a thoughtful Morton alone at table, eating a cold supper. He offered her some but she declined, then sat across from him stealing morsels from his plate with her fingers, and smiling mischievously.

"But what was your sense of Rokeby? Did he act like a man who'd committed murder?" she demanded as she nibbled on a bit of his mutton.

"Well, after all, he has. Several times."

"I mean, did you think he was hiding something?"

"Rokeby is always hiding something—his low birth, to begin with. But whether he was hiding anything about Glendinning, I cannot say. What seemed more important to me was his reaction to Louisa Hamilton's name, and there he did betray a little emotion." Morton paused to swallow a final piece of bread. "There was definitely anger. But whether there was enough..." He looked at Arabella and shrugged.

"You should have had me with you. I could have told you in a moment."

Morton smiled and wiped his mouth with his napkin. It was one of Arabella's more endearing qualities, he thought—this complete and utter confidence in her "intuitions."

"Perhaps the most interesting thing was that he bothered to speak to a Runner at all," he remarked. They rose and went into the other room. "I certainly could not have compelled him to. What did he expect to get out of it? Did he want to know how much Bow Street knew?"

Arabella tilted her head in thought at this, but said nothing.

She reclined on Morton's scroll-ended divan, her lovely chin propped on one hand, and Morton sat opposite, smoking a cheroot and tranquilly admiring her beauty in the lamplight. The translucent gleam of her skin, the gracious curve of her stretched-out form. How good it was to be at peace with her again, to think of her only as he most liked to do. To remember last night, and anticipate another such.

"And what of you, Mrs. M.? How go your enquiries?"

She crinkled up her eyes in the delightful way she had. "I have made only a little progress as yet. I cannot simply knock on a door, wave my baton of office, declare I'm from Bow Street, and begin asking questions. I must drink tea and gossip and listen to women prattle on about their insufferable children. Dear God, Henry, some of these women!" She pushed back her thick red hair with a languid hand. "But I have learned a few things. Halbert Glendinning was well enough respected in his own circle. There are a few who believe he had some real talent for verse. He was destined for a military career—the Glendinnings have been Royal Navy for generations—but his constitution wasn't up to it. At Oxford he fell in with the literary set and made something of an impression on his tutors, if his friends are to be believed. A little over a year ago he began paying

visits to the Hamilton home—at first to see Peter Hamilton, with whom he had been vaguely acquainted for
some years, and later...Well, you know whom he
sought out later. Nothing earth-shaking there. Louisa,
however, is another story." She met Morton's eye.
"There is a rumour that some number of years ago she
was under the care of Dr. Willis."

"Who?"

"Dr. *Willis*. The one who treated old King George,
when...you know, he was talking to the plum trees and
so on."

Morton stared. "Are you saying she was mad? That I
have taken two hundred pounds from a woman who is
not of her right mind?"

Arabella shrugged. "I could find out no more than
that. Her mother, and this is no rumour, self-murdered
years ago—when Louisa was a girl. The Hamilton children, Louisa and Peter—who was the product of a first
marriage—were raised apart, by relatives. Their father
went into retirement after the death of his second wife,
and was almost never seen by his children. And it seems
his death was dubious too: He drowned, and no one can
say if it was really an accident." Arabella shook her
head. "Not a family blessed with calm nerves, one
would have to say."

Morton rose and stepped about the room in agitation.
He remembered the veiled woman who had visited him
two nights before: her odd way of looking at him and
her slightly wandering eye. But she had not seemed
mad....

Arabella followed his movements closely, green eyes
glistening in the lamplight.

"And what of Richard?" he turned and asked. "Have

you found out if that was her pet name for Glendinning?"

She shook her head. "No one has ever heard it was." She drew her lower lip between her teeth, and stared past him. "But you know, Henry, there is another moment of intense ... *emotion,* when women have been known to call out the wrong man's name."

Chapter 17

Sir Geoffrey Bush, Halbert Glendinning's city solicitor and agent, occupied chambers on Lower Thames Street just across from the cluttered bulk of the new Customs House. His second-story window afforded a clear view of the works, with its bustle of wagons and swarming builders. The constant clink of iron tools rang audibly through his panes.

Sir Geoffrey welcomed Henry Morton with great civility, apologised for the construction dust that sifted everywhere, warned him that it was entirely impossible for him to divulge information about his clients even to Bow Street and then, hardly waiting to be asked, proceeded to talk long and openly about the dead man, with the deep, happy relish of a born gossip.

Much of it Morton had heard before, and certainly nothing altered his basic idea of Glendinning's character. Sir Geoffrey dismissed the notion of his late client straying into dens of iniquity with a worldly wave of his hand, a tolerant smile.

"Absolutely out of the question, sir. No one on this

earth would have been less likely to do such things than young Mr. Glendinning."

Morton had begun to wonder what kind of man people thought did slake his lust on female children. Everyone seemed so certain of the kind who didn't. But he let it pass. If Halbert Glendinning had had a secret, he'd kept it well. But then, if one had that particular secret, one would.

"Sir Geoffrey, do you know any reason for Mr. Glendinning to have been distressed? Were his affairs in order?"

"Certainly he had no money worries or the like," the solicitor allowed. "Mr. Glendinning did not gamble or make risky investments. That part of his life was quite in order." He looked a little grim, and sighed. "However, I will admit to you, Mr. Morton, that I was often left with the impression that his relations with Miss Hamilton were not all . . . how shall we say? Moonlight and balmy sighs. There was something not quite right there. Mr. Glendinning confided in me," he lowered his voice a little, "that he sometimes wondered if Miss Hamilton would ever be able to forget her earlier attachment."

Morton sat up straighter in his chair.

"What attachment was this, Sir Geoffrey?"

"Has no one mentioned it? Miss Hamilton, you see, was engaged to be married once before."

Morton needed only to look interested, and the lawyer rattled blithely on.

"It was a most tragic affair, Mr. Morton, most tragic, for I believe she was a bit mad for her first fiancé." He smiled sadly at Morton and shrugged, leaving the Bow Street man to reflect on the choice of words. "I think poor Halbert felt he could never measure up to his late rival, and I fear there were intimations from Miss Hamilton, if not in so many words, that this was so."

And here Sir Geoffrey raised the fingers of both hands in an eloquently poignant gesture. "This other man...he served his King, went abroad, never to return."

"Was his name Richard, perchance?"

Sir Geoffrey looked at him in surprise. "I thought you knew nothing of it. It was, in fact: Richard Davenant. Died in Spain in 1811, at Albuera. He was a captain in that Sussex Regiment they were all part of, the men from down there. The Thirty-fifth Foot, I think. The terrible irony, though, was that this 'hero,' the captain of Miss Hamilton's heart, did not, it seems, die the death of a hero."

Now Sir Geoffrey was clearly waiting to be asked, so Morton did.

"How so?"

"The word is, Mr. Morton," and the lawyer's voice sank to a whisper as he leaned forward slightly, "that he bolted. The bullet that killed him was lodged in his back, when he ran from the French at the height of the battle."

He sat back again, a sad, satisfied smile playing on his lips.

"Halbert suffered, as did many who were willing but unfit for service. In some strange way I think he believed that a coward who went to war was better than a worthy man who could not. Do you see what I mean?"

Morton nodded. He did. He could also see how a shy, young country gentleman might have been lured into revealing so much of his private life to this garrulous urbanite, with his welcoming manner, his seeming wisdom, and his easy willingness to talk of such things. Sir Geoffrey Bush enjoyed other people's confidences. He took pleasure in hearing them, and he took pleasure in repeating them. Poor Glendinning indeed. And poor Louisa.

"What happened to Louisa after Davenant's death?"

Sir Geoffrey raised his hands. "I cannot say. I am not a confidant of Miss Hamilton's. In fact, I have met her but once."

"And Davenant? Did you know him?"

"No, I had the story from Robert Bromley, the regimental surgeon of the Thirty-fifth at the time. Offices in Golden Square, should you want to talk to him. He saw the fellow's body, apparently, and was in a position to say. Though, I have to admit, I have heard it once or twice repeated by others."

Morton considered a moment. "Do you think matters between Mr. Glendinning and Miss Hamilton had deteriorated so badly that your young client had fallen into despair? Was he melancholic, do you think?"

This seemed to sober the old gossip a moment, and his face might actually have expressed a degree of genuine sympathy. "He was not born with an immense capacity for happiness, our Halbert," he answered. "As to his relations with Miss Hamilton . . . I think she did not appreciate him as she should. But even so, they were to marry. I don't know how joyful a union this might have been, Mr. Morton, but Halbert had all his hopes tied up in it, that is certain."

"Then you knew them to be engaged? Was it common knowledge?"

"Well, I don't know how common, exactly. I certainly

knew, and Halbert repeated it the last time I spoke with him—but two days before he died."

Morton touched his fingertips together. "Did you think it out of character that Mr. Glendinning fought a duel? To your knowledge, had he ever done such a thing before?"

"Oh, I'm quite sure he hadn't," Sir Geoffrey said quickly. "As to it being in character, he did not have an aggressive disposition, Halbert. He had a romantical one. Fighting a duel to protect the honour of the woman he loved?" His eyebrows raised. "It was, perhaps, a way to make himself a hero—perhaps even more of a hero than her former love."

"He might easily have been a dead hero. His opponent was the most notorious duelist in London."

"A bit of bad judgement, that," Sir Geoffrey admitted.

Something occurred to Morton. "Did you advise him to engage in this duel, Sir Geoffrey?"

The man looked wide-eyed at Morton. "Certainly not!"

"Excuse my suggesting it," Morton murmured evenly. "Can you tell me," he went on, "who benefited from Mr. Glendinning's will?"

The man looked at him a moment. "Only his own family, Mr. Morton, and I'm sure they'd rather have him back than have his money, which came from them anyway."

Morton rose. "I thank you for your time." He stopped as he pushed his chair back. "This surgeon, Bromley, I believe you said, is acquainted with Mr. Glendinning's set?"

"Oh yes, he's thick with many of them, although I've never understood how he managed it. Rather a paltry chap." Now the lawyer's smile became sly. "Indeed, Mr. Morton, you mustn't believe quite everything he tells you."

Morton returned a somewhat sour version of the same smile. "I make a rule of that for everyone, Sir Geoffrey."

Chapter 18

Arabella Malibrant chose the early visiting hour to call on her lover's new employer and was shown into Miss Hamilton's personal sitting-room upstairs, a comfortable place full of delicate rosewood furniture done up with ormolu—all very elegant, if a bit subdued to an eye accustomed to the livelier style of Drury Lane.

In fact, Louisa's refined tastes were everywhere; her books lay scattered about, and an easel in the corner displayed a half-finished, and rather heroic, drawing of a young man whom Arabella recognized as Halbert Glendinning. On one wall were two finely executed oils of military men—family members, Arabella assumed—while beside the window was a portrait of Louisa. And what a portrait! Lit by a soft golden light, she appeared almost to glow. Her startling blue eyes gazed out directly at the viewer, shining with such naked emotion that Arabella was almost embarrassed, as if she'd accidentally seen something deeply private.

She had only been looking at it for a few moments when the lady herself came in.

"I do hope I've not intruded too soon," Arabella said warmly, as they took each other's hands.

Miss Hamilton beckoned to an armchair and sat down on the sofa opposite.

"No, I welcome company just now." She gave Arabella a wan smile. "It is a pleasure to see you again, Mrs. Malibrant."

"And you, Louisa."

Louisa Hamilton simply and graciously bent her head in response. She seemed not to resent the rapid adoption of her Christian name.

Arabella settled herself. "More important, is there any way I might be of help?"

"You have already done me a real service," said Louisa softly, "in directing me to Mr. Morton."

"It was a small thing. I hope his efforts will bring you some peace."

Louisa Hamilton nodded. "He is not quite what I expected, your Mr. Morton," she observed.

Arabella wondered about "her" Mr. Morton. "No, he is not quite so rough as his fellow Runners." She smiled.

"Indeed, I found him reading Byron!"

Arabella felt a tingle of blush in her cheeks as she recalled the circumstances in which Henry Morton had received that volume. And the inscription she had quite forgotten it contained.

"He attended Cambridge for a year, and has certainly made efforts to improve himself. He is his own creation, Henry Morton. As much as any character I have fashioned for the stage."

"If he was at the university he must be of good family...."

Arabella hesitated. Suddenly she found this interest rather too intent. "His father was of good family," she said, lowering her voice.

For the briefest second Louisa looked confused. "Ah," she said, realisation dawning. "But of course such things should not be held against the child. And he seems to have found his way in the world."

"Exactly my thinking."

Arabella could not see a delicate way to work into the conversation the fact that Morton's mother had been an unmarried maidservant, so she let it pass.

Louisa Hamilton was looking at her now, head tilted slightly away, the one eye wandering almost imperceptibly. It was a penetrating gaze for all its indirectness.

"I will tell you, Mrs. Malibrant, that there are moments when I cannot believe that Halbert was murdered. Moments when I think I must have fallen into fancy and delusion, just as people are saying. I know that men are murdered in London every week—but not gentlemen. And certainly not gentlemen like Halbert Glendinning, who wished harm to no one." She hesitated. "My brother Peter thinks I am . . . that my spirits are . . ." She did not finish.

Arabella regarded her steadily, thinking of the rumours about Dr. Willis. Suddenly she found she could not quite believe it. But she knew the way people, this brother for example, rushed to conclusions. Always to protect the woman, supposedly, bundling her away into the sickroom. They would no more listen seriously to what a woman told them than they would to a child.

"If Henry Morton believes there was foul play, Louisa," she said firmly, "then you need not worry that it is a product of your distressed state of mind. Henry

Morton has an intuition and skill in these matters that is unrivaled by any but Mr. Townsend himself."

Louisa looked up with a flash of gratitude, and her hand went out impulsively to touch Arabella's arm. Arabella's hand covered hers, and for a moment there was no need of words.

"Better to concentrate on the matters at hand," Arabella said, "than worry about things that are illusory. Was there anyone other than Colonel Rokeby who might have wished Mr. Glendinning ill?"

"I can't believe anyone at all could wish it—not even Colonel Rokeby." Louisa's features contorted suddenly, and her voice began to break. "Whyever did poor Halbert agree to fight that foolish duel!" she cried out.

Miss Hamilton rose and went to the window, concealing her face from her visitor. The casement was opened to the early summer air, and from the street below came the clatter of carriages and tradesmen's carts rattling hollowly over cobbles. Louisa looked very striking in the light filtering through the plane trees, the darkness of her dress and hair contrasting with the paleness of her braceleted arms and delicate neck.

"I will tell you the worst of it," she said without looking round, her voice calmer. "I might as well have sent Halbert off to fight that duel myself." She paused. Arabella Malibrant waited, saying nothing. "Always I compared him...never praising his accomplishments, chary with my compliments, parceling them out as though I had only a few to spare. I was horribly cruel, without ever uttering a word that could be construed as hateful." Louisa seemed almost to pant out her guilt now. "But Halbert knew. He felt the sting of it. And then he went out to fight that senseless duel, challenging this

cad Rokeby, who meant nothing to me, so that he might
prove himself worthy. So that I would think him brave.
That I would find him worthy of my praise and my affections."

Arabella could see her shoulders shudder.

"Perhaps I hoped Mr. Morton would discover a murderer so that I might blame someone other than myself."
It was almost a sob.

"But Halbert wasn't killed in the duel," Arabella re-
minded her quietly. "He was killed later. The two matters might have no connection."

After a long moment Louisa turned, her cheeks glistening. "What has Mr. Morton's enquiry uncovered?"
she asked faintly.

"He has been to the Otter House in Spitalfields."

"This is the 'flash house' he spoke of?"

"Yes. It seems that Halbert was there that evening,
just as the jarvey claimed."

Louisa shook her head. "And what does that mean,
pray?"

"Only that he was there, but we know not why."

Miss Hamilton did not respond for a moment.

"Did he go out that morning seeking death?" she
asked suddenly, "because he despaired of ever winning
my favour? Is that why he went?"

It was not a question Arabella Malibrant could answer.

"But what of Rokeby?" pressed on Louisa. "Was I not
perhaps too harsh with him, earning his enmity? And
look where that led."

"You take too much on yourself. Colonel Rokeby and
Mr. Glendinning were men, making decisions such as
men do. If Henry Morton went out tomorrow and were
killed in a duel defending my good name I should mourn

him, and think him a fool, but I should not take the blame. Mr. Morton makes his own way in the world, as did Halbert Glendinning. And you were likely not so cruel to him as you think. I hardly think you capable of real cruelty."

Louisa glanced at her, birdlike. "More capable than you think," she muttered.

Arabella decided to change her approach. "Besides, I always say that if a woman hasn't had at least one duel fought over her she should begin to question her charms. I've had three fought in my name."

Miss Hamilton smiled bleakly at this attempt to cheer her.

"I suppose one of them," went on Arabella, "was more about my husband's debts than about me, strictly speaking. But that's another story." She looked directly at the other woman. "No one died in your duel, Louisa. If Halbert was murdered it was in a less honourable way, and you can hardly take blame for that. Indeed, as I said, it might have nothing at all to do with you. It could have been a case of mistaken identity."

Louisa's eyebrows raised at this. "You are being very kind," she murmured, but there was appreciation in her voice.

An uneasy silence settled around them, punctuated by the street sounds echoing up from below.

"May I ask you a question, Louisa?"

Arabella received the smallest shrug in answer.

"Who is Richard?"

Very casually, Louisa put out a hand to the window casing. "Why do you ask?"

"On the stair, that evening at Lord Arthur's... you called out the name Richard."

Louisa shook her head as though in disbelief. Then

she turned and went to one of the military portraits. "Richard Davenant," she said, her voice warming noticeably. "We were engaged to be married, but he gave up his life at Albuera in 1811."

"And he is the man to whom Halbert was always compared... ?"

Louisa nodded.

"You must have taken his death very hard."

For a moment Louisa only stared at the portrait, and then managed a nod.

"It is a fine portrait," Arabella said, unable to bear the woman's distress any longer. "You have a significant talent."

"It is my brother Peter's work," Louisa said, drawing herself up a little. "Richard was his dearest friend, and brother-in-arms. You see, we have both lost terribly...." But she did not go on. Instead, she turned to Arabella. "One can be overwhelmed by grief," she said firmly, "and not be mad."

Chapter 19

Surgeon Bromley's waiting-room was rather a dismal place, dark, lined with hard wooden benches, but empty of patients. Military surgeons frequently set up in private practice upon their discharge from active duty, and in fact many of them did not wait for that formality. Stories were told of doctors who blithely informed their commanders that their other patients left them no time to go on campaign. Morton wondered if Robert Bromley had really succeeded to this degree. The address was good, but the premises seemed a trifle shabby for a physician who'd made any serious inroads on fashionable society.

It was rather a well-dressed gentleman, however, who presently emerged from the inner sanctum, picked up his hat and cane, and departed. A few moments later Bromley's sallow apprentice ushered the Runner in and pulled the door closed behind him, leaving the visitor with his master.

Across a polished table the two men stared at each other in surprise.

"Well, Dr. Bromley; I have the pleasure of meeting you again."

The other nodded curtly, and scowled.

It was the same small bald man, the same surgeon, who had been in attendance at Portman House when Morton had examined the body of Halbert Glendinning.

"You're one of those bloody Bow Street people. I've forgotten your name."

Morton grinned mirthlessly, and introduced himself. Bromley made a curt gesture toward a chair and they both sat.

"I've not changed my view," immediately announced the surgeon. "The man died of choking, on his own vomitus, brought on by intemperate use of alcohol, and other dissipations, doubtless."

"Doubtless," softly echoed Morton.

"I can tell you nothing more. Miss Hamilton is better out of it, I daresay. The man was clearly another lowborn blackguard, pretending to be a gentleman."

Morton wondered if this odd statement was an accident or if it was aimed at Morton. But now Bromley fell silent and merely glared at him, folding his arms defiantly over his small chest.

"Was Mr. Glendinning your patient?"

"He was not. My clients tend to be better bred . . . and not shirkers," he said, keeping his eye fixed on Morton.

"We do not all serve in the same way," Morton said evenly. "If he was not your patient, then how do you know of his 'dissipations'?"

Bromley tossed his hands up briefly in impatience. "No, I know nothing, just as you say. Like everyone else, I've heard it murmured, I cannot recollect when or by whom. But there were the appearances, on the night you and I saw him, after all."

"Are you intimate with the Hamiltons?"

"What is this in aid of, sir? I am a casual acquaintance of both families, no more. I was at Lord Arthur's entirely by chance. I made my diagnosis as a courtesy to my host. And I stand by it. There is an end to it—unless of course you have found some way to make some silver out of this poltroon's death."

Morton ignored this, letting his eye run casually around the room. The place was decorated with a series of sentimental oils depicting fallen British heroes, inevitably mourned by their comrades against darkening sunsets. Odd fancy for a former military surgeon, he thought.

Morton turned back to the little doctor. He let a certain threat slip into his voice. "It certainly is a curious chance, sir, that you seem to have attended at the deaths of both gentlemen to whom Miss Louisa Hamilton has been engaged."

The surgeon looked startled, but Morton did not quite know how to read his expression. "I had not thought of that. But I suppose, as you say, it is true. I had quite forgotten about the other. Or rather, had forgotten her misguided preference for him. That milk-livered soldier."

"Richard Davenant."

"Yes. I believe that was him."

"You were, in fact, there at his end?"

"At Albuera, during the peninsular campaign. Yes. I was regimental surgeon to the Thirty-fifth at the time. But he was dead when he got to me. Just like this other one."

"Why do you say he was milk-livered?"

"He ran from the enemy."

"How do you know this, Mr. Bromley?" A growing dislike had put a certain coldness into Morton's tone, of which the other man, in his apparently habitual ill-humour, seemed oblivious.

"He had a bullet squarely in the back of his head. He was supposed to be advancing. What conclusions would you draw, sir?"

"In a battle, surely many things are possible."

"They who brought him in confirmed it."

"You did not examine Davenant where he fell?"

"Nay, sir," snapped Robert Bromley. "It was not my role to go where the shot fell. Would you have me amputating limbs under cannon fire?"

Morton looked steadily back at him without answering.

"Sometimes," the surgeon went irritably on, "the men would wrap a fellow up in a blanket or some such matter and carry him back to me. The army discouraged it, as the folk who did this were often shirkers. They carried some 'beloved' comrade back, and then, strangely enough, never quite returned to their rightful places in the firing line."

"Was Richard Davenant carried back to you this way? You just said he was dead already."

"It was a battle—if you had ever been in one you would know that much is lost in the confusion. Perhaps he still had a faint pulse when he reached me. But it didn't last long."

"Could he speak?"

"No, sir, of course he could not, any more than you could under the same circumstances." The little man put his fingertips together and stared up at the ceiling.

"Some of his fellows were blubbering and making a great show of their grief about him, but it was clearly a ploy. The truth soon came out: The man had blanched at the sight of the French, and bolted, shamefully, at the moment of greatest peril. I've told others this, sir, and I'm weary of telling it. He was far from the only one. Some of these puffed-up tin soldiers, with their fine uniforms and their lies of glory, they weary me. I've seen them when they've not been so proud, sir. I've heard them scream and beg when I've had them on my table and taken a leg from them, or an arm. And I've seen many a wound that no one ever got from charging the enemy direct. No, sir, anyone who has been where I have been and seen what I have seen knows how rare true bravery is. And I will tell you something about the men who possess it, sir. They tend also to be the men with the best blood and purest pedigrees. The old, true stock of England. Not ill-bred bastards or the sons and grandsons of tradesmen and grasping, time-serving Scottish interlopers!"

Morton found himself wondering, not in a cool impersonal way, how a swiftly delivered uppercut would affect this vicious little doctor's opinions. He had already intimated Morton was a shirker—though apparently aiming this insult elsewhere—and passed judgement on sham gentlemen.

What were the real sources of Bromley's resentment? Could he have imagined himself a rival for a woman like Louisa Hamilton? But there were so many other possible reasons. A more plausible sweetheart stolen by one of these same tin soldiers. Or the fact that he could never have been a soldier himself. The Duke of York's height requirement, though hardly stringent, would certainly have eliminated this near-dwarf.

The man, at any rate, was cramped, bent, fairly curdled within by his hatreds, his jealousies. They reeked from him, like an offensive odour. Morton could barely stand to be in the little man's presence, and found his own anger welling up.

"In so great a battle I'm surprised that you remember the death of Richard Davenant. There must have been so many."

"I knew Davenant somewhat," Bromley admitted grudgingly.

"And did not like him."

"I didn't know him well enough to like or dislike him. But he was known to me by reputation."

"Who was it told you that Richard Davenant had run?"

Bromley threw up his hands. "I was hardly on a social footing with the whole Thirty-fifth Regiment of Foot!" he snapped back with what seemed unnecessary vehemence. But then, "It was some captain or other. I'd only recently been posted to the Thirty-fifth, and did not stay long. I went to the First Guards after that, which is a much better regiment in every respect."

A more fashionable one, at least, Morton reflected. And coincidentally enough, Rokeby's regiment. "Colonel Fitzwilliam Rokeby was not also in the Thirty-fifth Foot at that time, by chance?"

"To my knowledge, the Colonel has always been a member of the First Guards. Now, sir, if you please. I have much better ways of using my time than in idle discussions."

Morton made no move to leave.

"You disapproved of Miss Hamilton's impending marriage to Mr. Glendinning?" he asked.

"I disapprove of any comely woman throwing herself away on a coward."

"How do you know Glendinning was a coward?"

"It was all around town that he went out to meet Colonel Rokeby and near swooned from his fear."

"Unlike you, sir, who would go out to meet a man like Rokeby as though it were a ride in the country?"

The surgeon's face suddenly turned red. "What are you saying, sir?"

"That if you ever found the dark eye of a firearm peering at you, Mr. Bromley, I daresay you would be as frightened as young Glendinning. And if you don't think so, send a friend to call on me and I will aim a pistol at you and prove my point. Good day to you."

Morton gravitated back to the Golden Apple for his midday meal. Jimmy Presley wasn't there, but it was the haunt of several Runners and he had not been sipping his bitters long when a familiar voice interrupted his meditations.

"Now what is Henry Morton on to, going about London looking so thoughtful?"

Morton glanced up to find John Townsend smiling down on him benevolently.

"The people of London aren't used to men looking so contemplative, Morton; you will confound them. Perhaps frighten them. You might even make them wonder, if they still be capable of it."

Morton gestured to a chair and the venerable Townsend settled himself. Morton smiled, and only partly from the pleasure of Townsend's arrival. The eccentric veteran had turned out his short, corpulent

person in the most peculiar collection of ill-fitting clothing, some of it once very fine, none of it even remotely in
harmony. But although he certainly was no dandy, Morton had always thought he had the face of a stoic
philosopher.

Morton liked John Townsend immensely, and not
just because he had begun at Bow Street as his protégé.
The old man exhibited such courtly charm, and such an
avuncular concern for all his younger colleagues, that
Morton invariably found himself cheered in the man's
presence. And despite his apparent oddness, Townsend
was still the most effective Runner Bow Street had ever
known—even at his great age, he was formidable. He
knew the city and its denizens like no one else, and was
familiar with both princes and flash men. He was usually present when the Prince Regent entertained, and
when His Highness gambled John Townsend held his
money, releasing it as required. It was rumoured, of
course, that the old Runner had accumulated a great
fortune over his many years of profitable service. And it
might even be true. But Morton also knew the strength
of Townsend's integrity.

"So, Morton, what is it that has sent you so deep into
this foreign region of the mind?"

"I am reflecting on the place of coincidence in the
lives of men."

Townsend grinned. "Now there is a fitting subject for
an inquisitive mind," he said, twisting around and
searching, for the publican, apparently. "But I suspect
you aren't really being so philosophical.... There's
something more specific in Henry Morton's thoughts, if
I know the man at all."

Morton sipped his beer again and released a grunt of

agreement. "Did you hear about the duel at Wormwood Scrubs the other morn?"

"The one Mr. Vaughan and young Presley so rudely interrupted?"

"The very one. But did you hear that the man who had challenged Rokeby died that same evening?"

"Well, rumours of such a thing reached me," Townsend said. "And that is your coincidence?"

"Only in part. The man, whose name was Glendinning, was about to become engaged, perhaps that very evening. The woman he was intent on marrying had been formerly spoken for, but her previous gentleman was killed at Albuera in the year eleven."

"Ah, both her paramours died tragically," Townsend said.

"Yes, but even that is not the whole of the coincidence. The surgeon who saw her first man die in Spain was also present the other evening, when Mr Glendinning arrived dead in a hackney-coach."

"Well...!" Townsend said enthusiastically, and raised the brimming glass the barkeep had just brought him. "To coincidence!"

"But it goes even deeper than that. After her first fiancé died, the lady briefly indulged, then spurned, Colonel Fitzwilliam Rokeby, who was the duelist who stood against Glendinning. And later this surgeon, who saw her first man die in Spain, transferred to Rokeby's own regiment."

Townsend sipped his ale and considered a moment, his eyes losing focus. Just when Morton had begun to worry that age had chased their conversation from the old Runner's mind, he stirred. "Well, Morton. Coincidence and I have an uneasy accord. She is like an out-of-pocket relation. When she comes rapping at my door on rare occasions, I am as ready as anyone to tolerate her presence. I do my best to accommodate her, even welcome her, in fact. But when coincidence starts to become too familiar, to appear too often... Well, I find her a more and more disagreeable companion. What you have here is coincidence dropping by a little too often even to be offered tea, if you take my meaning."

"I have been thinking the same thing. But what it means I cannot yet fathom."

The veteran Runner produced a long-stemmed pipe and tobacco pouch and motioned to a servant to bring him a lamp. He lit his pipe reflectively, obscuring himself in cumulus. "Was Rokeby in Spain?" he asked.

Morton gazed at him thoughtfully. "Well, Mr. Townsend, I cannot answer that question. He is in the First Guards. But somehow the idea of Rokeby involving himself in anything as unprofitable or disagreeable as a real campaign seems unlikely."

"First Guards *were* in Spain, mind you," remarked Townsend. "But I can tell you one thing, Morton," he said, emitting a luxurious puff of scented smoke, "you've something more than coincidence, here. I am confident you will sort it out if you persist. However, you should take care about this business with the lady. You should take care. I'd not have any ill befall my favourite young colleague."

"It seems a reasonable enough commission," said Morton after a moment, "and 'tis very well rewarded."

"Oh, I daresay. But your Magistrate warned you away from it, did he not? He is not pleased with you now, and may become even less so. And it appears to involve you in a matter of vengeance, which is always, in my experience, an unpredictable and dangerous sort of a matter. Perhaps it is the revenge of the lady upon Rokeby, or Rokeby upon her. Or perhaps it is the revenge of some other person entirely, upon one or both of them. But in any case, 'tis a question of the passions, of woman and man, and such things are ever treacherous."

Morton said nothing, but felt a certain sense of the world moving around, as though Townsend had seen something he had not considered. Could he be in danger?

"This new lad, Presley," Townsend went on after several slow, satisfied puffs and a swallow of his ale, "what do you make of him?"

"Jimmy has a future at Bow Street, I think."

"Well," Townsend drawled, "not if he takes after our Mr. Vaughan, he doesn't. Now, Presley seems friendly to you, Morton; perhaps you should have a word with him. George Vaughan already has a follower or two too many at Bow Street."

Morton gazed at him in sober silence. Townsend clearly knew of the bribe paid by the duelists on Wormwood Scrubs. Had Sir Nathaniel even alerted him, asking Townsend the same questions he had put to Morton as they rode to meet the Glendinnings? And what had Townsend answered, Morton wondered.

Just then the door opened, admitting two men in a quick fan of light. Beside the bar a muttering conversation ensued. This grew in volume and began to flit from table to table like flame passing down a street, from one house to the next to the next.

"What is it?" Morton said to a man returning from the bar.

"Haven't you heard? Bonaparte fought the Prussians before the Duke of Wellington could join them, and he beat them, beat them terribly, at a town called Ligny.

The Prussian marshal, Blücher, was killed, and what's left of his army is running for the Rhine."

"Dear God," murmured Morton.

"Yes," the man said, "and the Austrians are nowhere to be seen. Now there's just the Duke left in the field against him." He shook his head. "We'll see what the British soldier is made of now."

As the man went off to his table Townsend eyed Morton. "Do you know what our Duke calls his brave British soldiers, Morton?"

"I do not."

"He calls them 'the scum of the earth—the very scum of the earth.' "

Chapter 20

So, you told Rokeby you would arrest him if he challenged you, then proposed he meet you at Gentleman John's for fisticuffs. And after that you challenged the little surgeon to a duel?" Arabella was both incredulous and delighted.

"I did not challenge him to a duel, I only said he might challenge me."

Arabella laughed. "Ah, well, that's all right then. Colonel Rokeby, I understand, is not extended this same courtesy?"

"You are intentionally refusing to understand," Morton said, exasperated and a little embarrassed by what he was admitting. "You are being forward and... and... I could not allow Rokeby to challenge me, because I am a Bow Street officer and mayn't duel, for it is against the law, but Bromley would never have the temerity to challenge me, because he is a fainthearted little man."

"That is all very convenient," Arabella said quickly. "The *duelist* may not challenge you but the *coward* may, though of course he won't, for he is a poltroon."

"It is exactly this kind of thing," Morton fired back, "that sent young Glendinning out to fight Rokeby."

"Is that what it was? Confronted with reason, he was driven to dueling?"

Morton threw up his hands. "That bitter little surgeon is like many a man who has never faced a loaded firearm—he believes in the myth of courage. I have had a pistol primed and aimed at my heart, and I can tell you there are only two kinds of men who don't know fear in such situations: those too stupid and insensible to realise what might happen, and men like Rokeby, who are unnatural, born without capacity for either fear or conscience. I could not bear the little—" Morton stopped before he used an extremely impolite term.

Arabella clapped her hands together and laughed. "Oh, Morton, you do charm me when you are so . . . *human*."

"And I am usually somewhat less than human, I collect?"

"Oh, no: You are more, and it's madding."

Morton shook his head. "Well, I shall try to be less perfect in future, as you find my faults so captivating."

They were at Arthur Darley's, Arabella as a somewhat scandalous guest, and Morton on paid duty to keep watch over the ladies' precious baubles. Morton had at first been inclined to refuse employment with Lord Arthur, thinking that the aristocrat was sending him a less than subtle message about their relative places in the world, but then he had decided he would accept, and show not the slightest sign of intimidation.

Lord Arthur, however, had greeted Morton as a welcome guest, been more genuine and gracious than Morton had any reason to expect, and left the Runner wondering what exactly he had fallen into. One would think Lord Arthur unaware that they were competing for the affections of the same woman. They *were* competing, were they not? But if one went by Darley's behaviour one would be forced to conclude they had come to some gentleman's agreement to share the lovely woman in question. Did gentlemen make such agreements?

Morton still could not fathom it.

Lord Arthur's guests were not quite typical of fashionable society. Poets, painters, and rather scruffy-looking journalists were as common as lords and ladies, and there was a certain paucity of soldiers. The scraps of conversation he overheard suggested, furthermore, that the military news was not foremost in their minds. Instead, they were talking about Lady Caroline Lamb's latest indiscretion and the rumours she was writing a novel about her affair with Byron.

As he mingled in the chattering rout, Morton had more than once been engaged in conversation himself—he was, after all, dressed as a gentleman—and when it came out that he was a Bow Street Runner, he even encountered some polite interest, as well as the usual hints of embarrassment and distaste. One writer of a certain celebrity had questioned him at length, listening raptly to Morton's stories of criminal ingenuity.

Now, however, as Arabella was visibly summoning up her wit to continue teasing him, Morton noticed with relief another man hovering nearby, clearly wishing to speak with one of them. It was Peter Hamilton, Louisa's half-brother.

"Mr. Morton, may I have a word with you when you are quite free?"

Arabella gave them both a fetching smile and swept off.

"Mr. Hamilton," Morton said, giving a slight bow. The man was dressed in black, though Morton knew that this was as much fashion as a sign of mourning.

The man looked warily over his shoulder to be sure that they could not be heard. "Mr. Morton, may I ask you again who has engaged you to look into Halbert Glendinning's passing?"

"I'm sorry, Mr. Hamilton, but I have been charged by my employer to reveal his identity to no one."

Hamilton raised his eyebrows and blew out a sigh of exasperation. "Let me just say this: If it is Louisa, pray be aware that she is not—" He shook his head and looked down at the carpet in embarrassment. "She has had, in the past, bouts of... distraction, or shall we say... nervous collapse... brought on by grief and loss. She is prone, at such times, to believe that she is persecuted and that there exist plots against her, even among those who care for her most. It is more than distressing. I tell you this, Mr. Morton, because I believe you are a man of character and would not take advantage of a woman in such straits."

"I am not in the habit of taking advantage of women at any time, Mr. Hamilton," Morton replied evenly.

"No, of course, Mr. Morton. Of course."

Peter Hamilton looked off over the crowd. Morton observed that the man's fists were tightly clenched.

"Dr. Bromley is my physician," Hamilton then said. "He assures me that Halbert expired of aspirating his own gorge." He took a long breath, as though to calm himself. "It is a sad thing to admit, but I fear it is the truth. As I told you, Halbert could be intemperate at times, and after the stress of that awful day..."

"But he came here from a criminal house, Mr. Hamilton, and the people at that house are most anxious to hide what occurred in their den. I know this, for I have been there."

Hamilton looked at him. "Mr. Morton, I am only asking you as a man of conscience, to consider my poor sister. She does not need someone stoking her delusions at this time. She needs only the truth."

"And Mr. Morton is concerned with nothing less," came a voice from over Morton's shoulder.

He turned to find Arthur Darley approaching.

"Do forgive me, Peter, I could not help but overhear." Darley nodded graciously to Morton. "I assure you, Peter, that if Mr. Morton believes there was foul play involved in Halbert's death, then you may be confident that this is very likely the case." He turned to the Runner. "You will excuse me, Mr. Morton, but I have had a very good character of you."

Morton merely nodded gratefully. What could one say to that?

Hamilton stood a moment, as if unsure how to proceed, and then asked Morton, "But have you found out why Halbert was in this den of iniquity?"

"Not as yet, Mr. Hamilton, but be sure that I will. There is always someone in such places willing to peach on their fellows for a little coin or if the right persuasions are applied."

Hamilton bowed his head in acquiescence. "Well, I suppose if the thing is to be done," he sighed, "it is best to press on and do it promptly. Find out for sure. Find out everything. The sooner it is all behind us, the sooner

Louisa may begin to forget." The skin of the man's face drew suddenly tight and he blinked quickly. "The sooner we may all begin to forget."

The evening's entertainment was over and Morton sat with Darley and Arabella drinking claret in the library, a room Morton coveted. What books! This was how a man should live.

Darley and Arabella both seemed completely at ease and Morton was determined not to be outdone in this. He lounged in a chair, delicately sipping his claret.

For her part, Arabella appeared every inch the lady in these surroundings. Of course she was an actress, adept at her craft, and certainly she had played ladies enough on the stage. But gone was the Arabella that Morton knew. She of the uninhibited laugh, the outlandish wit, the bawdy jest. Morton hardly knew this elegant creature, perched so primly on the edge of her chair.

"It is curious that you both uncovered the identity of Richard Davenant," Lord Arthur said. "You need merely have asked me."

"You knew him, then?" Morton said.

"I never had the pleasure of actually meeting him, but his mother was my wife's second cousin. He was a young man with a future, or so it was believed. In the Davenant family, the world revolved around Richard. And what a soldier he was! Do you know, he refused advancement so that he might not be removed from the heat of battle? That is the kind of man he was. Men would follow him through the halls of Hades, I was told. It is difficult to imagine that such a man would break and run from the French."

"Men do break," Morton said softly. "Even such men as you describe. But could this all be family myth, do you think? Some families do make heroes of their lost sons."

Darley shrugged. "I cannot answer that, though I have heard this of Richard Davenant from others as well. Bear in mind also that these charges of cowardice, of fleeing the enemy, were never officially stated. It was a whispering campaign, perhaps by some jealous comrade."

"Or someone who was competing for the attentions of Louisa Hamilton," Arabella added. "The poor woman has suffered the rumours of Davenant's cowardice until even she has begun to have doubts—and this has burdened her with a terrible sense of guilt and betrayal."

Morton nodded agreement at this. "Is it not odd that there are rumours about the characters of both these men Miss Hamilton favoured? Richard Davenant was, in the end, a coward, or so we're told. Glendinning was something worse, if we believe he was in the Otter for the reason that most are there." He paused to reflect. "It is as though there were someone out to ruin the good name of any man Louisa Hamilton might choose. This might be coincidental, but it might not."

"Well, it is clear that this vile man Bromley is behind both these campaigns," Arabella said firmly. "He declared Glendinning dead from choking after drinking himself senseless, and Richard Davenant dead of cowardice."

"Yes, it does seem so, and he was later the surgeon for Rokeby's regiment, though I cannot quite make the connection there." Morton turned to Darley, who appeared lost in thought. "Do you know this surgeon, Bromley, well, Lord Arthur?"

"Only vaguely. He is actually a physician, and reputedly a very good one. His practise is largely composed of retired military officers and their families, and these people cannot say enough good about him, apparently. I know a number of people who are his patients and they concur, though I confess, I find him a sour little man. He came that night with someone—I cannot recollect whom—though it was all the same to me. I keep a somewhat open door here at Portman House."

Yes, Morton thought, how else would you explain a Bow Street Runner and an actress taking their leisure here at this hour?

"Has he known Louisa Hamilton long, do you think?" Morton asked.

Darley regarded him gravely. "You don't really think that Bromley has something to do with this?"

Morton shrugged. "He is a physician, and if I am not wrong and Glendinning was poisoned, then who better than a physician to administer the final draught?"

"But Bromley was here, not at the Otter.... Of course, I see—you aren't speaking literally. He might have supplied the poison to some confederate." Darley looked over at Arabella and raised an eyebrow.

"Does this let Rokeby off, then?" she asked, disappointment clear in her tone.

"I have let no one off," Morton said, "for I fear we are not near the truth yet. I have been meaning to ask, Lord Arthur: Glendinning's manservant told me that his employer received a note the afternoon of the duel. It was delivered by a boy. This might have had some relevance to Glendinning's later actions. Would it be possible to ask his parents if such a note was found among their son's belongings?"

Darley shook his head. "I hardly think they will cooperate, given their feelings about the matter, but I could ask if you think it important."

"One can never tell what will be important. Often, in these matters, it is some scrap of knowledge you have had all along that proves the culprit's undoing. Something you have looked at a dozen times and noticed nothing amiss."

Lord Arthur shook his head, though it was in admiration, Morton suddenly realised. Was Arthur Darley a little bored with his coddled life? Did that explain the risqué company, the stage-actress mistress? And now, his apparent interest in the efforts of a Bow Street Runner?

"How will you proceed, Morton?" Darley enquired. "I'm not sure how you make your decisions."

"Nor is Henry, Arthur," Arabella added quickly. "Why, I have seen him make decisions that surprise even him."

Chapter 21

His next decision actually did surprise Morton. He did not pay another visit to the Otter in Spitalfields, as reason might have dictated. He was not yet ready to go there again. Instead, when he rose the next morning it seemed to him there was something else he wanted to know more badly. Something that had its seeds in the conversation with Arabella and Darley the night before.

He rented a handsome bay hack, and was on the road leading south into Sussex by seven.

It was a pleasant day for a ride, with high summer rapidly approaching, and billowing white clouds spotted motionless in the blue sky.

If not for the threat of war that hung over England like dense fog, Morton would have been almost lighthearted. But even among the country-folk he met as he went, there was a palpable anxiety, and when they learned he had come recently from London, they asked what news, and then looked like people bracing themselves for the worst.

Morton could say little. The news of the Prussian defeat had spread out into the surrounding countryside as quickly as a horse could speed.

It seemed to Morton that England was like the country people he encountered along the way, bracing itself for the worst. Bonaparte was like a phoenix—he rose up from the flames of war again and again. Morton wondered if an end could ever be made of him.

Once into Sussex, he began stopping. At every country tavern or inn he asked the same questions, and slowly but surely was pointed in the right direction.

The country-folk, he soon discovered, were intensely, possessively proud of their regiment. This came as rather a surprise to Morton, who had been all too familiar with the cynicism of the metropolis, and it began to become more clear to him how Britain had fought this long, terrible war with French ambition. Londoners had laughed about the common people telling their children that Bony would come and eat them, perhaps believing it themselves. Radicals and poets claimed the humble were being exploited for a struggle that was not their own. But in fact ordinary men and women seemed to have been filled with a fierce, unselfconscious patriotism, a determination to preserve the Britain they knew—that the sophisticates in the capital hardly imagined.

So there was no lack of willingness to talk about the Thirty-fifth. By the end of the day the Runner had been directed to the Queen's Head Inn in the town of Mayfield, where a certain veteran by the unlikely name of Sempronious Stretton was said to hold court on a nightly basis. Stretton had come back from Spain without one of his legs in '12 or perhaps '13, people said, but had been with the regiment for fully thirty years before

that. If he couldn't answer Morton's questions, no one
could.

By the time Morton reached the place, it was night-
fall. He swung from the saddle he had kept for many
hours and consigned his horse to a shuffling, apparently
speechless ostler. Then, groaning a little in relief and
stretching, he walked through into the back garden
where the patrons were taking advantage of the warm
summer evening to sit out on benches or upturned
stumps, drinking their pots of cider and ale and drawing
on pipes whose coals glowed and faded in the dusk. The
dark shapes of the elms that surrounded the inn rose
above them against a deepening azure sky in which the
first stars were beginning to glitter.

For a good while Morton smoked and said nothing,
enjoying the peacefulness of the garden, the palpable
contentment of the place, and the slow rhythms of country speech that rose and fell in the soft evening air, as if
time, too, had slowed, and hours such as this would drift
on forever and there would never again be any need for
fretfulness or impatience. But then finally, in one of the
longer lulls, he murmured to his neighbour, asking if he
knew Sempronious Stretton.

"Oh, aye, friend. There's he a-lighting his pipe; he of
the peg leg."

He indicated the man who sat near the center of the
gathering. Stretton was a greying man of perhaps fifty,
his cheeks stubbled, but his chin firm and his blue eyes
bright. He had been speaking little, but Morton had already noticed that when he did speak there was immedi-
ate deference.

"Sergeant Stretton?" Morton took the opportunity to
politely hail him. He had expected, with so strange and
seemingly learned a name, that the man might be one of

the occasional "gentlemen rankers" whom want or eccentricity had driven to enlist as private soldiers. But when he saw him, he knew that this after all was a man of England's old peasant stock.

"Aye, sir?"

"Am I told aright that you served a captain by the name of Richard Davenant?"

There was a silence, and Morton could feel the curious eyes of the whole gathering upon him while Stretton bent his head a little in what seemed to be deep contemplation. Then, slowly, the old soldier beckoned to Morton to come and join him. The man sitting nearest vacated his place unasked, and Morton made his way through to sit where he had been invited.

"Who art thou who asks?" wondered Sempronious Stretton quietly.

"Henry Morton. I have come from London and am a friend of the lady Davenant was to have wed."

Stretton stared at him a moment, and though the gaze was not entirely unfriendly it was certainly suspicious.

"There are those up in London-town who have spread lies about my captain and fouled his fine name," the old soldier said, his voice dark.

"I am not one of them. These rumours have been repeated so often that they have begun to acquire the lustre of truth. I would gladly gainsay them but I was not there, at Albuera. What can you tell me of Richard Davenant and his last hours, that I might tell his lady?"

The man gazed at Morton a moment more, only the insects pulsing in the invisible fields beyond, the gathered men drawing on their pipes and watching. Then Stretton nodded, turning his gaze away.

"Captain Davenant commanded Third Company,

First Battalion, for some two years. That was my company, and I did know him, I knew him well. He was a fine officer, the finest I ever served, and most every man he commanded would say just the same. He was a gentleman of true generosity and tested valour, who cared for the lives and comforts of his soldiers. He was the soldiers' friend, sir, and that was not to be said of every man who held a commission. He fought with honour in a dozen engagements in Portugal and in Spain, and he died at Albuera, in May of the year eleven."

He finished speaking, and a deep quiet fell over the men in the inn yard. Here and there a red glow brightened as men had thoughtful recourse to their pipes.

When Morton felt it proper to break the silence, he asked: "Were you there that day, Sergeant Stretton?"

"I was there," the man replied, still not looking at Morton.

"Did you see him fall?" Morton asked very softly.

Sempronious Stretton took a long breath, then he began to speak again.

"The battle fought at Albuera was a very terrible battle, sir. We were under the command of General Beresford, who was a good soldier, but not so able a field general as the Duke of Wellington, who was in the north at that time. We were facing Marshal Soult, who was the best the French had in Spain. The weather was hot as a smith's forge, and the place where we fought was covered in tall grasses—so dry that the flame from the muzzles of our muskets set the grasses afire. Even as we engaged, the ground was burning, and men who fell were sometimes burned to death before they could be helped—or they died of the smoke, which was harsh and thick. It was here that Colborne's brigade was lost, and where Myers was killed and most of his fusileers destroyed while taking the center. It cost them all but fifteen hundred of their six thousand. We were on the right flank, and we lost close to half, and more than half our officers. All through that terrible afternoon Captain Davenant was calling for us to go forward, and we did go forward. Again and again he rallied us and called to the other captains to bring up their companies, even when matters seemed to be going very hard for us. I saw him, sir, before he died, but I did not see him fall. I was in the wing squad, second rank. I saw him go ahead into the smoke, he and all those with him, and be swallowed up in it."

Silence again left Morton wondering if that was all Stretton had seen. After another long moment, he asked: "Were you amongst those who carried him back?"

"Nay, sir, I was not. I was in ranks all night. I heard later that he had fallen. Like so many others."

"I am told, Mr. Stretton, that there was a captain and some other soldiers who carried him back to the dressing-post."

"It may be so. I did not see it nor ever hear of it."

With reluctance, Morton decided he must press the issue even further.

"The battalion surgeon, Bromley, claims that the men who carried Captain Davenant back said he was shot while fleeing the French."

"He did not flee," Stretton said firmly, more than a little menace in his voice. "He did not flee. I know men who were near him at the end—men I would trust with my life and whose word I would never question. They were there, and Captain Davenant was before them."

Morton gazed quickly about the gathering. Men

shuffled their feet and looked down at the earth. Some
muttered to their fellows. But he was here to find the
truth and he would not leave without it.

"But he received his wound in the back," Morton
said.

"What of it, sir?" Stretton said, his voice clearly angry
now. "Many a man is shot while helping another, or
turning back to call others forward. Some are shot by
their own in the thick of battle, and there was no battle
in which such a thing were more likely to happen. The
smoke was thick as night at times, and men from both
sides shot their own—more times than any would care
to know.

"You may tell this man Bromley he'd best not come
into Sussex, and repeat his lies here where men know
better. And you may also tell Captain Davenant's lady
that she should keep his memory bright. You may tell
her, and you may tell all of those who have heard the
lies, that Richard Davenant was as brave a man as I
have ever known—and I have known many. That is all I
have to say about it."

Next morning Henry Morton rode back to London
through the shining green and chestnut countryside
with a lighter heart. Always he had gone forward, Captain Davenant, urging the men on. Fighting, calling to
the other captains. Until . . . he had disappeared into the
smoke.

No more was possible, but it was surely enough.
Enough to tell Miss Hamilton, and enough for Morton
himself. Some malice—and not an aimless malice—had
determined to tarnish a good man's name. It might have
needed only a few words spoken at the right time and

into the right ears. Then the usual avidity with which people took up and spread such a story took over, and soon enough the damage was done. A thousand pities that London would never hear the simple eloquence of private soldier Stretton.

Why had Morton ridden so far to hear this? Because if Richard Davenant was being defamed, whoever was responsible was a man whose other activities Henry Morton wanted to look into further.

And who else might that be than the little dispenser of poisons, Dr. Robert Bromley?

Chapter 22

It was too late to carry the good news to Louisa Hamilton, so Morton had Wilkes return the hackney-horse to its livery, bathed and changed, and went down to Drury Lane for the last act of Arabella's new production of Dibden's *Revenge*. As he strode up to the theatre he saw a dark, solitary figure looming through the fog, seemingly awaiting him on the front steps under the marble portico. It proved to be Vickery, another of his brother officers from Bow Street, who had obtained Morton's old job of guarding on performance nights. It was in this function that Morton had first met Mrs. Malibrant, retrieving a valuable ring that had been snatched from her in the foyer.

"Well, Mr. Vickery, any excitement?"

James Vickery was a sober, slow-spoken man.

"Well, Mr. Morton, the flash crowd are out and about on a dim night like this, that's sure."

"Oh, aye?"

"A lady's diamond bracelet taken, just an hour ago, but I saw the dab and gave him chase."

"Nab him?"

"Aye, I did. Ran him down in Little Russell Street. The lady gave me a guinea for me trouble, too. But then the management of the theatre here comes out and abuses me for deserting me post."

Morton laughed. Typical enough! The private parties who hired Runners for a specific service seemed to think they should drop every other demand of their profession. But no one, as Morton's colleagues would often say indignantly to each other, ever promised these clients exclusive use of an officer of justice.

"What are the swells saying about the new play?"

"Well, Mr. Morton, you know I don't listen much to their prattle. Sounds as if they approve Mrs. Malibrant, though."

Morton smiled and gave him a friendly slap on the arm before going in.

Henry Morton approved Mrs. Malibrant too, as he told her an hour or so later, backstage. It had been a few days since they'd had this kind of privacy and the kisses tasted particularly good, the look in each other's eyes as they held each other out for inspection particularly warm.

"Let's retreat to my little castle and have a supper" was Arabella's suggestion.

There'd been a full house and out on the front porch there was still near-pandemonium in the fog. A huge press of carriages struggled to move down the narrow street to the theatre doors. Competing with the coachmen and the private lackeys calling out to try to locate clients and masters were the link men with their torches, bawling *"Who goes home!"* to offer their services as escorts.

"Perhaps we should just stroll down to the Strand and see if we can get a cab there," suggested Morton.

But then a hackney-driver hailed them, seeming to make a superhuman effort to barge his way past his competition to reach them. Other potential fares shouted at the man in indignation but he was determined to give Morton and Mrs. Malibrant the benefit of his exertions. Morton smiled. The jarveys took pleasure in serving the beauties of Drury Lane.

A few minutes later they had struggled free of the crowd and, in the intimacy of the coach interior, after a few more kisses of reacquaintance, Henry Morton brought his fair companion abreast of his efforts.

Arabella seemed to regard Morton oddly as he told her what he had done with his last two days. "Well, if nothing else comes of it," she offered flatly, "Louisa will be glad of the news." She eyed Morton. "I should think she will be very grateful indeed."

"Now, Arabella," Morton said, sensing the drift of things, "I did not do it for that reason, as you well know. There could easily be some connection between Davenant's death and Glendinning's. You remarked on it yourself."

She nodded thoughtfully. "Yes, I suppose. But do be aware, Henry, of your propensity to rescue women in distress—especially troubled women. And if they are comely into the bargain . . ."

"If I did not know better I would say you were jealous."

"You do know better," Arabella answered, pulling her shawl about her, and in doing so, moving imperceptibly away from him in the carriage.

Morton did not quite know how to retrieve his last remark, or save the situation, and they rode on in silence for a time.

"I suppose it comes back to this man Bromley," he said at last.

Arabella glanced at him, and then quickly away, but then she relented. "I suppose it is the unavoidable conclusion, though I will be disappointed to see that rogue Rokeby go free. Did you not say that Rokeby, Davenant, and Bromley were all in the same regiment?"

"Nay, Bromley transferred from Davenant's Thirty-fifth to Rokeby's Guards, and that is odd enough. Then Bromley ruins the reputation of Louisa Hamilton's dead fiancé. Rokeby makes a play for Miss Hamilton, but she refuses him. Some months later Rokeby provokes Glendinning into a duel, and when that fails someone with some knowledge of physic administers a draught of poison later the same evening."

"Well, then Bromley has assisted Rokeby," Arabella said, though without her usual enthusiasm. "How else can you read this book?"

"I fear this is a book with too many possible endings. If you consider—"

"Where on earth are we going?" Arabella suddenly interrupted.

Morton stared at her in surprise for an instant, then twisted round and peered out the coach window. They had turned into a narrow stone passage that neither of them recognised. This was not the way to Red Lion Square and Theobald's Road.

"Henry," said Arabella, looking out the other side.

They came swarming out of the foggy shadows as the coach rolled to a stop. Four, perhaps five of them, silent and swift.

Morton reacted before he thought.

As the first man wrenched open the coach door, the

Runner braced himself and lashed out with his foot as hard as he could. The blow caught the man squarely in the chest and he reeled backward, colliding with his fellows. Morton knew he had to get out of the tight confines of the coach. He was aware of Arabella's shrill cries behind him as she grappled with someone on the other side. He lunged forward and leapt out into the night air, meeting another of them head-on and bowling the man back with his superior weight. An iron bar clashed and rattled on the cobbles as it fell from the hand of his assailant. A sharp blow hit Morton on his shoulder blade, and he whirled and caught the attacker's arm before he could strike again. Wrenching this man around, he thrust him tumbling into the path of another. But there were too many.

"Do him, do him! Smash his pate!"

The frightened cry was coming from above, from the driver, who was struggling to control his pitching, neighing horses. Morton turned and vaulted up onto the swaying body of the coach. Hands grabbed his legs from behind but he kicked out savagely, breaking free and ripping his tight breeches as he did. The jarvey saw him coming and struck down at him with his whip, cutting Morton a searing hot lash across the cheek.

Roaring with pain and fury, Henry Morton seized the driver's wrist before he could draw back, and holding his own position with one hand, hauled the man bodily down over his shoulder. The jarvey cried with panic as he tumbled headfirst toward the cobbles. Morton scrambled with frantic energy up onto the seat, slamming free the brake as he did.

"Arabella!" He glanced down the far side of the vehicle as he fumbled for the reins, and saw his mistress hanging half out the door, struggling with a man who was trying to pull her into the street. Morton lashed the reins and the frightened horses bolted forward. The man holding Arabella still clung to her, being dragged along.

But then some instinct warned Morton of danger on the other side, and he pivoted. Another figure, lithe and athletic, was bounding up toward him, arm raised. Morton squirmed away, seeing the silver flash. The blade cut through his coat and stuck hard into the wood of the carriage frame close beside him. The attacker did not let go of his weapon, and for an instant he and Morton looked into each other's faces. Morton had a vivid impression of snub features, cheeks deeply pitted with smallpox, a shining bald head. Then he swung his arm and struck the man a tremendous blow with his free hand, catching him squarely in the face, feeling all his strength behind his fist. The man went limp, his eyeballs tilted upward, and he dropped away.

On the other side of the coach there was a cry of pain from a male voice.

"Filthy blowen!"

"Prigger!" howled Arabella.

Morton glanced down to see the figure of a man sprawling on the cobbles behind them. He urged the horses on. Obstacles loomed ahead in the dark passage but he drove straight at them. The carriage bounced crazily over whatever littered the narrow way, but kept its wheels, and in a few moments shot out into the comparative brightness and space of High Holborn.

Chapter 23

He drove Arabella up to Theobald's Road. When he opened the carriage door he found her calmly using a fine linen handkerchief to wipe the small dagger she'd used to stab her assailant.

"Have they harmed you?" Morton asked.

"Not so much as you," Arabella said, reaching out to his bleeding face.

Morton winced, and she offered him her already stained handkerchief.

"I'll be but a trice," Morton told her.

Once Arabella was safe in her house he drove rapidly back through the thickening fog to Bow Street and there found Vickery and a couple of other officers. By the time they returned to the little alley, however, it was deserted but for a single figure, lying motionless in an impossibly awkward heap on the filthy stones, like an abandoned doll. It was the hackney-coachman, and he was dead, his neck broken when Morton had thrown him from his seat. A few dribbles of fresh blood were the only other sign that anything had happened here at all.

Although a weary hour of police procedures passed
before Henry Morton could return, he found Mrs.
Malibrant still awake, clutching a glass of brandy in her
upstairs parlour. White and shaken, she looked much
worse than when he'd left her. He sat beside her and re-
arranged the shawl over her shoulders. When the maid
had gone out, he reinforced the effect by putting his arm
around her and drawing her close.

"It is strange," she said tonelessly, "how it takes a time
before one feels afraid."

"You were magnificent," Morton told her.

"I don't know what came into me," she said in vague
wonder. "Some sort of fury. I'm frightened out of my
wits now, just thinking about it. Is that what men feel in
scrapes and battles and so on?"

"Perhaps. When they're finally into the thick of it."

Now she looked at him with sudden solicitude, and
reached again to gingerly touch his face.

"Poor you. Does it sting?"

The line where the coachman had whipped him was
rising into an ugly welt, pulsing fiercely and bleeding a
little in one corner. The blow had caught Morton across
lips and nose and one cheek, but by great good fortune
had missed his eye.

He winced again. "The man who gave it me got
worse," he remarked quietly.

"Dead?"

Morton nodded.

Arabella seemed to grow even paler, but then deliberately turned away from her thoughts. "A poultice it
needs," she said firmly. "Christabel! She must make you
a poultice."

And for a while Morton let her minister to him, as it seemed to help her as much as it did him. He knew she was recovering when she began to laugh and make bawdy jests with her maid Christabel about the rather revealing rip in Morton's best breeches.

Then they talked about it, both with a glass at hand, Morton lying back holding the dressing across his tender face.

"They must have corrupted the jarvey," he said. "He was so ready to take us at the theatre, you remember. And then he drove to where they were waiting. But my guess is that he wasn't really one of them. He seemed to have little enough stomach for the business, once they'd begun."

"He's past regretting now," remarked Arabella.

"Aye, a pity too. He could have told us much."

"But who were they, and...and...*why*?" Arabella sounded a little fragile still—the shock that evil intentions should come so close, personally, to her.

"Robbery seems unlikely," he said, thinking aloud. "There were plenty of better marks, and they didn't go about it like highwaymen."

"I don't suppose it could have been directed against me?" Arabella asked in a small voice.

Morton gave her a painful, but he hoped reassuring, smile. "I trust you haven't been saying anything too intolerably cutting to your rivals, Mrs. Malibrant." When her look showed she was trying seriously to remember, he laughed affectionately. "Nay, it was no theatrical tiff," he told her. "They were after Henry Morton, and it was only a shame that you were with me."

"Then whom have *you* antagonised, Mr. Morton?"

This needed real consideration.

"A Runner has no end of foes," he remarked. "The question only is, who hates him most? Whom has he thwarted most recently?"

"And...?"

"I suppose, especially after the attack on my lodgings, that the friends of the Smeetons come to mind. Yet I cannot feel that they would be so well organised, so patient and cunning as these were." Morton knit his brows, but even that hurt.

"Who else?"

"O'Doyle, Raggles, Thurtell, Otley," he wearily rhymed off. Arabella looked at him in alarm. "And these are just a few of the men I've had transported, or sent up to prison, and who've cursed me for it."

"Lor'," breathed out Arabella. "You ought to have warned me when we met."

"Then there's Rokeby." Morton's eyes narrowed as he thought. "I insulted him at his club, but he's not like to meet me at Gentleman John's. If he cannot line up a man to shoot him with a pistol, perhaps this is what he would do. He certainly has the resources to pay for it. And if he did, then his poisoning of Glendinning suddenly seems more likely. Is he so vengeful, do you think?"

"Perhaps he does not like it that you are enquiring into the death of Halbert Glendinning."

"Perhaps not," agreed Henry Morton. "Or perhaps, at any rate, *someone* doesn't." They sat musing in silence awhile, and then his eye lit on the dagger on the walnut side table at Arabella's elbow. It was only a few inches long, almost an ornament really, contrived to dangle discreetly within her outer garments on a fine silver chain.

"I never knew a woman to bear such a thing," he said.

She looked back at him innocently. "If you did," she said, "we'd have lost the element of surprise, wouldn't we?"

Morton smiled in acknowledgement.

Arabella abruptly turned quite businesslike. "Now that we know the truth about Richard Davenant," she said, "how do we proceed?"

"Well, Miss Hamilton's to be informed, I suppose. I expect that in itself is worth her two hundred pounds. And another visit to the Otter is in order."

"I should look out of place in the Otter," Arabella said decisively. "So I will bear the good news to Louisa."

Morton opened his mouth to object but then thought better of it.

There was a sudden hailing and din of raised voices from the street, and Morton and Arabella went to the window, casting it open. People were spilling out of doors, and all along the street windows were being thrown open.

"What is it?" Morton called down, and a boy of perhaps sixteen, catching sight of Arabella, stopped in his flight.

"Wellington has been defeated," he cried breathlessly. "At Quatre Bras. The army is routed and retreating in tatters. Bonaparte is marching on Brussels!"

Chapter 24

Morning light revealed a Bell Lane that looked little different from a thousand other small, unfashionable London streets. Heavy drays rumbled down its narrow length with barrels from the brewery, and it was otherwise crowded with ragged but apparently innocent commerce. There were even the usual milkmaids in their white pinafores and black taffeta bonnets, pails dangling from the yokes across their shoulders. From a particularly pretty girl Henry Morton bought a cup of milk and flirted for a few pleasant moments, finding that, despite the neighbourhood, she was the very pattern of modesty.

The Otter's door stood open, airing, and he stopped a moment to inspect its strong and polished Bramah lock. Aside from it, there was no bar or other fastening.

When he went down he found the barroom deserted except for an old crone wiping the tables. Constellations of dust motes hung in the beams of light that angled from two basement windows high in the wall.

"This house be closed, yer worship," said the old woman in a toothless mumble.

Morton looked around thoughtfully. He wondered what secrets the rest of the place might hold. What would he find if he went up those stairs behind the bar? But even for a Runner, armed only with a clasp-knife and his baton, it might be ill-advised to mount them alone and unannounced, especially when no one at Bow Street knew he was here. His could be the next corpse found floating facedown in the Thames.

But then, even as he pondered, a small figure came tripping unconcernedly down that same staircase. The little serving-wench he'd seen before: Lucy.

She stopped when she reached the bottom, and for a moment they regarded each other. Then Morton smiled at her, and was rewarded with a tiny, grimacing kind of half-smile in return. She looked nervous, but also curious, and Morton was struck again by the air of extraordinary intelligence that seemed to play over her sharp little features.

He turned and sat down on one of the benches along the wall, in the light. Continuing to smile at her, he patted the bench beside him with his hand, and invited her with a motion of his head to join him. After a moment's hesitation, and a wary glance at the old woman, she came.

She sat down a little farther from him than he had indicated, and did not look at him. The sickened thought passed through Henry Morton's mind that she had probably obeyed such a summons from other gentlemen many times before, and for other purposes. Yet, yet, that look almost of trust she had given him perhaps meant that she understood he did not want what other men had wanted. And she probably knew that men rarely came to the Otter for carnal pleasures at this hour of the day. The crone stood hesitating, motionless, regarding them both suspiciously, apparently trying to decide whether to object again, or to go and alert someone.

Morton casually fished a shilling from an inside pocket and tossed it in her direction.

"Do thy cleaning, Mother," he told her. "The kinchin and I will only work our jaws a space."

Muttering something unintelligible, the old woman bent for the coin and did as she was bidden. Morton turned back to the little girl.

"Thou art called Lucy?" he asked in as friendly a tone as he could command, and once more smiled.

She nodded, still not looking at him, and rocked a little on the bench, tapping her heels against the wall behind her. She was dressed as she had been before, in shapeless dirty rags, but in this better light Morton could see them to be scraps of cast-off adult clothing, a bit of ruffle visible here, an odd little length of pleated hem there. She seemed to have tidied her hair slightly this time.

"How old art thou, Lucy?"

He hardly expected any real answer, but she screwed up her face in a considering expression.

"My mamma told Joshua I was born at Michaelmas," she replied, in a high, clear voice, like a bird's, "in the year before the year when Admiral Nelson was shot by the French. Joshua told me that this happened a *decade* ago, which is a word meaning ten years. So, I will say that I am going on to be eleven years and a half a year old, but I cannot tell it for certain, because neither Joshua nor my mamma are entirely to be trusted.

Although for different reasons. I have been here at this house for a year and seven months: This is a true fact that I know, as I have recorded it myself."

Morton blinked at this extraordinary speech.

"You work it out very well!" he remarked.

Now she looked at him and smiled a quick, proud smile, before resuming her former attitude.

"Does your . . . mamma come here to see you?"

"Oh, no. Joshua gave her thirty shillings for me, but she had to promise not to come back. And she promised it."

Morton shuddered and tried to think what else he could ask her that might serve his purposes. He did not want to know anything more about her life. He wished he didn't know as much as he suddenly did.

But before he could, she looked up at him and asked her own question.

"What happened to your face?"

His hand went up automatically to the painful red streak that disfigured his features.

"A man mistook me for a horse," he ruefully told her.

"He mistook you for a *horse!*" cried Lucy with a sudden silvery peal of delight. "How could he be so daft!" And she laughed again, immoderately, as if Morton's answer had appealed to a deep enthusiasm for the absurd. The old woman peered over at them and scowled bitterly.

Morton joined the girl's laughter.

"Now, Lucy, can you tell me something?"

"You don't look like a *horse!*"

"No. Now, can you remember something for me? Do you remember seeing a man last week, a gentleman it was, dressed in dark clothes and a high white neck-cloth? You might have been taking him drinks. Maybe many drinks."

But now the mood abruptly changed. The old woman was staring very hard, and Lucy, glancing anxiously at her, suddenly blanched with an expression of pure fear. She said nothing.

Morton saw, and quickly retreated. He'd not do this little soul any further harm, whatever the needs of his investigation.

"Ah, well, no matter. I'm sure there were many gentlemen. Who could tell them all apart?" He reached for his hat, which he had set down on the bench beside him. But in the moment he was turned away he felt a light motion at his side, as a quick hand pulled the volume he had left in his coat deftly from its pocket.

He turned in surprise, then could not but smile at the look of helpless fascination with which the little thief was gazing at the treasure her fingers had been unable to resist. She cradled it in her lap like some precious offering before an altar. His surprise turned to astonishment, however, when she delicately opened it to the title page.

"LORD . . . BY-RON . . . HEB-REW . . . MEL . . . O . . . DIES," she pronounced slowly and carefully. Then looked up at him, wide-eyed. "What is that?"

"Poems," he murmured. "You can read this, Lucy?"

"I am learning," she whispered, confidentially. "I began with my mamma. Now Joshua shows me sometimes, and sometimes the gentlemen do." This suggested a side of both Joshua and "the gentlemen" Morton would hardly have credited. But then, there was something particularly appealing and determined about the gaze in this child's eyes. "I am collecting things," she added. "Papers with writing on them, so I can practise."

"This is extraordinary," he murmured appreciatively.

"But I don't have..." she went on, hesitant but daring, "I've never had...a *whole book*." The pure, passionate need with which she said it, the naked childish greed, made Henry Morton shake his head.

"Take it, Lucy. Take it. It's yours."

Morton wondered if he had ever in his life seen true happiness. It startled him. Was there really anything in the world to warrant such ecstasy? He would not have believed it possible.

In an instant she was gone with her prize, bounding lightly up the steps into whatever terrible world lay above, joy in the very spring of her limbs. The old crone bent darkly muttering to her task again and Henry Morton was left by himself, fighting back inexplicable tears.

Chapter 25

There were more people in the Otter that night than Morton had seen on either of his previous visits, making it feel more like a normal public house in a shabby quarter of town. Men were crowded along the walls and played cards at both of the tables amidst a clutter of gin glasses and beer mugs. Pipe smoke hung in a dense cloud along the low wooden rafters.

As he stepped into the room, baton prominent in his hand, he listened to the voices abruptly die away. There was an uncomfortable silence. Joshua glowered resentfully from his place behind the bar again, but Morton did not see either of the other men who had been present the first night.

He felt his anger begin to rise within him, his disgust at this place. The destruction of children, murder, theft—what crimes had not been fomented here? It was always best, and safest, to be aggressive and confident in these situations, but for Henry Morton tonight there would be little need to pretend.

"I am an officer of police on His Majesty's warrant,"

he announced loudly. "No man is to part these premises until I've had speech with him."

"There's no call for this," objected Joshua from his place. "My customers are law abiding. You've no right disturbing them."

"I'll disturb whom I please," retorted Morton coldly. "And God help him who tries to stop me."

"You've no actual warrant to—" began Joshua again.

But Henry Morton's rage flared and he brought down his baton on the nearer tabletop with a furious crash, splitting the flimsy board and sending the cards and coins and glassware spilling noisily onto the floor. The men who had been sitting at it scrambled up anxiously and backed away.

"You'll hold your peace!" Morton bellowed. The silence now was complete. He looked around the dim room. "This is a den of vile corruption, and any man here for its filthy commerce gets no consideration from me!"

He stepped forward, slapping his baton against his gloved palm, and letting his words sink in.

"A gentleman was murdered out of this house last week, and every one of you is under suspicion for it. I want each man here to come to this table and tell me his whereabouts on Saturday last, and how he can prove it."

The men at the other table made way, snatching up their drinks and other belongings. Morton took a place from which he could keep his eye on the doorway and sat, laying his hat and baton down before him. He looked over at Joshua and pointed at him.

"You first. The rest of you keep off and give us room."

Joshua reluctantly came and took his place. Morton kept his voice low, if still full of menace, so that it could not be generally overheard.

"I asked you about a gentleman who visited this house, and I am going to ask you again. This time I want the truth. I have a dozen witnesses who heard the jarvey say he picked him up here. Respectable witnesses, do you understand? Gentry-folk."

"Happens there may have been such," muttered Joshua now. Morton regarded him closely. Was he intimidated? Or had his instructions changed?

"What was he drinking?"

"Happens maybe brandy wine, if 'twas him we're speaking of."

"When did he arrive?"

Joshua's eyes narrowed, and he hesitated.

"I've heard lies enough in my time," Morton told him evenly. "So do not think yours will pass me. I'll have the truth, Joshua, or you'll be coming with me to Bow Street where we have a cozy little room where the truth always comes out."

Joshua paused a moment more, then spoke.

"Early in the evening he came. I've no notion what o'clock 'twas."

"What did he want? Why was he here?"

"Wot else did he want but wot most coves want?" The publican jerked his head briefly, to indicate the upper regions of the house. "That and his brandy. He was half-seas over when he left, but he was content. Coves leave here content, now, don't they?"

"Are you telling me positively that he went upstairs with one of these … children?"

"Aye, he did. Two on them, before he was done. Just as do plenty of you swells. . . ."

The Runner restrained his disgust.

"Did he drink enough to vomit?" he demanded. "Did he flash the hash?"

The barman dourly shook his head. "Not while he was here."

"Whom did he keep company with?"

"None was with him."

Morton considered Joshua coldly. "Had he ever been here before, this gentleman?"

"I know not. But I'm not always here, am I?"

Morton stared a long moment. The barman's eyes were full of concealment, that was sure, but Morton believed he'd told all he would without further persuasion. He waved him away, and pointed to another man at random.

His reference to Saturday had been deliberately misleading. In fact, Halbert Glendinning had died not on Saturday, but Friday. Morton let the Otter's customers make their denials for the former day, argued with them awhile, and then as it were casually asked them whether they had been in the house on the latter. Frequently enough they were glad to admit it, as if such a concession would make the Runner more likely to believe them on the first account. Then he came at them hard.

"Did you see a gentleman in here that night, dressed all in dark clothes and drinking brandy?"

"Nay, yer worship. No such cove."

"And are you blind? Is that what you will tell me next? I say he was here, and you did see him, and maybe you helped murder him, too!"

"Nay, yer honour! I swear to you!"

"What good's the oath of a liar? I know he was here. Did you see him, or shall I clap you in irons and haul you down to Bow Street?"

But as much as he pressed them, he could squeeze little of the wine of truth from such worthless mash. A few might really have seen Glendinning. A few of those seemed to confirm that he had really been drinking brandy—although it was anyone's guess how much. All of them were lying about at least part of their story, of that Morton was certain. Some of the folk here couldn't open their mouths at all without lying, even if they had no cause to. They were certainly being as secretive as they dared now. Indeed, there was something a bit more brazen about them than Morton usually encountered when he made a visit like this to a flash house. They were afraid, he thought. But not of him. Not enough.

Then his luck changed. The man who sat down across from him broke into a crooked smile.

"Hello, Mr. Morton, sir. Haven't clapped eyes on me in a twelvemonth, have you?"

"Valentine Rudd," murmured Morton in recognition.

"It's me. Been down in Cornwall, sojourning with me cousins there. But I did miss London-town, Mr. Morton, I'll say that."

"Are you back cursing the moon?"

Morton had known Rudd at Drury Lane the previous year, where the big countryman had employed himself as a link man, carrying a torch and offering protection to the patrons on their somewhat dangerous nighttime trip back to their homes. Such men were called mooncursers, as bright moonlight supposedly made their services unnecessary. Rudd was not a man of much wit, but Morton had always liked him.

"Nay, I'm 'prenticing now, with a locksmith in Brick Lane."

"What brings you into a wretched place like this, Rudd? I always thought you were a man of decent habits."

Valentine Rudd looked a little crestfallen.

"Well, Mr. Morton, here's the way of it. It's rather a

strange yarn, I'll admit to you. True, this house is not for
the likes of me. But I wandered in here by chance, soon
after I got back. I didn't know what it was, Mr. Morton,
this place. I went upstairs, as all I wanted was a regular
bit o' laced mutton, as I'll say to you I do indulge in
from time to time, when the inclination arises. You'll
understand that, sir, and not think too much the worse
of me?"

Morton shrugged.

"Well, I goes up, just for the usual knock or two. But
there she is, the sweetest little mort. Not as I expected
at all."

"But a kinchin-mort, Rudd. A child!"

"Nay, she's older than she looks!" He blushed. Then
blurted it once and quickly. "And she's all my heart
now!" He grinned helplessly at Morton. "I come back to
see her when I can, and I tell her when I can raise
enough from my toil, I'll buy her free, and we'll be wed.
So I promised her, and so I'll do, too, God help me."

Morton shook his head in wonder at this odd roman-
ticism. However, he knew of other marriages in the city
that, against all likelihood, had begun this way, and
even succeeded. Then a troubling thought. "Is the one
you're nutty on the little wench Lucy?"

"Oh, nay, Mr. Morton. Mine's named Marie, my little
charmer, French-like. And she's nay so young. Full fifteen year she is, just she looks younger." A furrow of reflection passed across his broad brow. "Nay, that Lucy's
a deep one. That Lucy's not for the likes of me."

Morton pondered.

"How much money do you need to get your girl free?"

"Oh, be..." he calculated, "some twenty shilling
more."

Such a small price! The child was not strictly the

property of the Otter, of course. Hers was probably some kind of informal indentured servitude, and the sum was a debt owed the Otter either by her parents or herself. If Morton simply removed young Marie and defied them to take her back they might, or might not, resist. The law was murky in this area, as in so many others. But it would probably be cleaner for her, and for Rudd, if they got their money.

Morton leaned forward slightly, to be quite sure they were not overheard.

"Very well, Valentine Rudd. You help me, and it'll be worth twenty shillings to you. Now listen here—and don't look too happy while you're talking to a horney."

Rudd grinned in incomprehension, realised what Morton meant, and belatedly attempted to look grim.

"I need two things," went on Morton. "I need a little information I can trust, and I need a key to this house. The lock's a Bramah, so the key will be small and easily enough pinched. Can you do it?"

Rudd thought, then very slowly nodded.

"Mayhap, we can. If Marie can fetch the key for me, I can get a copy made at our forge. We've done Bramahs before."

For what purposes? silently wondered Morton, but made no more of it.

"Wait outside for me, at the corner of Bishopsgate and Union streets, nigh the Charley there. I'll not be more than an hour more, and we'll speak on this." He sat back and said in a louder voice: "You're even stupider than the rest!"

And Valentine Rudd seemed prone to demonstrate this by looking, at least for a moment, genuinely hurt.

There were only a few more to speak to. When he was done, Morton called to Joshua, who was morosely surveying his deserted tavern. Each of his customers had beat a hasty retreat once Morton had talked to him.

"I'll take another dram of your brandy before I go."

Joshua looked black, but complied and, as Morton had hoped, called for Lucy to deliver the order. Lucy brought it as before, but when her back was turned from the bar she favoured Morton with a brilliant, conspiratorial grin. So, it appeared she had not been harmed. With any luck, the old woman had not reported Morton's early visit at all.

He was rewarded with something more than this reassurance, however. As she carefully set down the drink before him, the girl leaned very slightly forward, and in a clear quick whisper, said:

" 'The Ass-syr-ian came down like the wolf on the *fold*. And his co-horts were gleam-ing in pur-ple and *gold*!' "

Morton laughed aloud in surprise, and with a joyous flash of her brown eyes she darted off again.

His anger had drained away. Joshua's goodwill might preserve Lucy from any consequences of this suspicious fraternisation with the enemy, so this time Morton paid for his drink, and even added a few coins to compensate for the broken table and glassware before he left.

Valentine Rudd was waiting as instructed, chatting in friendly fashion with the aged "Charley," one of London's notoriously ineffectual nightwatchmen, who had crept for a while from the safety of his sentry box. Morton took the Cornishman by the arm and they walked along Bishopsgate, passing from the shadows into the yellow glow of the lamps and then back into the darkness again.

"Were you there in the Otter on Friday last, Rudd?"

"Nay, Mr. Morton, I weren't. But there's a cull who

surely was. He's there most every night. I've never gone
but he weren't there."

"Who is that?"

"Wardle, Amos Wardle. He is a confectioner, and
has his shop at the corner of Osborne Street and
Whitechapel, just by us. Seems he has a weakness for
the kinchin-morts. Brings them candy. He's a mutton-
monger, sure."

"Married man?" wondered Morton.

"Oh, aye," replied Rudd emptily.

"Any daughters?" asked Morton, bitterly.

"Oh, aye," replied Rudd, "I seem to recall." And his
surprised glance at the Runner's face told Morton that
the simple man did not see the point of the question.
Morton changed the subject.

"What can you tell me about the Otter itself? Who is
the owner? Is it that cove Joshua?"

"Nay, I can't say as I ever heard anyone say who
owned it." Rudd scratched his head. "Now, Mr. Morton,
sir, I suppose I didn't really have my eyes about me in
there. I only had my eyes one place, that's the truth."

Morton tried to describe the burly man he had seen
before, from whom Joshua seemed to be taking his instructions.

"Oh, him, aye. I think I know the cove you mean.
He's called Bill, I think."

"Bill who?"

Rudd looked at him helplessly. Morton saw one of the
infrequent hackney-coaches coming down the street
toward them and decided he had enough for the moment.

As he flagged the cab, he turned back to Rudd, reaching into his pocket.

"See if you can find me Bill's name. Here is ten

shillings. Bring that key to my lodgings by the forenoon tomorrow, and there will be ten more left for you with my landlady. See that you go promptly and buy out your Marie, too, and get her clear of that place. I shall come and look for you in Brick Lane soon enough, to hear what else you can remember." And he gave Rudd his address and climbed into the cab, telling the jarvey to take him to the hotel in Mayfair where he was to meet Arabella for a late supper.

Valentine Rudd gave him a hearty wave and started to stroll off into the dark, whistling as he went, a man at peace with the world.

As soon as he dropped back into his seat, Henry Morton, by contrast, began to brood. He began to wonder why only one child should be rescued from the Otter. He thought of the little girl who, in such a place, was resolutely going about learning to read, of all things! But was he going to rescue them all? And then, what about all the rest scattered about London? And in every other city in the land? But why stop there? The world was full of mistreated females.

"Bloody Sir Galahad," he muttered aloud, and stared unhappily out at the dark shapes passing in the shadowy streets of London.

Chapter 26

Morton was rather slow to rise the next morning. Even the steaming coffee that Wilkes brought him did little to clear his head, or soothe the rawness of his mood from the previous evening. The Otter had been unpleasant enough. Then he and Arabella had quarreled in the hotel dining room, green-eyed jealousy once again raising its head, and she had gone off to Darley instead of coming home with him. Morton in turn had sought other distractions, primarily of the liquid sort. Now he sat on the side of his bed, rubbing his face as his manservant arranged his shaving bowl and razor and laid out his clothes in tactful silence.

Finally, Henry Morton looked up.

"How would you take to a little jaunt in the country, Wilkes?" he asked thickly.

"I believe it would answer for any number of reasons," Wilkes replied. "Where shall we go?"

"Down into East Sussex. But I shan't be coming. Get a hack from Master Toller—" But there was something about the look on Wilkes's face.

"I can no longer ride, sir," the old man murmured apologetically. "It's my hands—the horses cannot bear the shaking."

"Ah. I should have thought. No matter, just take the Brighton Diligence." Morton closed his eyes a moment. "There's an old veteran down there—man with a peg leg—Sergeant Sempronious Stretton...."

Morton spent much of the day loitering about the Old Bailey, waiting to give evidence in the trial of three simpletons who had attempted extortion and then murder—failing notably at both. The three were so benighted that Morton hardly thought it fair to hang them—they had not the wit of a single man amongst them. But their lordships were not so moved by this lack of God-given reason. They were condemned, and the thief-taker found himself enriched by thirty pounds for his part in their downfall.

The whole business left him in an even lower humour than he had begun the day.

As he emerged from the Old Bailey, someone hailed him, and at a distance he thought for a moment that it was Byron. But as the man drew near Morton realised it was not the poet, but Peter Hamilton again.

"Good day to you, sir," Morton greeted him.

"Hello, Mr. Morton."

Hamilton looked out of sorts, too, Morton thought. But the precincts were not cheerful, and the business that brought folk here was rarely of a pleasing nature.

"Nothing untoward, I hope?" Morton nodded toward the grim grey structure behind them.

"Not at all. A friend of mine is a barrister." Hamilton

fell in beside Morton. "It is fortunate that I ran into you. I confess, I have been wondering how your investigation was going."

Morton was reluctant. It seemed Hamilton wasn't entirely in his sister's confidence—and after all, she was paying for Morton's efforts, not he.

"I have discovered a number of things, though they don't yet sum to very much," Morton admitted.

The other man bobbed his head thoughtfully. "Ah," he said. Then: "Darley told me that Lady Caroline let him glance through Halbert's effects, but he found no letter."

Morton had not yet heard of this. He tried to hide his frustration. "Unfortunate," he muttered.

"I'm sure. I wonder what happened to the letter? Do you suppose his valet might have it?"

"No. I spoke with the man and am quite sure its whereabouts are unknown to him. It went into the trash, I suspect."

"Do you think you can still snare Rokeby without it?"

"You seem rather sure it was Rokeby," Morton observed.

"Well, I suppose he is the obvious villain. I should, however, not leap to conclusions. To be fair."

"That is rather noble of you, Mr. Hamilton," Morton said. "After all, the world is hardly fair."

"No, it is not," Hamilton agreed, his manner very serious. "Were it fair, Louisa would not suffer so. She would be with the man deserving of her heart and—" He looked up suddenly, as though surprised to find Morton standing there listening. He tried to smile. "And I would find myself addressed as Uncle, I suppose."

"May that yet come to pass," Morton said.

The other dipped his head. But the mute unhappiness in his face seemed to suggest that Miss Hamilton's brother took little enough comfort in the thought.

It was late afternoon by the time Morton reached the confectionery of Mr. Amos Wardle. The place was just where Valentine Rudd had told him it would be, in the better part of Whitechapel—though Whitechapel all the same—a modest enough establishment, but sporting the new low-silled windows at the front to allow prospective buyers to view a selection of the goods without having to leave the street. This was a clever innovation, Morton thought, but surely a lure to the flash men, especially in this neighbourhood. He wondered how many of these broad and tempting windows had been broken in London to date.

Wardle's shop was busy, and Morton saw the man himself helping his clerks tend customers at the far end of the counter that ran the length of the room. He made his way casually through the place, his baton tucked inconspicuously under his arm, until they were face to face. It was when the confectioner looked up that Morton remembered him: the fat man who'd brushed past him in guilty haste at the front door of the Otter on Morton's first visit. Wardle's small mouth drooped open in dismay. He apparently remembered Morton, too. Two worlds the man was usually able to keep separate had suddenly come together.

"Ssss..." He seemed to struggle to get his first word out. Morton watched him in silence, one eyebrow unsympathetically raised, waiting.

"Ssss...sss..." Amos Wardle changed strategies, his face red with the effort. "C-c-can I be of ass-asss-sistance, suh-suh, *sir*?"

"I expect you can, Mr. Wardle."

"Wh-whom have I the h-h-honour...?"

"Henry Morton. Bow Street."

The fat man's face suddenly shone with perspiration. He nodded hastily, thought to speak again, couldn't, thought better of it, nodded again, then raised a section of the counter and came out into the shop. He gestured to Morton to follow, and waddled rapidly to the back of the room where he opened another door, holding it for Morton to enter first.

They stepped into a small, heavily furnished parlour, in what were clearly the private apartments occupied by the shop owner and his family. With an anxious glance out at his customers, Amos Wardle pulled the door closed behind them, then hurried on and closed the other door that led into the rest of the house. Without waiting to be asked, Morton took a chair and folded his arms, looking coolly around him. Dogs, a Dutch still life, and, perhaps more significant given the predilections of the master of the house, a crude representation of the Spartan youth of both sexes at exercise, boys and girls alike stripped and glistening. His portly host hovered, struggling with what seemed to be the first words of various offers of hospitality.

"Sit down, sir," Morton cut him off.

Wardle obeyed, eyes lowered. But Morton waited until he had raised them again, and given the Runner a look of dread. Behind the back door they were both suddenly aware of female voices, laughter, and the clatter of dishes.

"I believe you frequent the Otter House in Bell Lane, Mr. Wardle." It was not a question.

Amos Wardle breathed out. "Softly, sir, please."

"You are an habitual indulger in its..." and Morton

let every particle of his disgust enter his voice ". . . pleasures."

Wardle sagged back into his chair, and there passed
over his countenance a curious expression, of defeat and
yet, somehow, relief. He nodded, and quietly said:

"Very well, sir. Very well." His difficulty with speech
seemed to have vanished.

"Very well, what, Mr. Wardle?"

"I know your business here," the other muttered.
There was another burst of feminine merriment from
behind the paneling, which seemed to make Wardle
shrink even deeper into his overstuffed armchair. "Let
us be quick about it, before my wife comes in. What will
buy your peace?"

Morton regarded him, his jaw tight with revulsion.
And, of course, this was what they all thought of the
Runners.

"I want something other than gold," he replied. For
the moment, he might as well keep the fear of blackmail
in the fat tradesman's mind.

Wardle gaped at him in a kind of dim, hopeless panic.
What could Morton mean? What unimaginable price
could the Runner be about to propose?

"That house is a legal house, sir," Wardle protested
faintly. "I've every Englishman's right to go where he
pleases. The Otter is not unknown to you people. It has
always been left in peace."

Morton looked thoughtfully at him. Had not Joshua
said something like this upon their first meeting? Some
suggestion of Bow Street's knowledge of the Otter. Did
some Runner indulge in its secret pleasures? Morton did
not even like to think who this might be. What would he
do if he met someone like Townsend there? Or worse—
Sir Nathaniel?

"I haven't offered you harm, Mr. Wardle." He smiled, with a soft and quite unmistakable menace. "Have I?"

Amos Wardle pulled at a handkerchief and wiped his gleaming face.

"I know it to be a vice in me," he abruptly started to confess. "I know it, sir, and I will tell you I take no pride in it. I abuse my understanding when I do such things, and I abuse my person, too, which my God gave me as a clean and perfect vessel for my spirit."

Henry Morton stared in contemptuous surprise as the man persisted.

"I know it is a low and vulgar indulgence, and that it shames me. I am a respectable man, sir, and a good supporter of my family. I am an honest man of trade, and except for this one matter I've no other vices. I have tried to prise myself away from its ... seductions. But it has been unavailing. It is like strong drink to me. I cannot do without it. And Mrs. Wardle would never understand that. She is ... she is a virtuous woman, sir. And she ... she ... is everything to me; the partner of my soul!" He had recourse again to his handkerchief, and loudly blew his nose and wiped at his watering eyes.

Morton continued to regard him in distaste. It was a sin, but only a sin in his own regard. As if he himself were the only person who could be harmed by it—to this particular father, the children meant nothing.

"I haven't the slightest concern for the well-being of your rubbishy little soul, Mr. Wardle," he said harshly. "I am only interested in some information you can provide. Do so properly and fully, and I shall gladly leave you in peace."

Wardle looked up hopefully. Morton's insults did not touch him. Deliverance was all.

"Were you in the Otter Friday evening last?"

The man had only to think for a moment. "Yes, yes, I was. I...I am, most nights."

"Did you see there a young gentleman, aged perhaps five-and-twenty, and darkly dressed?"

And finally, a simple, prompt answer.

"Yes. I recollect him. He sat at the table Bill usually sits at."

"He was drinking brandy?"

"Yes. Yes, in fact, we stood each other to a round."

Morton's heart speeded up at his good fortune.

"You spoke to him?"

"Yes, sir. Only for a few moments. There's not too many gentlemen to be seen in the Otter, and I thought to be civil." Wardle seemed to react as Morton's features hardened into an incredulous stare, and hastened to explain. "I assumed he was there for...the same reason as I. There were not too many places to sit down, either. I had come down...from above," and here Wardle looked ever more uncomfortable, and cleared his throat, "and the other table was taken by some low folk or other. I wanted to wet my whistle and I asked if I might join him. I ordered him a brandy, as I saw that was his pleasure. And so he ordered an ale for me, as that was mine. And we had a few words."

"Concerning what?"

"I asked him which of the little—" Wardle looked embarrassed, then hurried on, "but he said he was not there for that purpose."

Morton looked at him closely. "Did you believe him?"

"Yes, sir, I did. He was rather a shy young gentleman, and seemed unwilling to talk about the matter. He merely said no, such was not his pleasure, he was simply there to meet some folk, and they were late."

"Some folk?"

"Yes. Some gentlemen, I think he said."

"Did he name them, these gentlemen?"

"No, sir."

"What else was said?"

"Very little, sir. He was not talkative. I drank my ale and presently went back upstairs. When I came down a time later, he was still there, still alone. I went out then, sir, and came home."

"What o'clock was that?"

Wardle thought, his mouth open. "Could not have been later than half nine, sir."

"How did he seem to you? Did he seem drunk?"

"No, sir, certainly not when I spoke to him. When I came down the second time, he was sitting a bit lower in his chair, and staring, blank-like. He seemed not to see me, and I did not trouble him, but just went home."

Morton pondered. "Was the Otter busy that night?"

" 'Twas perhaps moderately so, at first. As I said, the tables were taken. But when I left it was nearer empty."

"Who is this Bill fellow? Is he the owner there?"

"It may be. Folk there talk very respectfully to him. I never had words with him myself. No one ever told me who he was."

"How do you know my people are aware of the Otter? What made you say that?"

Wardle looked at Morton in surprise. "Well, if you know nothing of it, Mr. Morton, then perhaps I'm mistaken."

"Something made you believe this," Morton said in irritation.

"Folk there say it," vaguely replied the shopkeeper. "I cannot remember when I heard it first. I have always understood it to be so, that the house was under the protection of ... some constables or members of the Patrol.

That is why I go to that particular house—for I've always believed I was safe from . . . you people. I—I presumed there was . . ." his voice dropped ". . . a consideration involved."

The house paid off someone from Bow Street, or perhaps some members of the Foot or Horse Patrol. At any rate, it appeared the Otter had a protector. Such arrangements were rumoured to exist with ordinary inns, and even sometimes with flash houses. But for a place such as the Otter, its profits stained by the most disreputable of all London vices? And now, out of the same house, a possible murder.

Then Amos Wardle said something very striking.

"Everyone knew. All the regulars. They only kept it from fools like Smeeton."

"Like *whom*?"

Wardle saw he had said something more significant than he knew, and that it may have been a mistake. His stutter returned.

"Th-th-that cove who was huh-huh-*hanged*. He came in, but the folk there laughed at him behind his back. They t-t-told him nothing. They all ss-ss-*said* he'd be hanged someday, he was such a cull." Wardle smiled weakly. "And he was, wasn't he?"

Chapter 27

Morton set out on foot westward along Whitechapel Road, his mind teeming with the implications of what he had just found out. He needed exercise, and air in which to think. Glendinning had not been drinking heavily; he had been waiting for someone—more than one person. He had not been whoring; he had probably never been to the Otter before. He may have died unaware that it was children one found up those stairs. The young country gentleman had been given an address and an hour. He might not even have known how infamous a street it was, or what part of the city it was in. He had simply given the instruction to the jarvey, and found himself in the tender care of Joshua and Bill and the flash men. But who had sent him there, and under what pretext?

Damn that vanished note! Could it have been the key?

And what was this about Smeeton?

He was in Aldgate High Street now, picking his way

along the side, avoiding the congested traffic, vehicles, horses, and men.

As he turned into Leadenhall, however, Henry Morton's attention was distracted from his musings. In the tight press around the corner he saw a vaguely familiar face coming toward him, already close. A half-formed memory made Morton duck back behind the edge of the brick building, tucking his baton into the waist of his breeches to have both hands free.

He had hidden himself before he'd even fully made the connection, before he'd identified the face. But he knew who it was by the time the man stepped around the corner and found himself nose to nose with Bow Street. Morton smiled as he reached out and caught him by the lapels of his seedy jacket. The bald head, the pockmarked skin, and the snub features, ornamented now with an ugly yellow-black bruise under the left eye, a souvenir of the blow with which Morton had knocked him off the hackney-coach two days before.

"You, bracket-face!"

"Grubbing horney!" growled the man, and with a convulsive movement wrenched backward. The flimsy coat tore in Morton's hands, and with the agility of an eel the footpad slithered free. In an instant he was off, bolting out into the busy street with Morton hot after him. People gazed at them both in surprise.

"Bow Street! Bow Street! Thief!" shouted Henry Morton as he ran.

"Filthy China-Street pigs!" was the solitary shout from someone in response.

The bald man rushed heedlessly into the path of a briskly trotting chaise and was knocked down onto the cobbles by the startled horse. But he bounced to his feet and set off again just as fast. Morton sprinted along the other side of the way, vaulted over a costermonger's low barrow, and almost succeeded in cutting off his quarry. Both skidded, nearly stumbling, only feet apart, as the man reversed direction and went haring back up Leadenhall toward Bishopsgate. Morton, hatless by now, was conscious of other running people, urchins, scraggy men, rushing along to watch the chase. A confused clamour of voices rose on all sides as the street world began to awaken to its newest little drama.

Morton made a sprint to close on his prey, but the pad put on speed and kept himself just out of reach, darting and dodging amongst the various animate and inanimate obstacles a crowded London street provided him. As long as the way was cluttered, the smaller, lither man had the advantage. But then, after a half a minute's furious pursuit, they came into a more open area, and the pad made a mistake. He tried to outrun Morton. Morton surged ahead with long, powerful strides and swiftly caught him up. With a strong push of his outstretched hand into the small of the back, he sent his prize sprawling into the street.

This time the man could not get up quite so quickly. But get up he did, gasping for breath and glaring back at the much bigger Runner, who now loomed over him. Unwilling to capitulate, the bald man made another mistake. He came at Morton with his fists. There was a ragged cry of enthusiasm from the knot of spectators who had come pounding up in their wake. A set-to! They quickly formed into a ring.

Morton circled, sizing his opponent up. Cries of encouragement for the bald man were coming from every side.

"Do him over, lad!"

"Aye, lad, he's got no pluck, blast him! These bloody horneys have no bottom!"

"Thrash him, man!"

"Aye, I'll—" grimly began the bald man, advancing, but he could not finish his boast before Henry Morton had hit him twice very quick and hard with his left and right hands successively. Directness of address was one of "Gentleman" John Jackson's most basic precepts, and it was a feature of his longtime pupil's style he'd never had occasion to complain of. Morton's opponent dropped with the suddenness of it, but he was not hurt badly, yet, and scrambled promptly back up, his lip and nose running fresh blood. He swung wildly at the Runner, charging him. Morton parried, defended, shuffled back for a few seconds, until the flurry had exhausted itself. Then he stepped up and hit the bald man again, harder, with repeated blows from his right hand, until he went down once more, his head bouncing once on the cobbled street.

Angry disapproval filled the air as the Runner drew breath, stepped forward, and pulled his victim to his feet.

"It's a cross! He hadn't a chance!"

"Grubbing trap!"

"Bully-boy!"

Morton pushed the dazed and stumbling footpad ahead of him, looking around for a hackney-coach to carry them back to Bow Street. But there were none in sight, and the circle of people around them was pressing closer, with increasing boldness, shouting imprecations.

"Keep you back!" Morton ordered them. "I am an officer of police on His Majesty's warrant!"

"You're a filthy horney, on your own bloody warrant!"

"Shit sack!"

"He's done no harm! Yer persecuting the poor men of England, you are!"

"Morris off!" shouted Morton with sudden vehemence, "unless you want to end up at Bow Street yourselves!"

But the situation was getting very tight. They were close enough now to shove at Morton, to wrench at his clothing. Others were pulling forcefully at the bald man, who was beginning to recover and trying to pull away as well. Morton was caught. If he let go his grip with either hand, he would lose his captive. But without his hands free he could not reach his baton, or push away the people who were besetting him. These people were getting bolder and bolder, taking confidence from Morton's relative helplessness, and they were growing in numbers. All the simmering popular anger against Bow Street seemed to be coming to a head. No threat or voice of authority he could produce was having any effect.

But Morton was also getting very angry. He thought about what his attackers might have done to Arabella. He was not going to let this miscreant go.

"Get back or I'll see you all in Norway neckcloths, so help me God!"

"Get him free! Get him free!"

"Filthy horney!"

Even as the bald man was in fact almost being wrenched out of Morton's grip, however, there was an irruption to the side of the crowd. People were being thrust back, and another deep loud voice joined the racket.

"Stand back! Stand aside! Bow Street! Bow Street!"

Elbowing his way forcefully toward the center was Jimmy Presley, bellowing all the while. In a moment he was at Morton's side. Together they hauled the captive in, and Presley laid his baton sharply over the wrist of the last man holding him, breaking his grip. With one hand free, Morton finally had his own baton out. At the sight of this reinforcement, the crowd drew back a little, cowed but not entirely beaten, and threw all their energy into their lungs. A few began pitching scraps of refuse and litter at the two Runners.

"We must get a coach," Morton grunted as they tried to force their way forward, with the bald man secured between them.

"There are always some up ahead, by the Bank."

They made their way. The crowd, after a lull, seemed to be building up energy for another effort. As they all came in a disorderly mass out into Cornhill, the distant line of coaches could be seen waiting before the blank stone mass of the Bank of England.

"Should we run over there?" Presley asked.

"Never, Jimmy. Never let them see you bolt."

Just then a heaved object caught Presley on the side of the head. Infuriated, the young Runner stopped and turned.

"Who was the coward who did that!" he roared. It was perhaps the loudest voice Morton had ever heard. "Who was it!" Presley seemed entirely taken out of himself with unselfconscious indignation.

This produced an effect. The crowd appeared to hesitate, almost abashed.

"You're Englishmen!" thundered Jimmy Presley. "You ought to be ashamed of yourselves, you should! Chucking things at a man, as if you were some foreign rabble!"

A kind of muttering, resentful silence was produced. But the mass of people slowly parted. Morton was allowed to stride ahead, pulling his prisoner along unhindered toward the coaches. Presley stood confronting the mob, glaring angrily from one side to the other, his beefy hands on his hips. At last he shook his head in sincere disgust, and walked after Morton.

Thrusting the bald man in before him, Morton ordered the jarvey to drive to Bow Street as he and Presley climbed in themselves. As they rattled away from the scene of danger, Henry Morton broke into a grin of congratulation for his young colleague.

"Now, you see, Mr. Presley, how much better a little confidence works!"

"I said what I meant," gruffly replied Jimmy Presley.

"Handy thing for me you were by."

"It's me neighbourhood," the younger man almost apologetically allowed. "I was just coming on duty."

Morton turned to their captive.

"Well, you cully bastard, it isn't five men to one today, is it? Who was it had you set upon me in the street?"

The man looked at him glassily, gaping.

"Answer me!" Morton reached over to seize and shake him.

"Never saw him but once," faintly mumbled the man. "Never heard th' cove's name. Paid us twenty guinea."

"What did he look like?"

The bald man shook his head groggily. "Little short cove. Gen'leman, appeared." His voice was a slurred mutter.

"And how did you meet him? Someone must have sent him your way." When the man did not answer, Morton slammed him hard against the back of the carriage. But this was not wise, as the bald man then

promptly leaned over and vomited all over their shoes.
Both Runners tried to keep their feet away and cursed
him.

"Sapscull!"

"Blasted simkin!"

Then Morton took it up again, even more angrily,
pushing the man's head back with his palm on his forehead.

"Who sent this cove your way?"

But the man's eyes rolled up in his head and he fell
limply sideways, sprawling on the floor. Morton had
seen men play at being unconscious before, but this was
no act. The Runner made a disgusted noise, and thrust
him roughly back into the corner of the compartment.

The Magistrates were not sitting when the coach arrived at number 4 Bow Street, so Morton and Presley
consigned the man to Constable Dannelly in the inner
waiting room. Presley had another matter to attend to,
but promised to return when the bald man was to be examined in Police Court at evening sessions. Morton
shook his hand.

"You did me a service, Jimmy," he said warmly.

"Aye. No matter," muttered Presley in embarrassment. He seemed to want to make no more of it, so Morton said nothing else.

Morton sat in the front room for a moment after Presley left, savouring his success, and considering. His satisfaction was growing. He had it now, did he not? A
short gentleman, with the means and the motive. That
was surely Pierce, on Rokeby's behalf. No point in
bearding them yet, until the bald man had told his
whole tale. But after he had done that, and after he had

identified Pierce in person, and after little Pierce had traded his unstretched neck for the truth, Morton would have the very considerable satisfaction of arriving at the Guards Club with a warrant for the arrest of the sneering Colonel Fitzwilliam Rokeby himself.

Then there would only be the matter of George Vaughan left to consider. George Vaughan, Caleb Smeeton . . . and the Otter House.

Chapter 28

Morton took the opportunity to seek out Arabella. He itched to bring her his splendid tidings, and imagined in advance her enthusiasm, how the news would sweep away the unpleasantness of the previous evening.

But she wasn't at home. And of course Christabel would not tell him where she was.

At this little reverse all his vexation came burning up again and their argument began to repeat itself in his brain. Blast it, but she *had* promised him yesterday evening! Perhaps he might be willing to share her affections, but he'd not be pushed aside at her every whim, or at Darley's slightest convenience.

Without any fixed pretext, Morton found himself gravitating in the direction of Bond Street and Grosvenor Square. Perhaps he was going to Jackson's, to take out his frustrations on some gentlemanly sparring partner. Some lady-killing poetic lord even. But he had already had a fistfight today, and in fact he knew perfectly well what his real destination was. Before long he stood in the gathering dusk, gazing up at the lighted windows of Portman House.

"You are acting the fool," he murmured. "The bloody fool. This is what women do to men in this world, and you know it well. You see it when it happens to other men. Do you suppose it's different for you?"

He was just about to go on his way when the door opened. Lord Arthur Darley came nimbly down the stairs, waving to Morton as though he were his dearest friend in all the world.

"Ah, Mr. Morton! What an unlooked-for pleasure. Do come up," Darley said, crossing the street as though Morton were not of another class of society at all.

Morton could hardly refuse now, and accompanied Darley silently up the stairs. "You have just missed Mrs. Malibrant," Darley told him, "and she will be unhappy to learn it. She was most set on seeing you today. I don't mean to pry, Morton, but I got the impression you'd had a quarrel. And poor Mrs. M. felt an awful guilt about it."

Morton shrugged. "Something of the sort."

Darley ushered Morton into the very room where he had first seen Halbert Glendinning lying, like a man dressed for a funeral. Morton soon found a snifter of smuggled cognac in his hand, and Darley served himself the same. They settled into chairs, Morton regarding his host rather warily. Why was the man so completely at ease?

"To the birds of the air, Mr. Morton," Lord Arthur said suddenly, raising his glass.

Morton must have looked puzzled.

"A beauty we can admire but never possess, Morton. I hope you feel as I do."

"Aye," Morton said, and then broke into a wry grin. "What choice have we?"

They both chuckled and tasted their cognac. They sat and talked, then, almost like a pair of old friends, strangely comfortable with each other. Darley asked about Morton's search for Glendinning's murderer and the Runner found himself telling all that had occurred.

"That was a stroke of luck, finding the villain who attacked you. If he can tell you who sent them to assail you—assuming it was related to Halbert's death—then you might well have discharged your commission, and with great dispatch, too. Perhaps that will lift the gloom from Louisa Hamilton." Darley raised his glass in salute. "Well done, Morton."

"If it turns out so neatly. Nothing ever seems sure in my profession."

"What kind of life would it be if everything was certain? I daresay, Morton, that you could have picked yourself a tame occupation, and had yourself a comely and constant wife. But you have chosen otherwise, and I must tell you, there are many who would envy you. No, there is much good to be said of uncertainty; believe me."

When he returned to number 4 Bow Street, the Public Office seemed unusually deserted. Then one of the clerks came running across the way from the Brown Bear, telling him he was wanted, that there was something amiss.

Inside the Bear the atmosphere was sullen. People were gathered in the gloom, sitting around tables, speaking in near whispers. Not the usual mood, that was certain. Jimmy Presley met him at the bottom of the stairs, his face full of consternation.

"Morton! There you are, at last," the young Runner said. "You'll not like what you'll see here."

"What's this?"

Presley beckoned for him to follow and pushed his way upward toward the second floor, where Bow Street, incongruously, rented lockup rooms for its overflow prisoners.

"It must have just happened...."

On the stair men stood smoking and speaking quietly, though they went silent when they saw Morton and Presley. The hallway above was choked with police and flash men and their fancy women. Sir Charles Carey emerged from one of the rooms, accompanied by a stranger.

"Waste of bloody—" he was saying, but then spotted Morton. "Well, Mr. Morton, you won't be arguing with the surgeon this time," he said as he passed.

Morton stopped in the doorway. The pock-faced man lay on the floor, arms akimbo, eyes glazed and gazing upward, mouth lolled loosely open. The dull light from a dirty glass chimney illuminated a pool of blood, quickly skinning over with brown.

"Sliced his pipes," Presley muttered at his elbow.

Morton took a long breath. "Who? Who did this?"

"Don't know. Bloody patrole was on watch, but he was in some back room looking to get poxed."

"Who was in here with him?"

"He was by himself."

"And no one saw anything?"

"Oh, I expect plenty saw, but you know this crowd. Won't be telling us, now, will they? Mr. Townsend's been sent for, but I doubt even he will find a soul with a tongue. No, this one's gone, Morton; anything he had to tell he'll be telling St. Peter."

Henry Morton banged a fist on the door frame in exasperation. It was certainly true that the whole matter of holding prisoners at Bow Street lacked system. They sometimes "wandered off," because no clear arrangement had been made as to who would watch them. Occasionally men even died at the hands of fellow prisoners in brawls. But no one had ever broken into a locked room and slit a prisoner's throat.

"One of us should have stayed with him," Presley muttered regretfully, and Morton nodded in grim agreement. Easily enough said now.

Evening Police Court was in session. Morton no longer had anything to bring before the Magistrates, but if he waited, he could speak to Sir Nathaniel Conant when he emerged in about two hours' time. He could start to tell the Chief Magistrate some of his ideas about the Smeetons, about Bow Street and the Otter. The subject would have to be broached sometime.

But Morton decided against it. He still had so little in the way of concrete evidence to present. And Sir Nathaniel's first question would be about the assignment he had given Morton, and he had nothing at all to tell the Magistrate in that matter.

Evidence. It was proving hard to find—and even harder to keep.

Chapter 29

He dined at Johnson's and did a round of the flash houses between the City and St. James, hoping to hear something about the murder in the Brown Bear. Or to hear anything at all that might be of use to him. But even his most reliable sources all came up barren.

It was well after ten when he wearily returned to Rupert Street, and as he did, a shadowed figure darted away from an empty doorway. Morton watched him go. There was no point in pursuing, and he had little enthusiasm for the game at this hour anyway. Often enough it happened that potential informants hovered about his door, then lost their nerve and ran off.

He went around the front of the building and in at the main entrance. Mrs. Budworth presented him with a small object wrapped in oilcloth: the copied key that Valentine Rudd had dutifully left for him during the day. It was a Bramah, sure enough, by its distinctive cylindrical shape. Slipping it into an inner pocket, Morton went upstairs.

Although Wilkes should not yet have returned from Sussex, lamps glowed.

"Wilkes?"

It was not his manservant but Arabella who appeared, backlit by a flickering lamp.

She came easily into his arms.

"What an awful bloody woman you've chosen, Morton," she whispered in his ear.

Morton shook his head, breathing deeply the fragrance of her hair. "It is the uncertainty," he said. "I'm told it is opium to me."

"What in the world are you saying?"

"Nothing, my love. Not a thing."

But their kiss was interrupted by a loud knocking at the door that closed onto the staircase down to the rest of the building. At the same moment they heard footsteps—numerous footsteps—on the balcony outside. They pulled away from each other in surprise.

"Henry?" Arabella whispered.

"I don't know," Morton replied. He stepped past her to an armoire and removed a pistol from one of its drawers.

The knocking was repeated; now there was hammering also from the back door that opened onto the balcony. Morton checked his priming, then stepped out into the hall with the weapon in hand.

"Who the devil is it at this hour of night!"

"Bow Street!" came the call from beyond. "Open, or we shall have this door down!"

"Vaughan? What folly is this!"

A second voice came then, quieter and more dignified. "Mr. Morton? No folly, sir. We have a warrant. Best open."

Morton breathed deep in surprise, and turned to

Arabella, who hovered behind him in the doorway. "It's Townsend! Townsend with a warrant!"

Morton set his gun down on the hall table and unbarred the door. In came trooping George Vaughan and several of the constables of the Night Patrol, with John Townsend apologetically in the rear.

Morton saw the hard, still look in Vaughan's face, and began to realise what was happening. Vaughan had somehow recognised how things stood, and had moved first. This was deadly serious.

Townsend was bowing in courtly fashion to Arabella Malibrant.

"Allow me to apologise, madam." Then he turned to Morton. "It wasn't my doing. Sir Nathaniel sent me along to see that things were managed properly." His voice and expression were rueful.

"What the devil is going on!"

Now, however, the old Runner was required to behave in an official manner, and he did. His voice became more formal. "We bear warrants to search your dwelling, Mr. Morton," he replied. "You may examine them. They were signed by Sir Nathaniel Conant but two hours past."

"Search? For what?"

Townsend solemnly pulled out another paper, and then his spectacles.

"Shall we not begin?" muttered George Vaughan.

"I will satisfy Mr. Morton first," Townsend retorted with noticeable coolness. He read from the paper. " 'Item: a fragment of marble, two and a half feet long by fourteen inches deep by three inches wide, carved in relief with a votive scene, portraying the goddess Ceres and—' "

"The antiquities stolen from Burlington House," interrupted Henry Morton. "What is this foolishness? I haven't found them yet, if that's what Sir Nathaniel is asking."

"Have you not?" murmured George Vaughan.

" 'Item: a fragment of—' "

"Spare me the recitation, Mr. Townsend! I know the particulars."

Townsend produced a neatly folded section of newspaper.

"From *The Morning Chronicle* of today's date, Mr. Morton. Permit me to read. '*Precious Goods*'—that is the heading—'*of ancient provenance. God of lightning and Goddess of the sickle*'—a clear reference to the images of Zeus and Ceres, but cunningly indirect—'*If grateful to a finder, apply upstairs, number seven Rupert Street, for hopeful tidings.*' " Townsend refolded the paper and turned his gaze to Morton, an eyebrow lifting.

"I did not place that advertisement, sir!" Morton said hotly. "Why on earth would I? It is absurdly inept! And to give my own address! What sort of fool do you think me?"

"That we shall discover," George Vaughan said. "Proceed!" he ordered the patroles.

"Mr. Townsend," Morton protested. "Anyone can place a notice in a newspaper!"

To which Townsend nodded gravely. "But search we must. I'm sure you see that."

Vaughan let the other constables in from the balcony. They had come in absurd numbers. As they began their work, Morton stepped back and watched, wondering for an instant if he had fallen asleep and into nightmare. Then he remembered the figure he'd seen run off from the empty doorway. Vaughan's man, no doubt. A sickening possibility was occurring to him, and its cold hand gripped his heart. He had sent Wilkes off to Sussex, leaving his rooms empty all day.

"Might we permit Mrs. Malibrant to return to her home, Mr. Townsend?" he asked quietly, hoping his anxiety would not be detectable in his voice. He felt Arabella look at him in surprise. "The matter hardly concerns her. The hour is late, and she was about to leave when you arrived."

"Nay," harshly said George Vaughan, stepping to the doorway from the next room. "They are together in everything. She's his whore, and as like they'll swing together, too, like that cully Smeeton and his sow."

At this Arabella went white to the roots of her red hair, and Morton wheeled on Vaughan in fury. Two constables stepped between them.

"You shall rue this, George Vaughan! By *God,* I'll make you rue it!"

Townsend looked from one Runner to the other, as though to weigh them, and then said softly to Arabella: "Madam would oblige me if she would tarry here just a moment longer."

It was not much longer. Within a few minutes there was a cry from the constables going through Henry Morton's bedchamber. From beneath the blue silk draperies of the four-posted bed frame they had pulled a heavy oblong of white stone. Marble. And then another.

Arabella's first remark was rather incongruous. "They're beautiful," she whispered.

The two white segments had been laid out for inspection on Morton's sitting-room carpet. About a foot broad, the sinuous half-clothed male and female figures formed a continuous pattern along the length of each piece of marble. Morton, too, as he gazed at them, was almost taken out of himself.

Townsend unnecessarily took the written description from his pocket and compared them carefully—giving Morton the benefit of the doubt—or perhaps he merely did it to aggravate Vaughan, who stood back a little, arms folded, an unreadable expression on his narrow face. Browne and one of the other constables hovered near Morton, not touching him but clearly ready to prevent him from fleeing, should he have a mind to try.

Henry Morton had no such notions. He spoke to the senior Runner. "These objects were placed here by some unknown person," he said. "I am the victim of an imposition."

Ignoring him, Townsend frowned slightly at his paper, looked once more at the reliefs on the floor, then folded the paper up and put it away.

"Well, Mr. Morton, you shall have to explain this to the Magistrates. But I must arrest you for the crime of thieving these valuable antiquities."

"The blowen, too," muttered Vaughan.

A pained expression passed quickly across John Townsend's round face.

"Madam," he said to Arabella, "permit me to ask if you have ever seen these objects before?"

Arabella quickly shook her head. "Never." She was carrying herself well, but Morton could see how frightened she really was. Vaughan's vicious remark about the fate of the Smeetons had done that.

"Have you any knowledge of how they came to be in Mr. Morton's possession? Had he ever spoken to you of them?"

"No. Never."

Townsend nodded sagely. "There is a carriage below, madam, which will convey you to your home. Pray remain available for the Magistrates' summons, should they wish to question you further on this business."

"She'll bolt!" objected George Vaughan. "She's as bad as—"

"You shall not offer insult to this lady again, sir!" Townsend cut him off, and everyone in the room was suddenly very still. Vaughan fell silent.

Arabella reached out toward Morton as she was escorted away, but the distance was too great. Then she was through the door and gone.

"Wrap up these goods and carry them down into the other carriage," commanded Townsend. "I shall not restrain you, Mr. Morton, if you give me your word you'll not attempt to flee."

Morton pulled himself out of his stunned distraction with an effort.

"You have it."

"You have no weapons upon your person?"

Morton shook his head. One of the patroles had already taken up the pistol. But his hands were clenched into fists, and he looked slowly over at George Vaughan.

"Mr. Morton..." Townsend cautioned. Vaughan's cold blue eyes met Morton's steadily. There was no bravado there. And no fear. There was not even any hatred—only purposefulness. It occurred to Henry Morton that this was what Halbert Glendinning really saw when he'd faced Rokeby down the barrel of a pistol. This was the way a killer looked.

Townsend said: "Mr. Browne, take possession of Mr. Morton's baton. It is no longer his to hold."

Chapter 30

Sir Nathaniel Conant had clearly been fore-warned, and awaited them in his private chamber. He sat massive and motionless behind his table as John Townsend lowered himself uninvited onto one of the side chairs. The rest of the men, including Henry Morton, remained on their feet.

"This is not a formal hearing, gentlemen," rasped out the Chief Magistrate. "The formal hearing will take place tomorrow morning in Bow Street Police Court, before the full panel. What we will do now is make a few preliminary enquiries, so that I can determine whether there be need to detain Mr. Morton."

He turned his gaze to Henry Morton. "I am disappointed to see you here, sir."

"I am disappointed to be here."

"The objects recovered from your lodgings correspond in every point to certain antiquities belonging to the Earl of Elgin and stolen from the courtyard of Burlington House on or near the seventh of June of the present year."

"I am sure they are the same," said Henry Morton. "But I did not steal them."

John Townsend inhaled snuff, and gave a loud, highly satisfactory sneeze into his handkerchief, his odd collection of clothing flapping once as he did so.

"How did they come to be in your possession?" demanded the Chief Magistrate, after an annoyed glance at the old Runner.

"My manservant was not at home for most of today, so my lodgings were unattended. Someone who wished me ill must have placed those goods there, just as they must have commissioned the notice in *The Morning Chronicle*."

"So might any thief claim," Sir Nathaniel said flatly. "Have you nothing more to say for yourself than that?"

"I have been looking into the doings at a particular flash house in the East End, sir, and twice I have been warned that the house was under the protection of someone at Bow Street. It seems very odd to me that I should discover this, and that almost immediately constables from Bow Street should find a notice *listing my address* and describing the antiquities I have been seeking. As you well know, I am aware of how such things are done—if I were a criminal I would not be such a fool as to list mine own address!"

John Townsend cleared his throat, and the Magistrate looked his way.

"I must say, my lord, that it does seem a scheme unworthy of Mr. Morton's intelligence. I have known him a good many years now, and have never had the slightest cause to doubt him." He looked over at George Vaughan meaningfully. "And I cannot say that of every man at Bow Street."

"You may have your say before the panel, sir," Sir

Nathaniel told him. "Mr. Morton is to be held in custody over the night, on my authority. Charges will be prepared, and he will answer to them tomorrow." He took pen and signed the document before him, blotted it, and handed it to his clerk. Then he rose, as did Townsend. Two of the constables stepped in an uncertain manner toward Morton.

"You were not eager to attend to this matter," Sir Nathaniel said to Morton as he gathered up the remaining papers from his table. "I remember that. You had no appetite for it, I seem to recall were your words."

Morton said nothing.

As Sir Nathaniel collected his papers, he knocked over a beaker of water, which spilled its contents across the oak-topped table, and down onto the floor. The Magistrate stopped, looking up at Morton. "I have long heard the talk about this Office, and about the Runners. I did not want to believe it. In particular, I did not want to believe it of you."

"There is still no reason to believe it of me, sir."

The Magistrate continued to stare at Morton, his hands brutally clenching a stack of documents. "You have all played me for the fool," he muttered bitterly, and strode out without another glance.

Townsend took Morton's elbow and, followed by a couple of patroles, escorted him as gently as he might across Bow Street to the Brown Bear.

Morton walked numbly, trying to take in what so swiftly and terribly had happened to him. He could not believe that he was now being escorted to the cells where he had led so many. So this was how it felt. And all at once he thought—with an awful vividness—of the Smeetons.

He could die. He could actually hang, there before Newgate like "that cully" Smeeton. Caleb Smeeton had been a fool. But Henry Morton had been a fool, too. Neither of them had understood George Vaughan until it was too late.

"Well, you are in the forge now," the old Runner remarked with a sigh as they walked. "What have you to defend yourself?"

"Little, it seems. The flash house I looked into—the Otter, in Spitalfields. That is the key to it. I need proof that it is Vaughan who controls it."

"Hard to get when you are locked up in the Bear."

Morton said nothing.

As they ushered him into one of the upstairs rooms, the old Runner leaned in the door. "You may sleep soundly, Mr. Morton. I'll have a watch set that you can trust."

Morton slumped down on the cot, staring at the thin crease of light that found its way beneath the door and spread like a stain across the filthy floor.

He must eventually have fallen into shallow slumber, because he was startled awake by the rattle of a key in the lock. He shielded his eyes as someone with a lantern came in, looming large and dark in the doorway.

"Who is that?" he mumbled. Suddenly he thought of the way the bald footpad's life must have ended, and he was on his feet, staggering from sleep.

The figure turned and quietly closed the door behind him. But it was a familiar voice that spoke.

"It's me, Morton. Presley."

Henry Morton grunted and slumped back down, rubbing his eyes. "Ah, Jimmy. Welcome to my little palace. I've no armchairs, but help yourself to part of my settee here."

Jimmy Presley hung his lantern from a hook and sat heavily beside Morton.

Morton reached around and placed an arm over the younger man's broad shoulders for a moment. "Thankee for coming, Jimmy. It's generous. What o'clock is it, by the by?"

"Near three."

"Ah. A bit longer I have to wait for my breakfast."

"What will you tell them?" he asked Morton.

"Tomorrow? Oh, I've a lot I can say. How much of it I can prove is the difficulty. And Sir Nathaniel is not just now of a mind to take much from me on trust."

Presley nodded glumly. "The beak's been getting angrier and angrier," he sighed. "I seen it. You've not been here, Morton, to hear him ask three times a day where you were and where that Elgin booty was."

"But others were," quietly remarked Morton. "Well," and he sighed now, "I refused to serve Sir Nathaniel, when he asked me to explain how Bow Street really works. This is a mess much of my own making."

"How did those marbles get in your lodgings, Morton? Have you really joined the flash crowd?"

"Do you think I have?" Morton laughed. "I'm surprised you're here!"

"Nay, I don't," admitted Presley. "But I don't see how—"

"Oh, it's no great puzzle *how*," Morton interrupted him. "My door was watched. When Wilkes went off, someone with the skill picked my back-door lock, and put them in there. There was even time to place a notice for the late printing of the *Chronicle*. How is no great matter. What is more to the point is why. And why *now*, exactly?"

Presley turned to look at him with a puzzled stare. "George Vaughan don't like you, Morton. I'll tell you that."

"It's a bit more than just not liking me, Jimmy. Who already knew my address? Why, the same man who knew it tonight, and yesterday, too, when the place was empty. Tell me, Jimmy, did *you* ever know where I dwelt? Did I ever tell you?"

"No," admitted Presley.

"No, I hadn't the habit of telling folk. But a Runner with a company of informants would not find it too hard to ascertain. That is, if he was of a mind to use them against his brother officers. And what about those pads who came after Mrs. Malibrant and me in the hackney-coach? D'ye think that was random?"

"The bald cove said they was commissioned by a short man."

"Aye, which led me in several wrong directions. Maybe 'twas so, and one of George Vaughan's minions is short. Or maybe it was just said to throw us off the scent. The main point is, they meant to get Henry Morton and Arabella Malibrant thrown off a bit more permanently."

"But why?" weakly asked Jimmy Presley.

"Well, now, Jimmy." Henry Morton sighed, drawing back and looking at him, "You've got your own notions by now about Mr. George Vaughan, don't you? That is why you're here with me in this stink-hole, and not out somewhere with the flash men raising a glass with Officer Vaughan and toasting your good fortune."

Presley swallowed and said nothing.

"Somebody didn't just nose on the Smeetons, did they? Somebody didn't just sell them to Bow Street. No, somebody went a distance farther than that. Somebody set up the whole scrap—recruited them, gave them the address and the time and even the tools to break in with, and then arranged to have his friends there to take the thieves in the act. Poor paltry thieves, those! But worth—what was it now?—seventy pound a head, all told. And for that the two cullies end up dancing on nothing, never knowing how it was done to them exactly, but suspecting, suspecting...especially by the end." Morton rubbed his face with his hands again, still trying to dispel his grogginess. "And it wasn't likely the first time, was it?" he went on. "Many another's swung from the same tree, I'd guess."

Jimmy Presley bowed his head in shame, but nodded all the same. Morton continued.

"Our George Vaughan has himself a little scheme that could earn him quite a few pound, or a Norway neck-cloth. You know it, Jimmy, and I know it, but what we don't have is proof.

"And maybe that's what's really puzzling me the most. I've been lying here trying to figure it. I may think I can see what Mr. Vaughan's business is, but I can't see that I have enough real evidence to do him any serious harm. So, as I said, why spring the trap *now*? Why try to put Henry Morton out of the way? Unless...unless I actually have more proof than I realise I have. Unless I'm closer to Mr. George Vaughan than I know. Have you ever been in the Otter House in Spitalfields, Jimmy?"

"Nay, thank God."

"Well, I've made myself familiar with the place in the last week or so, and there's a curious thing the folk there keep saying when I make my well-intentioned enquiries into their general state of health. They say, Mr. Morton, sir, it's kind of you to ask, but in fact, we're already keeping Bow Street abreast of all our news."

"Vaughan is *there*?"

"And, Jimmy, they were familiar with Caleb Smeeton, too, in the Otter. A low opinion they had of his wisdom, I must say. I think it's pretty clear the whole venture was set up right there. The Otter is George Vaughan's house, Jimmy.

"And you know who else paid a visit to the Otter House before he went on along to his maker, Jimmy? 'Twasn't just Smeeton. The Otter was the last place Halbert Glendinning is sure to have been amongst the living. And I thought, Mr. George Vaughan is not trying to work off Henry Morton because this Morton fellow suspects something about the safe-dead Smeetons. And he's certainly not going to do it because Morton knows he's excused some dueling swells a court appearance, for a modest sum. But maybe there really is one thing he can't quite forgive Henry Morton. Maybe he can't quite forgive Henry Morton for poking his unwelcome head into the Otter, and asking about Halbert Glendinning.

"Let's us put our minds to this Glendinning matter, Jimmy. George Vaughan knew that Glendinning had arrived at Portman House dead drunk, so to speak. Who told him that? And you remember the jarvey who drove the cove to Portman House and delivered him dead?"

"I misremember his name, but I know who you mean."

"Ralph Acton was his name. When I went looking for him down by Cartwright Square, the ragged folk there told me he'd gone off. But when I asked them why, they said 'twas because of the *horneys* coming about."

Presley blinked, not seeing it.

"Well, Jimmy, I thought they meant me. But I've since realized it could hardly be me. I hadn't but asked the man a few questions. And they spoke in the plural. Some other officer or officers had been to see our Master Acton before I got there, and given him a broad hint, likely some blunt, too, so he'd make himself scarce."

"Vaughan?"

Morton nodded.

"Working for Rokeby?"

"As like as not. But one thing seems sure: George Vaughan is afraid I can prove Glendinning was killed out of that house. He is afraid the murder of gentry-folk will be taken more seriously than that of petty criminals like the Smeetons. And he is afraid too many people in the Otter House know about it—that there are too many witnesses. He can't kill all of them. So he has to kill me."

"What would it take to get to get the proof you need, Morton?"

There was something very serious in the way Presley spoke. Morton regarded him carefully.

"It would be a hard task for you to take up, Jimmy, if that's what you're offering."

But the younger man was shaking his head.

"I could never do it." He lowered his voice. "But you see, Mr. Townsend sent me here. Said the guard watching over the hallway had disappeared and I should come look in on you to be sure you're all right. He gives me a key and says, 'No one will ever know where this key came from. You take my meaning, Jimmy? Say the same to Mr. Morton and take him my compliments.'"

Morton swore. "And we've been sitting here jawing?"

"Does he mean what I think, Morton? That I'm to spring you?"

"No, Jimmy, nothing so direct. But if you were to go out and leave the door unlocked...It's a risky thing, Jimmy. Are you sure you're willing?"

Presley nodded once in acknowledgement. "No matter about that," he said, low. "I've amends to make."

Morton looked at him a moment more, then clapped him warmly on the arm. "Right then. Go on down now and check there's no patrole in the taproom. If there is, come back up. But if none's to be found, then just continue on out. You need do no more than that. Mr. Townsend will have looked after the flash crowd. No one will see you come or go."

"But you, Morton; you'll need another along."

"Nay, Jimmy, that's more than I can ask. If I can't find the proof I need we'd be swinging together. Get along out and don't worry about Henry Morton. You've done enough. More than enough."

Presley stared at Morton a moment in the near dark and nodded once. Morton clasped his hand, neither speaking, and then the big Runner went out.

He waited for a count of a hundred and, when Presley hadn't returned, opened the door. The hallway was empty and lit by a single dingy lamp hanging near the stair head. In a moment Morton was on the steps, then down into the public room below. No one paid him any mind: In a dozen strides he was out into the open air of Bow Street.

Across the way a couple of constables from the Night Patrol were lounging in conversation on the doorstep of number 4. Morton bent his head and set off along the street at a brisk walk and in a moment was out of sight. Just another soul lost to the London night.

Chapter 31

Henry Morton walked a good distance eastward along the Strand and into Fleet Street before finding a hackney-coach to take him to the Otter. The summer night was warm and the stink of the Thames was particularly strong and foul, radiating in waves from over the housetops and out of the dark alleys to the south. It was a smell of vegetable rot, of human waste and tar. A smell, as so many Londoners before him had remarked, of putrescence and decay. A slow current of death moving through the heart of the living city.

With this ominous stench following him, Morton made his way through the city. It must have been close to four A.M. when he reached his destination. The streets of Spitalfields were silent at this hour, and Morton came up to the Otter House entirely alone. There were no lights in its windows.

He drew out the Bramah key that he still had in his pocket, and steeled himself. His hand went almost automatically to his waistband for his baton—and he remembered that he was no longer a Bow Street Runner. His best weapon, his authority, had been taken from him. Taken by George Vaughan.

Was Vaughan inside? Morton felt his anger rise. Well, that was good, because anger was all he had.

The Bramah slipped into the circular hole and moved easily in its wards. Murmuring a word of gratitude to the workmanship of Valentine Rudd, Morton drew the door closed behind him and stood in the pitch dark of the landing, trying to call to mind the exact layout of the place. Then, feeling ahead with one foot, he carefully made his way down the short flight of steps and located the stone arch that led into the main drinking room. From within, he could hear the rasping exhalation of a sleeping man.

A small tin lamp flickered on one of the tables, dully illuminating the familiar confines of the room, and a dark shape lying on the bench along the wall. It was the publican Joshua, his head pillowed on what looked like a rolled-up coat. Morton scraped a chair up to the lamplit table and the man on the bench raised his head and gaped at him.

"Bill . . . ?"

"Nay," replied Henry Morton curtly, lighting a cheroot from the guttering lamp. "You'll talk to me now, Joshua."

"I'll be talking to a dead man" was the muttered reply.

Morton gazed at the other's haggard face in the unsteady lamplight. "I think you're not so corrupt a man as the place you're in," he said, after pulling long on his cigar.

"What sort of man I am is nothing to you."

"Oh, it is something to me. Something indeed. Is George Vaughan upstairs, Joshua? Is Bill?"

Joshua looked as though he would not answer, but then he shook his head indifferently and laid it back on the bench, staring up at the ceiling. "What do you want of me?"

Morton had half a mind to seize the barkeep and shake the truth from him. But he'd seen men like Joshua before—not large or strong enough to force their way in this world, but inured to physical threats and violence, here, where they were the commonest coin of every transaction.

"I can set you free of this place," Morton said.

"And make a nightingale of me? I'm not much of a singer, Morton. And besides, I heard what happened to that cull you nabbed in Leadenhall Street. Someone set *him* free, now, didn't they?"

Morton stopped as he was about to draw on his cigar. "It won't be happening again."

Joshua shook his head wearily. "George Vaughan played you for a fool once, Morton. I'll not wager he can't do it again. It's a dim cully as bets against our Mr. Vaughan."

Morton could feel an edge of panic welling up, but he drew on his cheroot, trying to steady himself. He knew what happened to men who lost their nerve in this world. "You taught letters to that little kinchin, Lucy," he said.

A surprised pause.

"Small need to teach that one anything," the barman finally replied. "Wot of it?"

"You're her protector in here, aren't you, Joshua? And you've never laid a hand on her, have you? You've never laid a hand on any of the little ones."

Joshua muttered something under his breath. ". . . not for me" was all that Morton could make out.

"I could set them all free. All the sad little girls Vaughan is bringing to ruin in this house. Would that bring about a change of heart, Joshua?"

"Heart? He has no heart who labours in such a house as this." He said it savagely.

"Oh, you have a heart," Morton said. "It's beating in you yet. You know what goes on here. Vaughan had that young swell, Glendinning, poisoned. He arranged for the Smeetons to thieve that shop and then had them caught in the act. He hid the Elgin booty in my rooms so that I'd be arrested for theft. Theft over fifteen shillings, Joshua. That's a hanging offence."

"Aye," grunted Joshua after a moment. "A horney should know, shouldn't he?"

"So you know I'm in earnest. You can ask what you want of me, and I'll give it you."

"You'll say so, that's sure enough," muttered Joshua.

But there was concession in his voice. A long pause. Morton waited. He could not tell what Joshua was thinking, whether he would give another contemptuous refusal, or something else. Finally the Otter's barman spoke again.

"What would happen to Lucy and the others if you got them away?"

"To the others? An orphanage, I should think. Better than what they have here. Lucy? I think something better could be arranged for her. A home. What about you, Joshua? Would you like to set up somewhere else—in some other town—and raise a daughter?"

Morton could feel the pull of this on the other man. Feel it in his hesitation. "Nay," he said finally, "it's not for me to do. Girl needs a mother...and a father who can provide."

"We'll find you an honest trade, I swear. Will you do

it? Will you go before the Magistrates and tell them
what you know about George Vaughan and his foul en-
terprises?"

But then the smallest sound alerted Morton. A key
was turning in the lock.

Joshua's eyes met Morton's: a look of pure hopeless-
ness.

"Is there another way out?"

"Not for you," said Joshua.

Henry Morton threw aside his cheroot and leapt up,
snatching the chair by its back as he did. He stepped to
the door, raising his improvised weapon. When the first
man stepped through the shadows of the archway Morton brought the wood down hard, splitting it in two and
sending his foe abruptly to the floor. The man started to
scramble up, but Morton kicked him fiercely on the side
of the head, making him collapse again.

But the newcomer wasn't alone.

"It *is* the horney!" a voice shouted, and a second,
larger figure bulled in under the arch and struck the
Runner hard in the chest, driving him stumbling back.
As Morton regained his balance he found himself face to
face with the burly man he had seen on his first visit.
Bill.

Several other men crowded in behind and Henry
Morton saw that Joshua had been right. He was
trapped.

Vaughan was not amongst them.

"Hear me," Morton gasped out. "It's your master we
want to see swing. It's George Vaughan, not you. Give
evidence, and we'll let you be."

Bill was pulling a short silver cutlass from a sheath
concealed in his canvas trousers. The other men held

knives or cudgels. Bill looked over at Joshua, who sat motionless, his head bent, eyes on the floor.

"Did he ask you to do the same, Joshua, me boy? Did he sing you the same sweet song?"

"Aye," muttered Joshua, "but I told him I don't make deals with dead men."

Bill eyed him a second more. "Nor do I," he said. And with that Bill lunged at Morton with his blade.

Morton leapt aside, lashing out with his foot. The other man stumbled and tripped. Morton found himself circling behind the little table, which bore the only lamp in the room. Before he'd even thought it through, he knocked them both over. The lamp bounced off the bench and hit the wall; the flame instantly snuffed out, leaving them in utter darkness.

There was a little volley of startled shouts. Then Bill's voice, low and angry. "Guard the door, don't let him out!"

Morton had dropped to his knees and could hear in the air close above the whistle of Bill's weapon, cutting blindly out for him, but passing over his head. Scrambling crablike backward and to one side, Morton desperately got away from him in the dark.

Someone screamed as Bill's blade caught him, and then there was cursing and muttering. Morton could hear men shuffling about the room, searching for him. Groping behind him, Morton felt the bottom of the stairway. Up, he would have to go up, it was the only way. But then, as he reached blindly back, a hand gripped his hand.

A small, warm hand. Pulling him insistently another way. He followed. They passed not up, but behind the staircase. Morton struck his forehead a sharp blow on something overhanging. He bent lower, hit the top of his backbone even harder, but continued to scramble madly forward, half-stunned, on his hands and knees. A glimmer of light. In front of him a small, scurrying grey shape.

"There!" someone shouted.

"In after!"

They came, but Morton had scrabbled through into a low chamber whose entrance lay concealed behind the staircase. There was a tiny rush lamp here, and in its light he could see a stout door, perhaps three feet high. He seized this and slammed it shut. Groping in the shadows he found it had a bar, and he dropped this into its bracket just as they reached the other side.

Hammering and imprecations, and then Bill's calm voice behind, ordering them to desist and fetch a crow and his pistols.

Another streak of light now slipped under the door from outside. Morton turned around and found himself gazing into the pale face of the little serving girl, Lucy.

Chapter 32

It was more like a cellar than a proper room, and was crowded with the shapes of unidentifiable objects. Panting, Morton shifted a couple of small heavy barrels in front of the door, and then looked around himself. His momentary feeling of safety was quickly evaporating. There was no way out; the men beyond would soon have the door open, and now he had involved the child in his fate as well.

Lucy gave him a small, frightened smile, and said nothing.

"Thankee, girl," he breathed. "Thankee for that."

"This is where they keep the things they have stolen," she explained solemnly.

"Oh, aye," responded Morton emptily, "I suppose 'tis." He started picking about in the weak light, lifting and discarding objects, seeking for some sort of makeshift weapon to fight them with.

"It is also where they hide if they think the horneys are going to look for them. That's why it has a strong door."

"Aye."

He lifted a heavy object, and felt his hand slip over polished stone. The breast of a woman, her thigh. Raising his discovery into the anemic light, he saw that he held a figure sculpted in marble, about a foot high. A dancing, laughing goddess. A naiad. Part of the marble relief that had been stolen from the Earl of Elgin—the rest of which had been hidden in Morton's rooms.

"And it is also where the tunnel starts, so they can slip away if they need to," continued Lucy.

Morton turned and gaped at her, the marble still in his hand.

"No," she earnestly assured him, "it is."

It was certainly a feature of every flash house: some secret means of escape. A tunnel, or a route across the rooftops from an attic window, or a concealed door into a neighbouring building.

"If you want to go through it," offered Lucy, "I won't tell them that you did. I'll tell them . . . some story, while you make away."

"They'll be waiting by now, at the other end," breathed Morton, still trying to take it in.

"Oh, yes, perhaps. But also, perhaps not," said Lucy. "I think they don't know I know about it."

"I'm not even sure they saw you lead me in here," thought Morton aloud. Lucy gave a toothy smile, pleased. And he continued quickly to work it out in silence: They might not want to assault him through their tunnel, as it would probably be too awkward and too vulnerable a means of approach. It would be easier and safer just to break down the door.

There was a blow now on the other side of that wooden barrier, and a grunt of effort. Muffled voices.

Morton raised his finger for silence. He leaned close to the girl.

"Lucy, you show me where the tunnel is. And you come with me. They'll not be happy with you when they know you've helped me."

"Oh, no, Joshua will tell them it's all right. Joshua's my friend."

"Joshua will come away with us also. Later. But for now, you must come."

She stared intensely at him a moment, then scrambled off to one corner of the room. Morton followed, thinking she was going to show him the tunnel. But that was not her purpose. Out of the obscurity she produced her treasure. Tied round with string, stuffed full of other papers: Arabella's copy of *Hebrew Melodies*.

Morton shook his head. He realised he still held the sculpture and set it down. It had to be found here. To carry it with him would only compound his difficulties.

There was a rending, squeaking sound behind him. The men on the other side of the door were prising apart its boards.

"Show us the tunnel now, Lucy," Morton whispered urgently. Obediently, the child scrambled across to the far corner of the room and started yanking at a heap of stacked-up bales of cloth.

"I watched them once, when they used it," she explained as Morton motioned her aside and began the work himself. "They didn't know I was here. This is one of my secret places. There are ever so many spots in this house only I know about, where I can hide."

"Have you ever been through?" whispered Morton. She shook her small head.

In a few moments, Morton had made a space. Behind

it stood a flimsy piece of deal. Lifting this aside, he found himself looking into a dark hole hardly more than two feet high and the same width. A gush of dank, foul air spewed out of it. He recoiled. They would not even be able to take her weak little rushlight in its awkward holder. But there was nothing for it.

"Go first," he whispered, "and I will cover us up again." He glanced at her as he spoke, thinking how frightening this must be for a child. But Lucy crawled in promptly, practised at the motion, her Byron still in hand. Morton followed with difficulty, worming his way forward on his belly. He knew immediately that there was no question of twisting his large frame about inside in order to try to cover up the entrance behind them. He would have to leave it open. It would have taken their pursuers but a moment to discover their means of escape in any case. Speed now was everything.

Crawling forward, he felt the walls of the tunnel on each side. They seemed to be shored up with wooden posts, like the walls of a mine shaft. The floor was earthen and wet.

His face bumped into the soles of Lucy's shoes in the darkness. "Keep going, girl," he urged.

"But I can't see!" She sounded frightened now.

"It's all right, child. There's nothing to fear." He struggled to keep desperation out of his voice. "But keep going, Lucy, or we'll be caught and they'll kill me sure."

He heard her scuffle and he crawled after. He had to slew forward on his elbows, dragging his legs behind him, the space was so tight. A little wave of near-panic shuddered through him. It was like being buried alive. And suppose their enemies were coming toward them from the other end? He'd told the girl all was well. But what might happen to her in the dark?

After about ten yards he could feel brick instead of wood beside him, and the space seemed to be opening up above.

In the total darkness he could hear Lucy whimpering in terror.

"Lucy, girl, Lucy," he whispered, trying to grope forward. "What happened? Where art thou?"

"I fell!" The invisible voice was tearful.

"Stay where you are, child. I'll come up to you."

He was on his knees now, reaching ahead with his hands. Could he even perhaps stand? The surface below him was rough stone now, not earth. Somewhere in the obscurity before him Lucy was crying. He advanced cautiously, trying to find her in the darkness.

But careful as he was, he could not control himself as he went over an invisible edge. He lost balance, and his arms lunging out to the side for support suddenly found nothing. He toppled forward, chin first, down what seemed to be a short flight of steps, and landed on top of the child, who squeaked with alarm. He felt his face land against her gritty hair, and their skulls knocked audibly together.

"Good Lord!" he breathed, extricating himself, and feeling for her with his hands. "Have I hurt thee?"

A long pause. Then a small doubtful voice said, "No, sir."

He had her by the elbows and stood up, lifting her with him, setting her upright—he hoped—on what appeared to be a fairly level floor. He reached around until he could find her hand, then pulled her close beside him.

"You've served us passing well, Lucy," he whispered. "A brave bit of exploring. Now I shall go first, and you keep near me."

"Yes, sir."

"Do you still have your book?"

"Yes, sir."

He groped forward. At a guess, he imagined them to be in the cellar of an adjoining house. He must find the way out quickly, as it could only be a matter of moments before the men in the Otter understood what had passed and came racing around to the exit of their tunnel. If they had not done so already.

He started to his right, and moved in what he hoped to be a straight line until he reached a wall. Then he began to trace this. No blind groping in the centre of the room. Somewhere on the perimeter there must be what he was looking for.

It took them perhaps a minute and a half—an eternity. A door frame, a knob. Morton tried to turn it, but could not. He felt for a bar, but there was none. He hesitated a moment. If this was only a closet or another dead end, he ought not to waste time on it. But there was no way to tell, except by going through. He positioned Lucy behind him, told her to stay perfectly still, and released her hand. Then he lunged forward, shoulder first, slamming hard into the door.

It gave way on his second assault, and he went sprawling through, his left shoulder stabbed with a fierce flash of pain as he crashed heavily and loudly down on it. But to his inexpressible relief he knew he was out in the open air. There was faint light, the sky, the dark shapes of buildings on all sides. Gasping as he pulled himself to his feet, he staggered back through the now visible doorway to retrieve Lucy.

They hurried out into what seemed to be a small cinder-yard. Twisting round, Morton located the high bulk of Constitution Brewery behind him, which meant that they had come out of the Otter House on the northeast side, and that the row of houses before them probably faced on White Street. But there were people coming; he could hear their feet pounding behind the wall that divided this yard from its neighbour. He hurried ahead, pulling Lucy along with him, but unsure of where he was going, or whether he was rushing away from danger or toward it.

They crossed the wide yard and started to squeeze down the narrow alley between two houses. This, too, was dark, and almost as bad as the tunnel, but at least the safety of the street beckoned beyond it. If only they could get there before Bill got to the far end, they would be in the open, with a chance of other people being by, even a hackney-coach perhaps, and some hope of life.

But an inner sense told Morton they would not make it in time. Perhaps the barely audible sound of running feet, or just some intimation, some deeply working calculation of the number of seconds it would take the men on the other side of the houses to turn the corner and come around in front. Halfway down the alley there was a door frame, set a bare foot or so into the brick wall. Morton pulled Lucy into its shadows with him and desperately tried the handle. It was locked firm, with that immobile feeling that suggested a heavy bar on the inside. There was no time. Men were entering the far end of the alley.

Flattening himself against the door, pressing the girl close against it, Henry Morton laid his face against the wood and tried not to look.

They brushed by, literally within inches. Three men, hurrying. They needed only glance into the shadows, or reach to touch the dark space beside them as they slipped past, and they would have found their prey. But they didn't.

Almost as soon as they were past, Morton pulled
Lucy out and went on toward the street. He prayed
there were no more coming after, that they would not
meet them head-on before they got to the mouth of the
passage. A few terrible seconds of anticipation...and
then they were out into the open. There was no one
there. Not a soul, nor a coach, nor anything. He needed
another quick decision now. Which way? Where was
the nearest busy thoroughfare, and the hope of escape
from this dreadful quarter?

He picked his right hand, eastward and away from
Bell Lane, thinking to reach the nearest cross street and
then get down into Whitechapel. Running as fast as little Lucy could go, he headed toward the next corner. As
they ran he tried to listen for the sound of pursuit, for the
echoes of other feet than their own. He tried not to look
back.

They were only a few strides from the corner when
the first shot was fired. Lucy gave a little panted shriek,
and then with the second shot she fell, her small hand
wrenching out of Morton's grip.

Henry Morton bellowed, and staggered to a stop,
half-falling himself and propping himself up with one
hand. He scrambled up and rushed back, seized her up
bodily, flung her over his back, and began to run again,
her weight bouncing with agonising stabs of pain on his
injured shoulder. A few moments of violent effort
brought him around the brick wall of the nearest building and into cover. Only then could he dare to think
what might have happened. A great wave of unfamiliar
emotion was rising in him. If she was dead...

As soon as he set her down on the road, she bounded
back up, panting and gazing at him with bright eyes, her
Byron still clutched tightly in her small hands.

"I tripped when I heard that noise!" she gasped. "I'm sorry!"

He could say nothing but only nodded at her repeatedly. It was, after all, not surprising that Bill had missed. Pistols were highly inaccurate at any range above a few paces. Morton seized her hand again; in a few moments more, they were safe amongst the eddies of predawn traffic on broad Whitechapel Road.

Chapter 33

Morton had to hammer on Arabella's door for a very long while before a drowsy Christabel opened the peek hole. "Oh, Mr. Morton!" she said. "We were wakened earlier by Bow Street men searching for you."

Morton glanced anxiously back. Streaks of yellow and pink had begun in the east, but the street was still empty. "I have no doubt of it. Now let me in quickly before I'm seen."

There was an agonising moment of hesitation, and then the door swung open. The maid stepped aside, gazing suspiciously down at Morton's companion. "I'll call Mrs. M.," she said, and hurried off upstairs.

Morton led Lucy through into the parlour and set the tired little girl down in the centre of the sofa, where she perched uneasily, gaping about her. For his own part he paced back and forth in agitation until Arabella arrived.

"Morton!" she cried. "They were here, and said you had escaped and—" The words died on her lips as she spotted the waif, and for a moment she stared open-mouthed. "And who might this be, pray?"

"This is Lucy. She saved my life tonight."

Morton saw different feelings struggle in his mistress's handsome face, and waited rather anxiously to see whether maternal softness would win out.

"She has my Byron!" she said.

Lucy clutched the book even more tightly and gazed up at the actress with a mixture of defiance and awe.

"Did I not say I had given it to another woman?" Morton smiled.

Arabella burst out laughing.

"Can you keep her safe awhile?" he asked. "I have much that must be done if I am to prove my innocence."

Mrs. Malibrant nodded once, staring down at the child who still held hard to her book. Morton wondered who would end up with it.

"Would you like to stay awhile with me?" Arabella asked the girl.

Lucy gazed up wide-eyed. "If you please, m'lady."

Arabella flashed a smile at Morton. "Do you hear, Henry? She thinks me a lady." And then to Lucy, "Do you know, I once was a countess."

Lucy nodded, willing to believe anything of this vision before her.

"And yet another time a duchess. I was even a queen, though it was a brief reign. The critics pierced me with their quills and I vowed never to be a queen again." She offered her hand. "I think Christabel is making breakfast. Are you hungry?"

Lucy took the offered hand, but with her other kept the Byron behind her back. Apparently she knew something of exiled queens.

Arabella shot another bemused smile at Morton. "Be

off, Morton. I think young Lucy and I shall be the best
of friends."

"But I fear for you if you stay here. George Vaughan
will be looking for me—and her—and he is still a Bow
Street man. If he was to appear at your door again there
would be nothing you could do. Can you take her to
Darley? Vaughan would never dare to look for her
there."

Arabella considered. "I don't know what Arthur will
say to harbouring fugitives . . . but yes, I will go to him."
She looked at Morton, examining his torn and muddied
clothing, his haggard face, and for the first time he
glimpsed the depth of fear the actress was hiding.

"Henry?" she said quietly. "Do come back to me."

Morton leaned forward and kissed her, and for a moment she clung to him, before he ran off into the bustling
morning.

Morton found a hackney-coach in Red Lion Square.
The long ride out to Sir Nathaniel Conant's suburban
villa in Camden Town took an eternity, and the further
delay while Morton knocked up the porter and waited
until the Chief Magistrate was ready was almost as
maddening.

Sir Nathaniel finally received him, wigless, in his
modest study. Morton guessed that the visit had interrupted the Bow Street Magistrate's breakfast. The older
man's eyes smouldered, but he was too much the gentleman to commence with shouting or reproach, or to complain about the earliness of the hour.

"How is it you are at liberty, sir?" he demanded. "I
ordered you held until this morning's hearing of your
matter."

"I . . . procured my temporary freedom, sir, in order to obtain proofs of my innocence. But I am here, as you see, and am surrendering myself to your pleasure."

"This had better have been done at Bow Street."

"I did not do so because there are those at the Public Office who helped fabricate the evidence against me in the first place. I could hardly trust my new information to their hands."

Sir Nathaniel stared at him coldly. "I have little patience for these tales, sir. I will certainly not abide their recitation at this hour and in this place. You shall have your hearing, as originally scheduled, where you may make whatever claims you please."

Morton strove to keep his composure. Time was slipping away.

"I ask you to hear only this much. I've uncovered crucial evidence—evidence not merely to exonerate me, but that will reveal exactly the depth and extent of corruption in the Bow Street Public Office."

The Chief Magistrate had opened his mouth to issue another rebuff, but Morton's last few words made the older man reconsider. He bent his head and frowned, and stepped for a moment about his room, pondering. At length he looked up at Morton.

"If not for Mr. Townsend, I should refuse to countenance any of this. But he interceded on your behalf. Mr. Townsend all but swore an oath on his good name that you are not guilty of the crimes you have been charged with, and Mr. Townsend's oath I take seriously. His alone amongst the lot of you." Then he said: "What is the nature of this supposed evidence?"

"If you go now to the Otter House in Spitalfields you'll find it—but speed is all. Take a force of constables—men Mr. Townsend recommends. You will need men in numbers, because the folk in that flash house will defend themselves with desperation once they know that their Bow Street protector cannot save them. He—"

Sir Nathaniel interrupted him. "Name no names, sir! Not until you testify at your hearing. And then if you do, beware that you don't slander your colleagues without proof, as it will go hard for you."

"If I am unable to demonstrate my innocence, sir," said Henry Morton, "it will go quite as hard as can be."

"What shall I find at this Otter House?"

"There will be at least these two things. Firstly, in a concealed storeroom behind the staircase, you'll uncover a variety of stolen goods."

"We might well find the same on a warrant to search any flash house."

"But amongst these goods is an element of the sculpted antiquities stolen from the Earl of Elgin's collection at Burlington House."

"Very well. But you may have left or placed it there yourself. This flash house may be a place of your own resort."

"The second source of intelligence to be found at the Otter," continued Morton, steadying himself, "is a fully competent witness, who is prepared to testify as to what he has seen in that place. His name is Joshua, and he is the barkeep in that establishment." Morton hoped desperately that he was right in this: that Joshua would be willing to give evidence.

The Chief Magistrate grunted. "A respectable kind of witness." But his tone softened.

Morton went on. "He will swear to the origins of the goods in the house. Even more important, he will swear to the name of its true protector, the name, that is, of the

Bow Street officer who really does control and profit from that place. He will swear also to the kinds of crimes that—"

"That is quite enough." Sir Nathaniel's harsh voice was resigned now. He had listened. Henry Morton fell silent.

The Magistrate paced back and forth in silence a few moments more, his eyes down, and his hands clasped behind his back. Then he stopped and straightened himself, looking at Morton.

"I will instruct Mr. Townsend to assemble members of the Horse Patrol and go to this house on a warrant which I will sign myself. I will instruct these officers to proceed to the Otter House and make a search for precisely the goods you make reference to. They will also seek out *any* persons in the place who might provide information. Not merely the one whom you seem to believe will do you good. We'll see what they all have to say."

"But we must go quickly, this very moment, before the iron goes cold."

Sir Nathaniel Conant frowned, and then without further speech went out to give the necessary instructions to his household. Even so, it was some minutes more before the horse was harnessed and he and Morton were safely into his gig and headed for London.

The Magistrate chose to take the longer Saint Pancras road, in the hopes of seeing the incoming Horse Patrol from the north, but this manoeuvre proved fruitless. No other constables were encountered on the whole journey, despite Sir Nathaniel's spending several long minutes questioning the toll men at the Battle Bridge Gate as to their whereabouts.

"Damned useless system of patrol," he muttered as he climbed back up into the carriage. "Where would a man be if he was in any real need?"

Other than this, however, the Chief Magistrate kept a bleak silence throughout, and Morton made no further attempts to engage him in conversation. The portly man sat immobile as a rock, his jaw set, gaze fixed ahead, his hands gripping the traces hard.

At number 4 Bow Street, where they arrived with the sun fully above the horizon and the streets beginning to fill with early traffic, nothing could be done speedily either. The Horse Patrol had not come in, and Townsend was not about and had to be sent for. Morton was to be fitted with irons this time. The clerk had to start over several times writing the warrant, as Sir Nathaniel thought of changes he wanted to make.

Just after John Townsend arrived, so also did George Vaughan.

"Mr. Vaughan," suddenly announced the Chief Magistrate, seeing him, "you will accompany Mr. Townsend to the Otter House in Spitalfields."

Henry Morton, who was sitting half-forgotten in the corner of Sir Nathaniel's room, leapt up to object, his chains clanking as he did, but Sir Nathaniel silenced him with a look. "You, too, will accompany the expedition, Mr. Morton. But you are both to be observers of this matter, not participants. I wish you both to be satisfied that the business is properly done."

Morton looked at his superior in surprise. So, he had recognised what the choice was. Morton turned to George Vaughan, who returned his gaze steadily.

Then, in his usual drawl, Vaughan said: "Just as pleases you, Sir Nathaniel."

The Chief Magistrate regarded them both.

"I'll see one of you hang, gentlemen," he said. "Be certain of it. And believe me, I am perfectly indifferent which of you it be."

Soon after, the Horse Patrol came in and Townsend took charge. Now the operation moved forward with efficiency. The old Runner, for all his fussiness, knew what he was about. They were on the streets heading east within moments, the horsemen clopping in front in double file and the two coaches bearing the Runners and supporting constables close behind. All, except Morton and Vaughan, were armed with sabres or pistols. Morton was in the first carriage, beside Townsend. Vaughan came in the second.

Once they were under way, Morton said: "If you care to reach into my side vest pocket, Mr. Townsend, you'll find a key that will give you entry to the Otter House."

John Townsend looked at him in surprise.

"I cannot manage it myself," explained Morton, making a gesture with his shackles.

The other officer felt about until he retrieved the Bramah key, which had fortunately not been lost during Morton's various adventures over the previous evening.

"I must make the observation, Mr. Morton," said Townsend, turning the key over in his hand, "that your possession of such a convenience does not match well with your protestations of innocence in regard to the aforementioned house."

"Do you really think I have joined with the flash crowd?"

"No. No, Morton, I do not, but even so. Sir Nathaniel will find it most peculiar that you would have such a key in your possession."

"I shall produce a witness to testify that it was a copy made for me only days ago, from an original provided by one of the girls within the house."

Townsend stared at him a moment. "I pray this witness can impress the Magistrate with his integrity. For your sake."

For his own part, Morton prayed that matters at the Otter had not altered too much when they arrived. If Vaughan had been surprised by the preparations under way at Bow Street, Sir Nathaniel's canniness had at least prevented him from slipping ahead to warn his minions.

When Morton had made his escape a few hours ago, what would Bill have assumed? Perhaps that the disgraced Runner would flee the country, or even that he would make another attempt to intimidate someone in the house. But he would surely never have guessed that Morton would return to Bow Street and let himself be imprisoned again.

The Otter mob would not have known that he'd seen the stolen sculpture in their storeroom—perhaps they hadn't noticed that it was there themselves, that it had been left behind when the other marbles were removed. Had Joshua been able to persuade them that he'd not peached to Morton? With any luck, nothing fundamental would have changed in the shady little world of the flash house.

They were getting close. The familiar confines of Spitalfields were flowing past Morton's window, and he felt his chest tightening in anxiety.

As the carriages started moving up Bell Lane, they slowed to a crawl and then stopped dead. One of the mounted constables rode back to report to Townsend, his voice on edge with alarm.

"Trouble, Mr. Townsend! Trouble!"

And even as he spoke, Morton began to catch it. The acrid smell, the burning in his eyes. A man pelted past the carriage, dressed in a heavy black overcoat, a scarf tied round his mouth. A firedrake.

"The phoenix-men are here, sir, but it's too late, sure!" the constable cried.

John Townsend uttered a heartfelt, if somewhat antique, curse, and clambered from the carriage. Morton followed awkwardly. As soon as they were in the crowded street and trying to push their way forward through the excited onlookers, the smoke in the air became obvious. A few steps more and the flames leaping above the rooftops hove into view, and Morton's spirit sank.

The parish fire company had arrived, its unsalaried officers milling rather helplessly about in the narrow lane amidst a blizzard of swirling grey ash. The insurance company brigades were better equipped and more efficient, of course, but what likelihood was there that the owner of this particular property had ever insured it?

Not that anyone would have been able to do much now. Great hands of flame reached out of the windows and door frames of the Otter, grasping at nothing but air. As was Henry Morton at that very moment.

Chapter 34

This time Henry Morton was closely confined in a back room at Bow Street, shackled at wrist and ankle, a constable from the Horse Patrol constantly in attendance. Exhausted after a long day and sleepless night, dirty and unkempt, his shoulder throbbing from the injury received breaking out of the Otter's cellar, he slumped on a hard wooden bench against the wall.

Sir Nathaniel had postponed his hearing until the morrow, in order that the situation in Bell Lane be assessed.

Some time in the afternoon Vickery came in to tell him what had happened. A thundershower had assisted the fire company in its work. But by the time the blaze had finally been extinguished, three houses had been destroyed. In the ruins of number 12 they found five charred bodies: One was large, adult, and four were children.

They had sifted through the wreckage, and discovered the apparent location of the storage space, as Morton had described it. But there was nothing there. No stolen goods, certainly no marble sculpture. If there had ever been a tunnel, it had been covered forever in the collapse of the neighbouring house.

Morton nodded, slowly, seeing it all. There was little for either to say. Vickery went out, leaving his brother officer to the cold comfort of his thoughts.

An uncertain time later he heard shouting beyond the door. He and Browne, the constable who was watching him, both looked up in surprise.

"Order, what order! Who gave you such an order?"

"What does it concern you, you young fool, so long as they did!"

The voices were recognisable. The first belonged to Jimmy Presley. The second to the constable Dannelly, who was apparently mounting guard outside the room.

"I'll give you an order—with my fist, so help me God."

There was a silence, and then Morton heard the locks being worked. The door swung in, but instead of Jimmy Presley, Arabella Malibrant entered alone, and the door was pulled sharply shut behind her.

She strode unhesitatingly across the room to sit down beside Henry Morton, wrapping her arms around him and pressing her lips to his hair. He could hear Browne shift in discomfort, but Morton leaned against her, unable because of his shackles to put his own arm about her, and silently accepted her warmth, her embrace, the sweet familiar scent of her that filled his nostrils.

For a long moment they sat thus without speaking. At length she drew back, and quickly cleaned her wet cheeks with the back of one white-gloved hand.

"The Otter burned," Morton said at last, "taking all the children with it. The poor, misused children. Only Lucy escaped."

"And you," Arabella murmured.

"Yes, but only for a time. There was a man's body found there, too, in the ashes, and it will prove to be the barkeep Joshua, I've no doubt. He was ready to testify. They must have seen that. They took no risks."

Arabella pulled away so that she could look at him, her hands pressed against his chest. The lamplight shone in her hair, turning it the hue of failing embers, but her skin was very pale.

"But we have a witness still," she said. "Lucy has told me much. Much that I did not care to hear—and so naively stated. How could any girl's mother...?" But she let that sentence die. "Lucy knows everything, Henry, everything we need them to hear."

"She could know every bit of villainy George Vaughan had ever perpetrated and it would not matter to the Magistrates. She is a child, and a child raised in a criminal environment where lying comes as easily as the pox. They will not believe her, that's certain." Morton took Arabella's hands in his own. "I fear it will not answer." He gazed at her face, so filled with worry, and tried to change the subject. "But how is she? How is our young Lucy?"

"She is very well. I have her at Portman House still. She told me what happened last night, Henry, how you got her free from that place. She is a marvel. An absolute marvel. How could such a child have sprung from so corrupt a house?"

"There is a great spirit in that tiny body. At least I plucked her away in time, if nothing else. I wonder if Rudd got his Marie clear as well?"

Arabella stared intensely at him, her green eyes glittering. Then she took hold of his lapels and shook him gently. "Henry, you do not listen when I speak. Lucy can get you free. She recognises George Vaughan and can identify him! She heard him give orders for any number of felonies. Those people, the Smeetons—some man named Taylor was treated the same and hanged as well."

"Samuel Taylor?"

"That's the one."

"Vickery arrested him . . . on Vaughan's intelligence. I remember it." Her certainty was making some impression on Morton now. "Perhaps it is worth trying," he mused. "Like enough, the panel will prevent her even from speaking. And if she does speak, they will probably not believe her. But perhaps 'tis the best hope I have."

"It is the only hope. You'll see, when she begins to talk. She's rare, a prodigy, Henry. I swear she will make an impression on these Magistrates, if they have any heart at all."

Morton smiled a little in wonderment. Lucy must certainly possess something extraordinary to have won over the hard-to-impress Arabella so quickly. "Did they tell you the hearing is set for tomorrow morning?" he asked.

"Yes, and we shall have her prepared. Louisa Hamilton knows of your plight and has come to Darley's. She's taken up our young Lucy with a will, and is having some clothes fitted for her so she'll look well in Police Court. Henry, you won't recognise that child."

"And all this, at Portman House?"

Arabella nodded. "Yes, you have an admirer in Arthur. And now that he has heard Lucy's story . . . You are quite the hero over there at the moment."

"Lucy is the hero," Morton muttered. "Without her I would not have escaped."

"Nor would she have escaped without you. They would have left her to the flames."

For a second Arabella closed her eyes.

Morton caressed her cheek. But Arabella rallied, her eyes flicking opened, filled now with resolve. "We must think carefully about what we need to know from Lucy," she told him. "We must prepare for the questions she'll be asked. Arthur has offered his barrister, Oswald Barrington. He speaks very highly of him."

Morton smiled in gratitude. "Should I be bound over for Sessions Court in the Old Bailey," he replied, "I shall certainly need the best legal wizardry available, and I'll accept the offer. But a prisoner is not allowed representation at his Police Court hearing. He must speak wholly for himself, even arrange his own witnesses, if he has any. The Magistrates listen to the testimony, draw up documents, and make any decisions about the laying of charges. And actually, because the procedure is less formal, it's often a man's best chance to avoid an appointment with Jack Ketch. And so it might be for me."

"Then we must be very ready," said Arabella with determination.

For the next half hour she and Morton went over the possible course of the hearing, the dangers and the possibilities. While they consulted, Constable Browne stared emptily at the wall, without appearing to react to anything that was said. Townsend had put Browne in here, but Morton couldn't help wondering if Vaughan's influence in Bow Street was deeper than even the old man knew.

Chapter 35

When morning came, Morton was ready to rise and meet it. His warders were surprised at his demand that he be allowed to dress himself properly. Suspected felons were usually forced to appear before the Magistrates just as they were, unshaven, ragged, already criminal by their very appearance. But Morton loudly insisted that a barber be sent for and a messenger dispatched to Rupert Street to fetch him a change of shirt and breeches. Paying for everything with the last few coins in his pocket, he also ordered over a full breakfast from the Brown Bear. He had no intention of starting the struggle for his life weak from the lack of food.

A little sleep had gone a long way.

The shackles had to be removed while he was dressing, and several stone-faced constables stood in the room, arms folded and ready for anything as Morton was lathered and his cheeks scraped clean. Under the same scrutiny, he ate his sausage and black bread and drank his ale—coffee was too much to be hoped.

His clean shirt, and then his best dark green frock coat he pulled on—a painful operation over his aching shoulder—and the shackles were reapplied. Just before ten o'clock, a clerk looked in to inform them that the Magistrates were now entering court, and that the prisoner was to be brought. Morton breathed deep, and for the final time marshalled his thoughts.

And this was the moment Wilkes made his appearance. The old manservant was led in by Jimmy Presley.

"Good morning, Mr. Morton," he said, as though there were nothing out of the ordinary in the circumstances.

"The Brighton Diligence is a slow, mean way to travel, I collect?" Morton's irritation was beginning to rise, despite his fondness for the old man. Why had it taken him so long!

"But walking is slower still. I had only to walk a few English miles, fortunately."

"Come along, Mr. Morton, sir," said the constable.

"Did you find Sempronius Stretton?"

"I did indeed, and a great long tale I heard of his battles and service to England and—"

"But could he provide what I asked?"

"Indeed, Mr. Morton." And Wilkes handed Morton a folded sheet of paper, just as he was led away.

Police Court was held in the large, rather shabby central room of number 4 Bow Street, under the light of two aged chandeliers. A low wooden fence divided the room in two: one half for the judges and prisoners and constables, the other for the witnesses, those waiting their own turn before the panel, and the merely curious. The panel consisted of three Magistrates, perched behind individ-

ual raised desks on a platform that ran along the end
wall. Morton was brought in through the side door and
led to the railed box situated exactly in the centre of the
room. Here he was to stand—there was no chair—for
however long it took his fate to be decided.

He turned stiffly to look behind him. The other side
of the room was jammed full, and people leaned in at
the long windows that gave out onto the street. More
were packed into the corridor beyond the rear doors. All
craned for a view of this scandalous spectacle: one of the
famous Bow Street Runners finally accused of a crime!
The constables whose duty it was to control access to
the court must have been achieving substantial gain in
the small entry fees they were permitted to collect.

Morton scanned the faces. Arabella and Darley had
been able to procure a place near the rail—no doubt for
a price—and both immediately waved to him. Darley
was as poised as ever, but Arabella looked pale, and no
matter how much the actress in her projected confidence, Morton could see her fear.

Also close to the barrier were the reporters, whose accounts in *The Morning Chronicle* and even *The Times*
would start printing within minutes of the end of the
hearing, eagerly awaited by a city and a nation whose
resentment of their elite police had reached an unprece-
dented pitch. Just on the Magistrates' side of the barrier
there lounged a little knot of Bow Street men, arms
folded, waiting. George Vaughan was amongst them, his
face as inscrutable as ever, eyes half-closed but watch-
ful. Beside him were Dannelly, Mckay, Pelham, Vickery,
and Johnson. Was this, Morton wondered, Vaughan's
gang? But perhaps not. Vaughan would have been too
subtle to group his supporters together in plain view.
And Morton felt fairly certain that Vickery at least

was square, and probably Johnson too. Dannelly was Vaughan's man, though.

Farther along the wall, sitting alone on his own stool and unconcernedly perusing a newspaper, was John Townsend. Jimmy Presley was stationed in the doorway behind him, guarding the entrance back into the rest of the police offices. He tipped his hat briefly to Morton, and Morton nodded in response. Morton watched George Vaughan's narrowed eyes flicker to take in this little exchange.

The spindly-limbed clerk was calling the session to order, and Morton made one more swift survey of the room. He was looking for the one other face he had expected to see. But he could not find it. Louisa Hamilton was not there.

Sir Nathaniel Conant had taken his place at the centre desk and began to speak. The clamour of voices that had filled the room quickly quieted.

"The purpose of this hearing is to gather information, not conduct a trial," he told his court. "The panel will tolerate no evasions and no argumentation. All persons with relevant knowledge are commanded in His Majesty's name to present it fully and truthfully. The panel will record such material, decide upon charges to be laid, if any, and make a deposition to be conveyed to their lordships at Sessions House in the Old Bailey."

Sir William Parsons, the Magistrate on Sir Nathaniel's left hand, cleared his throat. Like many in his profession, Sir William was no trained jurist. In fact, he had been appointed, doubtless by his friends, merely because he was a gentleman and literate—his normal occupation was professor of music and Master of the

King's Band. Even so, Morton had attended his sessions before and had a degree of respect for his common sense.

"Does Mr. Morton have any opening remarks?"

This was conventionally a chance for the man in Morton's place to confess, and spare everyone time and trouble. Morton intended to make different use of it.

"My lords, I am exceedingly glad of this opportunity to penetrate a matter of importance, and I am confident that well-founded charges will indeed be laid before this hearing is concluded. I ask you only to keep your habitually open minds. I daresay the charges will not fall where you now imagine they should."

Across the panel eyebrows rose.

"The evidence will determine that," commented Sir Nathaniel Conant.

Townsend was the first to take his place at the witness stand, in front and slightly to the left hand of the Magistrates. In his eccentric and garrulous way, he testified to the discovery of the stolen marbles in Morton's lodgings, and he read aloud the advertisement placed in *The Chronicle*.

"You have served with Mr. Morton at Bow Street, Mr. Townsend?" unexpectedly asked Sir Nathaniel Conant.

Age had had its effect on the old Runner's hearing and the echo in the large room seemed to confuse it further. "How's that? Served with him? Indeed. Indeed, I have."

"How long?"

"Oh, a goodly time. Some seven years, I daresay. Quite long enough to make a determination as to his character."

"Thank you for anticipating my questions, sir," Sir

Nathaniel said dryly. "And what has been his character, as a man and as an officer of police?"

"Oh, excellent. I should not hesitate to say that Mr. Morton is a model of honesty and dedication to duty."

"But what is your view of the evidence you have provided? Is it not a clear sign of corruption?"

"It is a clear sign of corruption, without a doubt, but of whose corruption? That is less clear, I think."

"Have you any contradictory evidence to offer, Mr. Townsend?" William Parsons asked abruptly.

"Eh?"

"*Contradictory evidence,* Mr. Townsend," Parsons said loudly. "Have you any?"

"Oh, no, I'm sorry to say. Not at this time, Sir William."

Parsons looked over spectacles at Sir Nathaniel, who dismissed the old Runner. He then turned to Morton's box.

"How do you explain your possession of the Earl of Elgin's property, sir?"

"It was placed in my rooms by another person," replied Morton. "Without my knowledge, and while both my manservant and I were absent."

"And the notice Mr. Townsend has read us from *The Chronicle*?"

"Placed by another person, my lord. A clumsy attempt to attribute the crime to me."

Sir Nathaniel Conant pinched his lips together and made no response.

George Vaughan came next. He, too, testified to the discovery of the antiquities in Rupert Street, and to the advertisement which had led them there.

"What is your view, sir, of the moral character of Mr. Morton?"

Vaughan took his time answering. Henry Morton studied the man's expression, struck as never before by how obscure a countenance his really was. The eyes deep set, the lips habitually compressed tightly in a small, mirthless smile. Morton had often thought that George Vaughan was mocking his fellow man, that his attitude was carelessly contemptuous of most of humanity. But now he saw it differently: The man seemed to him to possess an air of alert stillness and waiting, of concentration, like some solitary predator of the forest.

"He always had a good name, my lord," said George Vaughan, and stopped.

"But does that reputation reflect your own opinion, sir?"

Vaughan paused again, seemingly with reluctance. He looked at Henry Morton, and Morton smiled coldly at him. *Tell your lie, sir,* he silently made the invitation. Vaughan's face remained expressionless.

"I never trusted him, my lord," he replied.

"Why not? What evidence did you have for this feeling?"

"The money he had. Things he let drop. Things the other lads let drop about him."

Morton loudly broke in. "This is innuendo and hearsay, my lords. Let these others testify if they have something of substance to say."

Sir Nathaniel pivoted angrily. "Keep your peace, sir, until it is your turn! The panel will judge the admissibility of testimony. This is not Sessions House and you are not a lawyer."

But Morton knew that his point had registered, and that everyone in the room was aware of it.

"Did you ever witness Mr. Morton committing any irregularity?" now asked Francis Beadwell, the third

Magistrate. He was a thin, quiet man, recently appointed, about whose character or abilities Morton knew little.

"He were too careful for that, my lord," quickly answered Vaughan.

"Confine yourself to direct answers to the questions, sir," calmly came back Beadwell.

"I saw nothing specific, my lord, until we searched his rooms these two nights past."

"Thank you."

Two other constables were called to testify as to what they had found under Morton's bed. Morton watched them, and concluded that they were not part of Vaughan's mob. This apparently was his technique—the same technique he had used with the Smeeton arrests. He arranged for unsuspecting and fully respectable men to provide an appearance of legitimacy to his operations. Townsend and these constables in this instance, and Presley and Morton himself on the earlier occasion.

Finally, Lord Elgin's private secretary assured the panel that the reliefs found in Morton's rooms were indeed the same as had been stolen from the courtyard of Burlington House.

"Excuse me, sir," then asked Henry Morton, "but are the pieces you have recovered complete and intact?"

The man glanced at Sir Nathaniel to be sure that he was right in answering questions from the man in the dock. The Chief Magistrate nodded.

"In fact, sir, an element of the smaller fragment appears to be missing."

"Would it be the image of a woman, sir?" asked Henry Morton. "A naiad with one breast uncovered and one hand raised, holding a wreath?"

The secretary looked surprised.

"Yes. Precisely so." As he stepped down, Sir Nathaniel Conant turned to Henry Morton.

"We have goods stolen, and appearing later in your possession, sir. We have your own apparent familiarity with these goods, even down to an unrecovered fragment. We have a newspaper notice apparently inviting the owners of these goods to contact your lodgings, presumably with a view to buying them back. Before I lay charges, do you have anything more specific to say in explanation of all this, other than that you are the victim of some monstrous plot?"

"I do."

"The panel," Sir Nathaniel told him, "will listen to no further testimonials to your character. The material evidence is so strong against you that no endorsement of your personal virtues would be sufficient to prevent the laying of charges. You must save such witnesses for Sessions House."

"I agree to forgo any such testimony, my lord."

"Then what do you have to tell us?"

"I have to tell you that you should arrest and charge Mr. George Vaughan for this crime, not me."

A stir went through the room. Vaughan's mocking smile broadened a little, while some of the Runners standing about him scoffed visibly. Sir Nathaniel Conant's face remained expressionless.

"Upon what evidence, sir?"

Morton turned away from Vaughan and looked into the faces of the panel members. "I am aware of the exact appearance of a missing part of the marble carvings at issue because I saw it, two nights ago, in the back storeroom of number twelve, Bell Lane, Spitalfields."

"Where is that missing fragment now, sir?" Sir William asked.

"I do not know. The denizens of that house have doubtless hidden it again, and have burned down the house to protect themselves."

"This is speculative."

"Informed speculation, my lord."

"Why should we not believe that it is you yourself who placed the sculpture there?" Parsons asked.

"The explanation is not brief, my lords," Morton said, and he described his last visit to the Otter, the fight there, his escape through the tunnel. As he did, however, he spoke only of himself, not yet hinting that anyone had escaped with him.

Beadwell asked the next question.

"You do not claim that Mr. Vaughan was amongst those you confronted in this house. Why are you accusing your brother officer in these matters?"

Morton proceeded, carefully and in detail, to relate his interviews with Wardle and Rudd, particularly with regard to their insistence that there was a Bow Street presence at the Otter. Then he told them about Joshua.

"This man identified the Bow Street officer who controlled the house, my lords," Morton said. "He identified him by name. And the name he gave was George Vaughan."

Into the rush of low voices that this produced, Vaughan interjected, sardonically echoing Morton's earlier objection. "Hearsay, my lords. Let this Joshua cove testify."

"He can't, my lords," calmly explained Morton. "George Vaughan and his accomplices have done him to death."

This produced an even louder burst of voices, so that the court clerk had to rap his rod hard against his desktop to restore order.

"What proof have you of such an outrage, sir?" demanded the Chief Magistrate. "What proof have you of any of this, except that you say other folk told it you? Other folk who are not here and cannot testify themselves."

"Wardle and Rudd can be summoned."

"That, too, will be a matter for the Old Bailey. If you cannot produce direct, independent proof of your claims, what possible reason do we have to accept them?"

Henry Morton drew breath. "The best possible reason, my lords. There is another witness. A witness who has seen and can tell this Police Court enough to have George Vaughan committed to Newgate a dozen times over." Now he turned his head in the startled silence and looked pointedly at Vaughan.

The other Runner was not quite impervious to what he had just heard. There was a certain fixity in his look, although the smile remained on his thin lips. Was he thinking, trying to imagine whom Morton might mean? One thing was certain: Morton had George Vaughan's attention now.

"What witness, sir?" demanded Sir William. "Can you produce this person?"

"I can. It is someone these men neglected, whose eyes and ears they probably never once considered as they planned and committed their crimes."

The three Magistrates regarded him wordlessly. Morton nodded to Arabella, who swiveled round and made a small wave of her hand to Merwin, Darley's butler, at the very back of the room. He disappeared, and returned moments later with Arabella's maidservant Christabel. Together they elbowed their way through the crowded room. Sheltered between them was a small person dressed in a white frock.

Arabella and Louisa had done a magnificent job. The girl had been reborn as a perfect little daughter of the gentry. Her hair, now that it was clean, proved to be a glowing honey colour. Her face shone with excitement, and she tripped forward with a light, childish spring that contrasted charmingly with her elegant muslin dress and reticule.

None of the men standing around Vaughan moved as the three reached the bar dividing the room. Even the clerk sat immobile, as if frozen, gazing open-mouthed. It was the courtly John Townsend who stepped promptly across to open the gate and let them in, even bowing slightly as he did. A few moments more and Lucy was ensconced on the witness stand, where she was given a chair to stand on, for she was too small to be seen over the rail.

Morton looked over at the partner of his escape and smiled encouragingly. He was favoured by a brilliant grin in return. Then she quickly settled her features into an expression of great seriousness, and looked expectantly toward the Magistrates.

"What is her name?" asked the clerk.

"Lucy Hammond!" came the clear, firm response from the girl herself.

Now Morton took time for another brief glance at George Vaughan. The face was still set, expressionless. But the small smile had vanished. Vaughan was watching now with the utmost attention.

"What is her—your abode?"

"I *was* living at number twelve, Bell Lane. But I am visiting now," she added with a certain complacency, "with friends in Portman Square."

The incongruity of the two addresses, as much as the poise and confidence with which they were announced, raised all three sets of eyebrows on the panel again in an almost comical fashion.

"Your age?"

"Twelve," promptly replied Lucy. Morton noted with an inward smile the rounding upward of this carefully worked-out number.

"Is this...place you formerly lived," now began Francis Beadwell, "also called the Otter House?"

Lucy looked straight at her questioner to respond. "Yes, si—my lord."

"How long were you living there?"

"One year and seven months."

"A maid like this!" now breathed out Sir William. "In such a place! Did she have any...did you know what sort of place it was?"

Lucy turned solemn eyes to him. "A very bad sort of a place, my lord. A flash house."

Now, however, there was a harsh interruption from the other side of the room. "Ask her what she did there," George Vaughan said scornfully. There was a low ripple of laughter from the men around him that spread after a few moments into the rest of the room. Male laughter. The clerk rapped with his rod.

"I carried the glasses to the tables," defiantly replied Lucy. "I cleaned and swept. And..." She faltered as Morton's heart sank. He did not want this, not even if it was to save his life. But they had told Lucy to tell the truth, and this was very precisely what she was going to do. She pressed bravely on. "... and only sometimes, if Joshua thought they were square coves and kindly,. I would go upstairs with the gentlemen, and—"

"You need say no more of that." Sir Nathaniel Conant gruffly prevented her from going on.

Into the hush came George Vaughan's sarcastic mutter. *"Only sometimes..."*

"Silence, sir!" The Chief Magistrate turned again to Lucy. He pointed one massive black-draped arm across the room toward Vaughan. "Lucy Hammond," he rumbled, "did you ever see that man, who just spoke? Did you ever see him in the Otter House?"

Lucy's eyes fixed on Sir Nathaniel. She knew the importance of the question as well as anyone else in the room.

"Yes, my lord. Many times. He was master there."

"Do you know his name?"

"It is Mr. Vaughan."

Beadwell came in now. "How do you know he was master?"

"Everyone obeyed him."

"Did he ever pass a whole night there?"

"Yes, my lord. Many times. He slept in the room at the top of the house."

"What about the circumstances under which you left that house," proceeded Beadwell. "How did you come to be in Portman Square? How do you come to be here?"

With no further prompting, Lucy began to tell the story of her escape with Morton. It matched exactly with the narrative Morton himself had provided minutes before, and Morton could sense the Magistrates registering this. He could sense, also, the growing amazement that was filling the whole court—an amazement, almost to the point of wonder, at Lucy's eloquence and self-possession. No matter where she came from, or how true her tale, this was clearly a marvelous child, an accident of nature.

Sir William described in overly elaborate detail the

sculptural fragment that was missing from the Elgin antiquities. Had she ever seen it?

"Oh, yes, my lord. It was part of the swag that Mr. Vaughan had Bill and the others steal from a rich lord. It was kept with the rest of the things they stole in the place under the stairs, until they decided to put some of it in Mr. Morton's rooms."

"My lord—!" Vaughan broke in scornfully, but Sir Nathaniel held up his hand.

"Peace, sir. You shall have your chance to speak." He went back to Lucy. "How do you know that they decided to do such a thing? Did someone in the house tell you that?"

"I heard them talking about it, my lord."

"You were a party to their discussions?" Sir Nathaniel allowed himself a degree of incredulity.

"I was in a little place I had in the room, my lord. They never knew I was there. Other times I heard things when I was carrying their glasses. They did not care what I heard."

"Who was there when this particular action—the one concerning Mr. Morton—was decided upon?"

"Mr. Vaughan. Bill. Joshua. And..." Lucy seemed to try to remember. "... some of their ... friends. I did not know what their names were. There were a lot of men I only saw once or twice."

Morton finally raised his own voice. "My lords. I believe that this witness can provide extensive information about an entire criminal ring, centered in the Otter House and commanded and organised by George Vaughan. She can tell of thefts arranged, and property sold back to its owners. She can describe abductions, murders, and other crimes arranged and often even perpetrated in that house. Such detailed testimony is perhaps not necessary for our present purposes. There are two specific crimes, however, I would like her to tell you about, as they would both demonstrate the considerable range of activities practiced by Mr. Vaughan in the Otter, and shed light on two matters currently being enquired into by the Bow Street Office."

George Vaughan was shaking his head in disgust. But Sir Nathaniel Conant seemed to have acknowledged that, at least for the moment, Morton had the upper hand.

"Proceed, sir," the Magistrate growled.

Morton turned to Lucy, who looked up at him with the same frank and ready gaze. Morton felt a wave of intense and grateful emotion for this wonderful girl. He breathed in deeply a moment, so that this feeling did not discompose him, then smiled again at her.

"Lucy, do you remember ever seeing a man in the Otter House named Caleb Smeeton?"

She nodded. "Yes, he was there many times."

"What was the opinion of Mr. Vaughan and Bill and the others of this Mr. Smeeton?"

"They thought him a cull. They called him Brother Hodge, or Captain Cully."

"A cull is a fool," Morton explained for the benefit of two of the Magistrates. "What happened to Mr. Smeeton?"

"Oh, they dished him up," calmly replied Lucy. "They did that to people. Mr. Vaughan called it putting a man in a play."

"What did he mean by that?" Sir Nathaniel bent forward to ask.

"I don't know, sir. But Mr. Vaughan would say, 'I think he's earned a part onstage.' And then the man would be arrested and hanged."

This caused whispering among the crowd, and the panel responded as well.

Morton took up the questioning again. "So what did they do to Caleb Smeeton? Mr. Vaughan and Bill and the others?"

"They told Mr. Smeeton there was a draper's panney that would be very easy to rob, and that he could make a pot of gold. They told him the address and they gave him the crow to break open the door, and . . . and something else. Oh, I know: the phos bottle to light their lantern with when they were inside. They told him to bring his wife to help. Then after Mr. Smeeton had gone home, they started to laugh, and made a plan to have them caught by the Bow Street Runners. Mr. Vaughan said he would set young Mr. Presley on him. And he would get Sir Galahad to be there, too, so it would look square."

Morton cleared his throat, his face slightly hot.

"Lucy?" Francis Beadwell said in a surprisingly soft voice. "Who was this? Sir Galahad?"

"I don't know, si—my lord. A man they didn't like, though. They often said so."

Sir Nathaniel raised an eyebrow to Morton.

"I believe it is a reference to me, my lord," Morton admitted, and there was a small titter through the crowd. Morton turned back to the baffled Lucy. "What happened to Mr. Smeeton, then? Did they talk about that?"

"Oh, yes, sir. He and Mrs. Smeeton were caught, just as planned. They were stretched—I mean hanged. And Mr. Vaughan told the others how much money they were going to get once the rewards were handed out. They got twice as much because there were two people. They were all very contented about that."

"And this sort of game was played at other times, you said?"

"Oh, yes, sir."

"And did no one ever consider the fate of the folk who were hanged?" Sir William cried out suddenly.

Lucy gazed at him, a little scared by his vehemence. "No, my lord," she said in a very soft voice.

Morton paused to let the rumbling of voices settle. He glanced at the panel. Beadwell was writing something. Sir William looked shocked and was slowly shaking his head. But it was Sir Nathaniel whose aspect most impressed. The Chief Magistrate sat motionless now, staring hard at Lucy. His face bore a look of such a depth of outrage, sorrow, and dawning recognition that Morton realised all at once that Sir Nathaniel had never truly been a cynic. He had believed, after all, in the basic decency of his officers. And what he was experiencing now was the deepest, bitterest sensation of betrayal. Morton felt his own breast fill with respect for a man who could feel such pain over the violation of trust.

"My lords," Morton drew breath and said, "with your permission, I shall proceed to the second matter upon which this witness can shed light."

Sir Nathaniel Conant gave him a very slight, wordless nod.

Chapter 36

Now, Lucy," said Morton, "I'll ask you to recall to mind an evening about a fortnight past, when you were serving drinks at table in the Otter House."

She looked attentive.

"On this particular night, a young gentleman came into the house. He was dressed in dark clothes, and you would have been taking him glasses of—"

Francis Beadwell interrupted him.

"Do not lead the witness, Mr. Morton." The Magistrate looked to Lucy. "Did you see such a gentleman?"

"Yes, my lord. It was not a fortnight past, however. It was exactly eleven days ago. He was drinking brandy. Mr. Morton asked me about him before. But everyone in the house knew we weren't supposed to talk about him, or say he had been there."

Beadwell looked thoughtful as he turned back to Morton. "Proceed, sir."

"Were you the one taking drink to this gentleman, Lucy?"

"Yes, sir. He were a very stylish swell, got up like Beau Brummell, Joshua said. But I thought him rather shy, actually."

"What was he doing there, besides drinking brandy?"

Lucy looked knowledgeable, and quite pleased with herself. "He was waiting for Mr. Vaughan and another man."

This startled even Morton. He did not quite know what to do with it. Beadwell filled the pause.

"How did you know that, girl? Did the gentleman tell you?"

"No, my lord."

"Then how?"

"He had a paper that I read. It was a letter that said he was to go to the Otter House and wait for Mr. Vaughan."

"You can read, child?" wondered Sir William Parsons in astonishment.

"Yes, sir. I was taught by my mamma, and by Joshua."

"She can read, my lords," Morton added. "I have witnessed this myself." He turned back to Lucy. "So you overlooked this letter, and saw that it told him to wait for Mr. Vaughan?"

Lucy looked a little confused by this, and instead of answering, she nodded.

"Did this gentleman . . . go upstairs, Lucy? Did he go with any of the other girls?"

"No, sir. He stayed at the table the whole time."

"Did he speak to anyone?"

She thought. "Yes, sir. For a moment. He talked to Mr. Sweets a little."

"Mr. Sweets?"

"Oh, that's not his real name, sir! He is a fat man,

who always brings candies and buns for the girls. He comes most every night."

Morton grimaced involuntarily at this reminder of the confectioner Wardle. "How much did he drink? I mean, the young gentleman."

"He had but three glasses of brandy, sir. I know because I took him them all."

"Now, Lucy, was there anything special about any of these glasses of brandy?"

"Oh, yes, sir. Joshua put something in each glass."

Now there was perfect silence.

"You saw him do this?"

"Yes, sir. I stood beside him, behind the bar, when he did it, sir. He told me to wait. Then he took out a little bottle and tipped some . . . water into the brandy, and stirred it with a spoon."

"Did you know what that water, or liquid, was, Lucy?"

Her simple shake of the head made it clear that she still did not know, or guess.

"Did Joshua say anything about why he was doing it?"

"No, sir."

"Had you ever seen him do this before? Add something to a man's glass?"

"No, sir."

"Now, Lucy, and this is my very last question for you: Did you see the young gentleman after he drank his last glass of brandy? Did you see him leave the Otter House?"

"No, sir. The house was near empty by then, and Joshua let me go back into the storeroom to sleep. I never saw the gentleman again."

"The panel will note," said Henry Morton, "that the

events described by the witness took place on Friday
June ninth, the date of the death of Mr. Halbert
Glendinning. I believe some of us have attended the
public lectures of Sir Benjamin Brodie, an authority on
poisons and their effects. The description of the barman's special liquid, and the condition of Mr. Glendinning's corpse later that evening, would indicate that the
substance Joshua added to Mr. Glendinning's drink at
the Otter House was oil of almonds, or hydrocyanic
acid—a lethal poison."

"Very well. Mr. Vaughan . . ." It was Francis Beadwell
who seemed to have taken control of the hearing. Sir
Nathaniel Conant sat heavy and motionless. "What do
you say in response to the testimony we have just heard?
Why should we not lay charges against you for these
crimes?"

George Vaughan laughed a brief, sarcastic laugh. He
raised himself from the half-sitting posture he had
adopted on the wooden barrier, and began to move into
the centre of the room, where Lucy Hammond still stood
in the witness stand. The girl shied visibly back. Several
men reacted at once.

Before Morton could speak, the deep voice of Jimmy
Presley rumbled out. "Stand clear of her!" The young
man had started forward from the wall, and John
Townsend was also quickly on his feet.

Vaughan mockingly raised his hands, palms outward, and stepped back a bit. "Keep your hats on, gentlemen," he said. "I'll not meddle with your little
duchess." He continued his stroll, till he settled on a spot
near the desk of Sir William Parsons.

"What have you to say, sir? Speak up." Beadwell's
voice was perfectly level.

"First off, my lords," and Vaughan's tone settled now

into a bored drawl, "as I'm sure you have guessed, I've never been in the Otter House in all my life. Mr. Morton and his squirrel are trying to put a noose about my neck, to save their own. They have been telling you nothing but lies from the start of it to the end."

The panel watched him. Beadwell and Sir William with attention, Sir Nathaniel Conant with a dark, smouldering detestation.

"I'm not an eloquent man, my lords. I've not been to a university, as your friend Mr. Morton has. But I know what is true and what is not." He pointed to Morton, in the box. "You have a man here, a corrupt officer of police. You find stolen goods in his lodgings. You find a newspaper notice. As Mr. Townsend himself likes to say—'When you hear hoofbeats, expect horses, not zebra.' The obvious is likely true: The man who possesses the goods, stole them.

"Now, these goods are valuable. English law says a man hangs for a theft of this value. Mr. Morton, caught with his hands still sticky, is like to dance on air. He's got to find somebody else to step in for him, hasn't he?"

"Pray do the panel the respect of getting along with your arguments, Mr. Vaughan," Beadwell interjected calmly. "It is entirely clear to us that either you or Mr. Morton is lying. The motive in either case would be transparent."

George Vaughan gave his mirthless smile. "Just as you say, my lord. Well, then, I must ask you: Do you have any proofs against me outside of what Mr. Morton and his little ... *friend* have provided? Do you have one solid piece of evidence?"

The trio of Magistrates stared wordlessly back at him, which Vaughan took as acknowledgement of his point.

"Nay, none at all. But you do have a solid piece of evidence against Mr. Morton, don't you? But, you may be thinking, the little duchess says some terrible things." He turned and looked hard at Lucy. Morton and Presley stirred, but Vaughan stayed where he was.

"Who is this *witness* who condemns me? This little parrot who repeats all that she's been taught? A child. And not a clean, respectable child, either. Do you not remember what you have here, my lords? Despite her one-day finery, and all the words she's been coached to say, do you not know what this is, here on your witness stand?" He continued to stare at her for a long moment. Then he faced the panel. "A whore," he said. "She told it you herself. And not just any man's whore, either." He pointed at Morton. "But this man's whore. How much has he profited from her labours, I wonder? How much socket-money has he pocketed?"

"My lords!" Morton struggled to keep his voice calm, as provocation was precisely what was intended. "Simply to voice such unfounded calumnies is not testimony! It is not argument."

"Confine yourself to what you have evidence for, Mr. Vaughan," cautioned Francis Beadwell.

"Yes, my lords," came back Vaughan, for the first time letting a little anger of his own creep into his voice. "They say to you that George Vaughan ran the Otter House. I tell you Henry Morton did, not I. I tell you that this is his fancy-girl here, testifying at his behest. Are you going to hang an honest man on the word of a little cesspool of corruption like her?"

"We don't hang anyone, Mr. Vaughan," replied Beadwell with the ghost of a smile. "The judges at Sessions House do that."

But now Sir William Parsons opened his mouth.

"It is entirely true, as many are aware," he pronounced, "that such licentiousness, especially at so early an age, cannot but have an unnatural, distorting effect on the female character."

George Vaughan nodded at him. "Aye, my lord, and officers of police have had occasion to see it many times."

Morton smiled bitterly at Vaughan's ability to make such a darkly ironic jest at a moment like this. The Master of the King's Band, of course, was oblivious.

"I must, on reflection," Parsons continued, "urge the panel to disregard the testimony of this young witness. Such things as she has experienced cannot but have a corrupting and perverting effect upon her fragile female nature. Nothing she says can be taken as truth."

Beadwell looked vexed, and glanced over at Sir Nathaniel Conant. But the Chief Magistrate stayed silent, as if he could not trust himself to speak. He merely stared darkly at Vaughan.

"I confess," Francis Beadwell began, "that I share some of Sir William's doubts on this matter. A female child of such age, and such a ... background, is indeed a slender reed upon which to build. I don't know if she could have been coached to say such things, but certainly she is a cunningly clever girl. Her ... unfortunate profession must count strongly against her in the mind of any upright man. This Police Court needs more solid, impartial evidence. Lacking such proof, I do not see how I can recommend any charges be laid except the obvious one against Mr. Morton for theft."

William Parsons nodded agreement. Sir Nathaniel sat glowering but, Morton realised, his views must essentially be the same. He might want the outcome to be otherwise, but he could not possibly allow himself to believe the word of a child prostitute.

The room had fallen eerily silent.

"The prisoner is to be bound over for trial, then," sighed Beadwell, "on the charges of—"

"My lords!" Jimmy Presley had risen, striding out into the open floor. His whole manner was stiff and awkward, like that of a furious child.

"What is it, Mr. Presley?" Francis Beadwell asked.

"It was me that pinched the Smeetons, man and wife, and I didn't note it at the time but it was not quite as square as it all seemed. Mr. Vaughan gave me all the information and told me to say that it came from my informant, so that I might get my appointment to Bow Street. I thought he was helping me, but I don't think that now. He told me to bring Mr. Morton along and even arranged to have Morton here at number four so that I'd not have to search about for him. 'You go by Bow Street and get Sir Galahad,' he said. That's what he called Morton. And then he said, 'They'll never doubt him.'"

The three members of the panel stared at him in disbelief. "Are you admitting that you gave false evidence in my court?" Sir Nathaniel demanded, incredulous.

Presley's gaze darted around the room, everywhere but to Sir Nathaniel. With a sinking heart, Morton realised Presley had spoken before he'd thought. A roar was growing in the room as the audience began to clamour in anger and excitement.

"Aye, he did for the Smeetons, just as we said!" someone cried out.

George Vaughan was adding his voice to those besieging the panel. "My lords! My lords! What has this to do—"

Beadwell and the clerk were calling for silence, while Sir Nathaniel continued to sit motionless, staring at Vaughan. It was only then that Morton caught sight of Arabella. She was pointing to Lucy, and calling out something.

"My lord!" Henry Morton shouted.

"Peace! Peace!" cried Francis Beadwell. "Mr. Presley, resume your place! This is not to the issue just now. We are not here to discuss the Smeetons, and to raise up the passions of this city again."

Presley unwillingly obeyed, but a scattering of voices continued to sound in the room.

"Nay, nay, you'll not have *that*!"

"You'll not have him heard, will you!"

"My lord..." Morton continued desperately to try to make himself heard. "My lord! My witness has not done."

"Mr. Morton, we have ruled on the value of the testimony of this—"

"Not testimony, my lord! She—"

"I have the paper," piped Lucy in a small, clear voice.

"No more of this—" scornfully began George Vaughan.

Suddenly Sir Nathaniel Conant rose at his desk. He brought his hand down with a crash.

"Quiet!"

And now there really was a startled silence. The Chief Magistrate heavily lowered himself into his seat again, and turned toward Lucy. "What paper, maid?"

"Maid!" scoffed George Vaughan, low and bitter.

"Silence yourself, sir!" Sir Nathaniel roared in a thunderous bellow of pent-up fury. The stillness of the courtroom deepened into a frightened hush. Lucy looked pale, but stood her ground, perched still on her

chair in the witness dock. The Chief Magistrate's voice was slightly unsteady as he once more asked: "What paper have you?"

"The letter, my lord. That the gentleman had. The swell dressed all in dark clothes."

"Mr. Glendinning?"

"Yes, my lord." And Lucy reached into the reticule she had kept tucked tightly under her arm the entire time. From it she removed a small volume, which Morton recognised at once as Arabella's Byron. With childish concentration she applied herself to the string tied around it, releasing the many bits of paper stuffed between its leaves. Her small fingers nimbly searched through these for the one she needed.

"Miss Hamilton told me not to forget to show it to you," Lucy breathlessly explained. "And I almost did forget!"

"Miss Hamilton?" gruffly wondered Sir Nathaniel.

"Miss Louisa Hamilton," quietly explained Henry Morton, "the fiancée of the late Mr. Glendinning."

"How did you come by this letter?" the Chief Magistrate asked Lucy.

"I was doing my cleaning, the morning after. It was on the floor under his table, in the sawdust. The gentleman must have dropped it. I took it because I like to have things to practise reading."

"Pass it to the clerk, girl. Mr. Smith, if you please."

As the reedy man got up from his desk and stepped to the witness box, Henry Morton turned his eyes toward George Vaughan. There was little obvious change in the other Runner's secretive countenance, but Morton saw the almost imperceptible sag in the shoulders, the calculating look in the eyes. Vaughan knew what was in this letter. And he knew what it meant.

"Let it be noted," said Sir Nathaniel Conant, taking up the document, "that the witness has produced a letter of normal dimensions, addressed on the outside, in a firm, adult hand, to Mr. Halbert Glendinning, Oxford Street." He unfolded the paper and turned it over.

"It is dated Friday, ninth June, 1815, and reads as follows:

> *Glendinning—*
>
> *All is arranged. Go to the Otter public house, by the old brewery in Bell Lane, Spitalfields, at nine-thirty tonight. This is our man Vaughan's ground, and he will meet us there. He will require twenty sovereigns, of which R. will already have provided ten.*
>
> *Pray, do not be tardy.*

"It bears no signature," concluded Sir Nathaniel in a businesslike voice which said much for the change in his mood. He turned his eye on Vaughan.

"I believe, sir, that you told this Police Court that you had never been in this house," the Magistrate said very deliberately. "I believe that was your testimony?"

Vaughan said nothing. He could certainly have objected, Morton thought, that the note, too, must be fabricated evidence. But the other Runner understood as well as Morton what Sir Nathaniel's view of things now was. Such an objection would be bootless here. No doubt he was already thinking of his strategy of defence at the Old Bailey.

Sir Nathaniel looked at the note again, and seemed to wonder aloud. "But who wrote this?"

Young Lucy, attentive in the witness stand, took it upon herself to answer. "The man who had Mr. Glendinning dished," she matter-of-factly proposed, and then shrugged to indicate she didn't know who that was.

But Morton knew.

Chapter 37

Events ran very quickly then. Sir Nathaniel ordered Morton released, and the same irons were used to bind George Vaughan—a proceeding Morton watched with a mixture of grim satisfaction and foreboding. For himself, freedom and vindication. But for his profession, and for Bow Street? The British public's worst fears had been confirmed.

Sir Nathaniel stood behind his desk regarding a contrite-looking Jimmy Presley and told him he could thank his Maker that he'd not been standing in the witness dock when he made his admission of giving false evidence.

Almost as soon as his hands were free, Morton took from his pocket the sheet of paper Wilkes had brought. Hastily he ran his eye down Stretton's list of the captains who had served at Albuera—Captain Frederick J. Dennis. Captains M. Moss and Richard Davenant. Captains Thomas Russell and Francis Galsworthy. Captain Peter Hamilton.

Morton stared at the name a moment and then closed

his eyes. He opened them to find Townsend by his side, clapping him on the back.

"John," he told the old Runner. "I will thank you a thousand times over for this day and more, but there is a matter, more than urgent, that I must attend to. Will you do me the great favour of finding Mrs. Malibrant and telling her to meet me at number seven Hanover Square? Can you do that?"

"It seems a small enough favour, providing she is still here. But what shall I say this is all in aid of?" Townsend asked.

"I cannot tarry to explain. In truth, I pray that I am wrong."

Morton grabbed Presley's arm, and the two pushed their way out the back of the Bow Street office, and into the nearest hackney-coach.

"What is this about, Morton?" Presley asked, but before Morton could explain, their carriage turned into High Holborn and found the way choked with people: a great flowing current of them with back eddies in every door and before every public house. Such a cacophony rose from this mass that it was like standing next to falling water.

"What's the matter?" Morton shouted.

"Haven't you heard?" the man nearest Morton's window bellowed. He waved a mug of ale, a drunken grin fixed on his florid face, jumping up on the spoke of a wheel of their now stationary carriage. "*Bony's beaten!* Wellington stood him off on a hill south of Brussels, and the Frenchers have all fled home!"

"Nay, ye gabbling ninny!" the man beside him shouted in a thick Scots burr. "It's but a rumour! The whole daft toon's turned out to celebrate a rumour! Nobody really kens aught at all!"

Morton looked over at Presley, who shook his head. Who knew? But whether it was true or not, Hanover Square was still a good distance off and they were stuck here in a flood of people, like a coach foundering in a ford.

"Let's leg it," shouted Morton over the bedlam.

They bounced out of the carriage, forcing a path through the crowd, Presley waving his baton, although this only seemed to amuse the few who noticed. They struggled ahead, setting their shoulders to the press, and finally made their way against the stream of humanity across Charing Cross and into the relative backwater of Sutton Street.

Everywhere they went people were out and in a high spirit. Kegs were rolled from inns and opened on the cobbles, publicans serving ale and cider by the dipper. Children seemed to be underfoot at each step, and twice Morton kicked at dogs that barked and snapped about his ankles, their dispositions seemingly affected by the madness around them. Soho Square was impassable, and they were forced south to Old Compton. Assemblies in Piccadilly and on Regent were thicker than they had yet seen, so it was a long and almost random route they followed to their destination, pushing, bulling, running when they could, diverted repeatedly by impassable throngs.

When they finally arrived, Hanover Square seemed almost hushed by comparison, the crowds apparently having gravitated to nearby Regent and Oxford streets. Morton and Presley were panting from their efforts as they pulled the bell.

No one answered.

Morton swore an oath, and stepped back into the street to look up at the windows. They stared blankly back at him.

"No one seems to be home," Presley said, employing the sensible action of trying the door handle. It was locked.

"We'll have it down, Jimmy," Morton said.

"Morton..." Presley cautioned.

"I will take responsibility."

Sensible of his tender shoulder, Morton and his young colleague stood side by side and kicked hard near to the lock. On their third try the jamb splintered; the door suddenly swung free.

Morton pushed in, calling out as he went, but only his own voice echoed back. The house seemed unnaturally still and silent after the chaos of the streets. The sun slanted in the windows and spread over the floor in perfect squares and shining rectangles. Dust motes spun in the angled light.

Morton did not like the feel of the place.

They found the rooms upon the ground floor empty, and Morton mounted the stair, almost afraid to speak or make a noise. The silence rang hollowly in his ears.

At the stairhead he smelled something faintly acrid, like a fire smouldering in a hearth that did not draw. The first room they looked into was empty, and seemed so perfectly ordinary that Morton almost wondered if his fears were unfounded.

But then he opened the next door and found Peter Hamilton, dressed in his habitual black and lying awkwardly upon the carpet. A stain of drying blood dyed the carpet around him, and a dueling pistol lay near to hand.

"Dear Jesus..." Jimmy Presley whispered. "Who's this cove?"

"His name was Peter Hamilton," Morton said softly.

"Did he do himself, do you think?"

"Perhaps," Morton said.

"This is what you expected to find?"

"No. No, this is not what I expected, but perhaps I should have."

A polished mahogany box lay capsized on the desk, its lid hanging open, the small locking mechanism twisted and broken. Across the desktop lay a scattering of loose papers. This small autumn of fallen white leaves spread onto the floor, where it seemed the wind had swept them here and there. Morton stopped and retrieved several pages, glancing at them quickly.

"What've you there?" Presley asked.

"Poems," Morton said. "Love poems."

He turned and went back out into the hall. He felt a chill within, a sudden loss of feeling, of contact, as though the essence of Henry Morton had been cast free of his attachment to his physical being. He walked as though in a disturbing dream. The appearance of objects was not quite right, as though illuminated by a strange, flat light.

"Morton . . . ?" Presley said, looking at him oddly. But Morton did not answer.

Before opening the door to Louisa's sitting-room, he knocked gently. When there was no answer he put his hand on the doorknob, but still hesitated.

"Shall I look for you, Morton?" Presley asked softly.

Morton shook his head, took a quick breath, and opened the door.

She lay there in the soft light filtering through the

trees outside, her hair wafting gently in the small breeze that found its way through the open casement. Morton turned away.

"Here's the matching pistol," Presley offered. "Did they both do for themselves, do you think, or did one murder the other first?"

"I don't know, Jimmy," Morton whispered. He leaned heavily on the back of a chair. "Better I had found nothing," he muttered. "Better to have failed in my commission than to have caused this."

Sounds came from the stairs just then. Voices calling, and then Arabella and Darley appeared, stopping, horrified.

"Dear God, Henry—!" Arabella said, but nothing more. Darley took her arm and drew her out. Morton and then Presley followed. They met Townsend and, unexpectedly, Sir Nathaniel, on the landing.

Presley nodded toward the room and the Bow Street men went in. Darley eased Arabella into a chair where she fanned herself with his hat, her white skin paler than Morton had ever seen. They heard Sir Nathaniel exclaim something from inside the room, and then he, too, emerged.

"Who is this woman?"

"Louisa Hamilton," Morton answered. "She was Halbert Glendinning's fiancée."

"There is a gentleman, too," Presley said, gesturing to the other door.

Sir Nathaniel poked his head in and emerged looking very grim. "I came along to offer my apologies—and find this.... What the devil has happened here, Mr. Morton?"

But Morton was already on the stair, and then out

into the street and into the light that filtered through the trees in the square.

Morton sipped the tea that Arabella had made. They could hear Nan moving above, seeing to the bodies of her master and mistress. The maid had come in not long after, a basket on her arm, having been sent on errands by her mistress—errands that had been difficult to discharge in the town gone mad.

The sight of Louisa had buckled her knees, and Morton and the other gentlemen had left her in the care of Arabella, hearing only the muffled sobbing and keening from above. But then some part of her, some part born of intense practicality and a lifetime of service, had set her to work, laying out the corpses, aided by Darley's silent butler.

A messenger arrived from Bow Street then, bearing the letter Lucy had produced in court—the one directing Halbert Glendinning to the Otter.

"I'll take it up," Arabella said, and went softly up the stair. A moment later she was down again, nodding to Morton.

"It is his hand," she said, passing the note to Morton.

"Perhaps now you can tell us what went on here," Sir Nathaniel said.

"I am not entirely sure myself," Morton replied. "The dead man was Peter Hamilton, Louisa Hamilton's half-brother. As I guessed, he wrote the note that Lucy read in court this morning—and was the man who commissioned George Vaughan to poison Halbert Glendinning."

Morton had not returned into himself completely, but

still felt the odd distance, the unsettling inner quiet and emptiness. But the others were gazing at him.

"It is for the most part conjecture," he continued, "but I think matters shook themselves out so: Peter Hamilton was obsessively and jealously in love with his half-sister. The poems, which obviously he had kept locked in the mahogany box, were all written to her or about her. The entire tragedy sprang from his unnatural passion.

"Hamilton *was* at Albuera, though he claimed to have been ill with fever in Lisbon at the time. Wilkes brought me a list of the officers who fought in the battle, and Captain Peter Hamilton was among them. That is what finally alerted me. I believe he shot Miss Hamilton's first fiancé, Richard Davenant, in the heat of battle. And, if that was not enough, he then spread rumours to blacken the dead man's good name. The regimental surgeon, Bromley, was his confederate in this, for there was no one like that vicious little doctor to go after a man who could not defend himself." Morton looked out the window to the bright day beyond. Hanover Square remained unnaturally quiet. "Bromley would not reveal Hamilton as the source of these rumours, for Hamilton was his brother-in-arms, and I suspect sent him patients from among the quality.

"I do not know what went on between Louisa Hamilton and her half-brother. And I do not care to speculate. But in due course, after Davenant's murder, Louisa met another gentleman. Lord Arthur told me that he thought Miss Hamilton and Glendinning were about to announce their engagement, and perhaps that was true, though there were always thoughts of Richard Davenant in her mind, which is why she cried out his name that night on the steps of Portman House, when Glendinning was found dead." Morton stopped to marshal his thoughts a moment, looking at the solemn gathering. He took up his story again.

"Peter Hamilton told Glendinning that Rokeby had slandered his bride-to-be—the Colonel had once courted her briefly—and probably pushed Glendinning into sending Rokeby a challenge. No doubt he believed Rokeby would do for Glendinning, and he likely would have, had Presley and Vaughan not interrupted this duel."

"There you are," whispered Sir Nathaniel.

"Vaughan, of course, turned the opportunity to account. He demanded a bribe not to prosecute the two parties. But George Vaughan was quite the man for recognising larceny in another's soul. And somehow, I would guess, he saw it in Peter Hamilton—or perhaps it was the other way around. The corrupt Bow Street Runner was too obviously the man Peter Hamilton needed. However it occurred, Hamilton paid our good Mr. Vaughan to murder Glendinning. But not just murder him—he wanted to destroy him in the eyes of his sister as well. So one of them hit upon the scheme of poisoning the man and sending him to Lord Arthur's in a carriage. The little surgeon Bromley just 'happened' to be there." Morton turned to Darley. "You said he had come with someone else, Lord Arthur, and I am willing to wager that it was Peter Hamilton." Darley shrugged, ready to concede the point.

"Bromley promptly pronounced the man dead of his own dissipations—I would think that he jumped so readily to this conclusion because he had previously been made aware of Glendinning's 'dissipations' by Peter Hamilton.

"After the duel that morning, Peter Hamilton had called on Glendinning, supposedly out of concern, but Glendinning's man had been left orders that he was not to disturb his master. Shortly after, a note arrived delivered by a boy. The note," Morton held up the slip of paper, "directed Glendinning to the Otter, but he didn't know Spitalfields so he carried it with him to be sure of the address. If no one had suspected foul play in Glendinning's death, that note would have meant little. It would appear he was paying off some Bow Street man for looking the other way after a duel. But once Arabella had decided that things were not as they should be, and I was called...the note became a terrible blunder, even if Hamilton had been canny enough not to affix his signature. He probably thought Glendinning had left the note behind, and in fact asked me questions that would have alerted me had I suspected him, which I did not.

"The note seemed to have disappeared, to Hamilton's great relief, no doubt—but we all know what happened to it." Morton glanced up at the ceiling, to the rooms above. "Lucy must have shown her papers to Louisa last night—she liked to show off her reading. Of course Louisa instantly recognised the hand. And so she knew. Peter had sent Glendinning to the Otter to be murdered."

Arabella plucked a thread from the skirt of her dress. Sir Nathaniel took a long, calming breath. Only Townsend looked unaffected; the Runner stared at Morton and nodded repeatedly, as though in admiration for his analysis.

"But what happened then?" Sir Nathaniel enquired.

Morton shook his head. "I don't know what happened in this house. I don't think we ever can know. Certainly Louisa Hamilton broke open the locked box and found the poems. Strange that she knew to look there....She might have confronted her brother, but whether he shot her or she him, I cannot say. Perhaps they both self-murdered. Perhaps she first in despair, and then he when he realised he would be tried and hanged for at least one murder—or when he found the opened box..." He looked over at Townsend.

"We'll never know," the old Runner agreed, but Morton could see the man had his own theories about what had occurred. He might even know something from observations he had made in the rooms above, but Morton would never ask.

Presley put his head in the door just then. "It's not a rumour any more," he reported. "Blücher wasn't killed, just wounded. He and Wellington were able to bring the remains of their armies together, and have defeated Bonaparte. The Duke's own messenger has come to the King."

But there was no joy among the party, nor would there be for many days.

Epilogue

Morton was standing in the wings at Gentleman John Jackson's, watching two men of limited skill but significant strength brutalise each other, when he recognised the man standing beside him, who was just making the same discovery.

"Morton, isn't it?"

"Yes. Lord Byron. An unlooked-for pleasure, my lord."

"We shall have to have a rematch, you and I," Byron said, smiling.

"I would like nothing better."

"Like to pummel poets, do you?"

Morton laughed. They both turned their attention to the contest in progress, until Morton turned again.

"Pardon me, Lord Byron, but did you ever know a man by the name of Halbert Glendinning?"

The poet looked away from the action. "Well, I will tell you, Morton, the name has a ring," he replied, "but I can't say where I know it from."

"Mr. Glendinning fancied himself something of a poet. He was of a Sussex crowd...."

"I *do* know who you mean. Yes, he had me to his rooms once to look at some verses. They were better than I expected," he remarked, as though this fact still surprised him. "Why do you ask?"

"Well, the poor fellow has died..."

"Oh, I am sorry to hear it. But he seemed a healthy young man...?"

"I'm sure he was. He was poisoned by a rival for the affections of a lady."

Byron winced as one of the boxers landed a heavy blow on the other, sending him staggering back. Neither man spoke for a moment, and then Byron said, "Do you know why I attend Jackson's, Morton, when I could be at the theatre or some other entertainment?" The poet did not take his eyes from the contest. "It is because here we do not lie about our intentions. When I stand toe to toe with a gentleman, I intend to beat him into submission. It is brutal but honest." He glanced at Morton. "Was there some service you would ask of me regarding this unfortunate fellow?"

"No, no. Not at all. I just wondered if you had met him, and I suppose I was curious to know if he had an actual gift."

"A gift? More like a curse I should call it, though I suppose the life of a scribbler is better than what has befallen your friend."

Byron raised his hand to someone he had apparently been awaiting, then looked back at the Runner. "Good evening to you, Morton."

"And you, sir."

Morton arrived at Portman House on time, not fashionably late, and found Arabella and Darley there.

"Well, Morton," Darley greeted him, "I see you have gone in for a Byronic look," and then he looked suddenly serious. "Or are you in mourning?"

"I have succumbed to style. It is my vain attempt to have Mrs. Malibrant notice me."

"Notice you, sir! She is mad for you. Talks about you all the time." Darley smiled and his eyes shone as he said this. The man had a charm that Morton had to admire.

"But to me she speaks of you, sir," Morton pointed out.

Darley laughed. "Is that not just like her, Morton? I ask you. Is it not?"

Dinner was served at a table that would easily have seated a dozen and a half, so the three clustered together at one end.

"What do you think the situation was between the Hamiltons?" Arabella asked. "Did she know Peter was in love with her? I mean, how could she not? Or was there even something more...?" She looked at Morton as though he were keeping the answer from her.

"I really don't know, Arabella," he said. "Nor do I want to know."

"Hear, hear," Darley agreed.

"That is the odd thing about men," Arabella said, annoyed. "You honestly do not want the answer. How can you not? Louisa might have been her half-brother's lover, and you do not seem to care! Have you no healthy curiosity?"

It was at this moment that the door opened and Lucy came in.

"There she is," Darley greeted her, "the heiress to the throne."

" 'Tis not a throne," Lucy said, surprisingly subdued.

"Have you heard, Henry? Louisa left a thousand pounds of her fortune to Lucy." Arabella swept the girl up into a warm embrace. Morton noticed how readily Lucy seemed to accept such handling. "There was a note on her escritoire," explained Mrs. Malibrant sadly. "Imagine her thinking of that . . . then."

"It does suggest she knew what might come. Or chose. Yet, the inheritance is splendid news," Morton said, for he had been wondering what would become of this child whom he had saved—and who had saved him.

"But she did not forget you, old saw," Darley told him. "No. Two hundred pounds awaits you at her solicitor's. Not half what you deserve, I think."

Morton did not argue this point. He had almost been hanged, and so thought the money fairly earned. Though if they finally hanged George Vaughan, that would be the most pleasant forty pounds he would ever make.

Lucy kissed each of them good night before her new governess shooed her out.

"But where will she stay?" Morton asked.

"I'm the administrator of her funds, legally," Darley answered. "And I suppose there are schools she must attend, and . . . well, any number of things. I cannot bring her quite into polite society, alas, for her earliest life will follow wherever she goes. In some ways I think she would be better going abroad, in time, where this sad history will not follow. Canada is a bit cold, I hear, but it will be a great land one day. Or America. We shall see. The child is perseverance itself, so she might just make herself a life right here in London. At the moment, for some reason, she is set on a career on the stage, of all things!" He looked at Arabella and they both laughed like two people who cared for and knew each other well.

Arabella finished her wine, and rose from the table. "I must go be read a bedtime story," she said, "which seems somewhat backward to me. If you will excuse me." She looked from Darley to Morton, her gaze seeming to linger uncertainly on each of them, and then she went quietly out.

Darley watched the door close behind Arabella, then turned to Morton. "Do you know, I cannot get the memories of Louisa and Halbert out of my thoughts." He gestured toward the wall. "I shall never enter my sitting-room without seeing poor Halbert lying there, already dressed for a funeral. I don't know about these young men going about dressed so—as though they have had some premonition." He looked at Morton. "You should not take up this practice," he said, almost hesitantly, then swirled the dark wine in his goblet, watching it stream back down the inside of the glass. "I was trying to recall those lines that Halbert wrote. Do you remember? You found them in his pocket that night.

> *"It will find you soon enough,*
> *The empty night after the day.*
> *Brief and filled with sorrow,*
> *Love will rise and slip away."*

Darley stared a moment more into his glass, then glanced to the door that Arabella had just used. He lifted his glass to Morton. "To the birds of the air," he said softly.

"Yes," said Morton, "to the very birds of the air."

About the Author

T. F. Banks lives in British Columbia, Canada, and is at work on the next Bow Street Runner mystery.

Look for the next
exciting Henry Morton mystery

THE EMPEROR'S ASSASSIN:
Memoirs of a Bow Street Runner

coming in summer 2003
from Delacorte Press